Dead Wrong

A Swanson Herbinko Mystery

Boston

Bathsheba Monk

Gift of author to Village Library, 2018.

Blue Heron Book Works

Allentown, Pennsylvania

Copyright © 2013 Bathsheba Monk
All rights reserved.
No part of this book may be reproduced in any form without the written consent of the author or publisher.

This is a work of fiction. Any similarity to events real or imagined is due to the uncanny skill and imagination of the author.

ISBN: 0996817719
ISBN-13: 978-0-9968177-1-4

Cover Design by Angie Zambrano
Cover Photo by Paul Heller
Cover Model Angela DeAngelo
Stylist Rose Ellen Moore of RC Moore For the Unique Individual

Blue Heron Book Works, LLC
Allentown, PA 18104

www.blueheronbookworks.com

DEDICATION

This book is for all the professional women I have worked with over the years: the first line of defense in the war for equal rights in the work place, each one of you the first woman to breach a wall for the rest of us to scramble over after you. All this while raising your babies and raising a little hell. If you see a little of yourself in Swanson Herbinko, it's no mistake.

Table of Contents

Acknowledgements i

Chapter 1: The Rich are Different 2

Chapter 2: Food For Thought 21

Chapter 3: Is That Your Gun? 33

Chapter 4: Just Because I'm Wearing Garters and Carrying a Whip Doesn't Mean I'm a Dominatrix 56

Chapter 5: When the Going Gets Tough, the Tough Go Shoe Shopping 73

Chapter 6: Double Dog Dare 88

Chapter 7: All Unhappy Families are Different 103

Chapter 8: What's a 7 Letter Word for Star-Crossed Lover? 120

Chapter 9: Behind Every Great Fortune There's a Crime 135

Chapter 10: Sloppy Seconds 149

Chapter 11: Love is All You Need 162

Chapter 12: Cat (and Dog) Fight 176

Chapter 13: Till Death Do Us Part 184

Chapter 14: Game Over 194

About the Author 202

ACKNOWLEDGEMENTS

Many thanks to Blue Heron Book Works for seeing this project through to the paper edition. And thanks of course to my husband, Paul Heller, who makes everything fun and every day an adventure.

Boston, Massachusetts, Summer 2002

Chapter 1

The Rich Are Different

I wasn't surprised when Matilda Stubbs called. Women like Matilda, hanging on with manicured nails as the whirlpool of middle age sucks them down, eventually need the counsel of a good attorney. Not that I can help them keep their youth. No law, not even our constitution, guarantees that. But I can help them retain at least half of their husband's fortune that would otherwise find its way to his new wife, usually a heartbreakingly younger version of the original.

That's why I keep a purse full of business cards to pass out at society lunches to which I am frequently invited as a representative of that most (to them) exotic species: the working woman. A lucky referral in the Lucy and Clarence Howe divorce a year ago propelled me out of my blue-collar orbit and onto the planet of moneyed divorce. I attend their luncheons, distribute my business card over iced tea and Milano Mint cookies, and tell them what I do, trying not to sound any alarms. Since the Howe settlement, I have received well-modulated inquiries on the phone about asset protection in the case of divorce. Sometimes the question arrives on suede-like vellum with a creamy raised monogram. During the past ten months I have heard from most of them. So, I wasn't surprised to hear from Matilda.

I kept tabs on her through the newspaper, as her husband, Carlton, being the biggest philanthropist in Boston or the biggest sonofabitch depending on whether you were the beneficiary of his charitable whims or the victim of his business deals, was always in the news. A month ago, Carlton was in the news for resurrecting the waterfront development project, abandoned twenty-three years ago when he refused to pay for the cleanup of Boston Harbor as a condition of development. The harbor was now an environmental success story, and the $125M his father left Carlton in trust almost 25 years ago was about to revert to him. His father, Harlan, had named Carlton's twin brother, Stone, as trustee. He would be allowed to distribute the money to Carlton before 25 years, if, in Stone's opinion, Carlton showed sufficient "maturity". But in 25 years, despite repeated petitions from Carlton to the courts, Stone hadn't seen fit to distribute the money. Now he would be forced to.

Matilda was a slight woman, attractive in the way that women of her ilk are: blond coif, Chanel costume, the reproduction jewelry they wear while the original stays in the safe deposit box. More to the point, the same plastic surgery choices, which made these women as indistinguishable from one another as Barbie Dolls. Matilda and I had balanced mineral water and small talk at cocktail parties together, so technically I knew her, and we had the same conversation every time we met. More than once I caught myself in mid-sentence, searching her eyes to see if it was really Matilda Stubbs under that eye lift or if I had mistaken another woman for her.

The last time I had seen her, though, it looked like Picasso had gotten hold of her smile and plastered it back behind her ears. I palmed her my card. That mouth was Exhibit A in a malpractice suit.

She told me on the phone to come to a place outside of Harvard, an affluent bedroom community 30 miles west of Boston. She was vague on the directions, so I spent a good half-hour lost in the winding woods of the exclusive area, spinning my tires navigating wrong—unpaved—driveways, and cursing her thoughtlessness. I used the time to stuff the last of a chocolate doughnut into my mouth, licking the melting sugar from my fingers so I wouldn't get the steering wheel sticky. I knew enough about society women to know she wouldn't have anything more substantial than a carrot to nibble on and I had already missed breakfast. It's okay for women who are basically inert ornaments to be thin and wan and not have enough energy to vacuum their own bedrooms. But a working woman like me needs strength.

I reached for a cigarette, then remembered I quit smoking 3 weeks ago. I rummaged in my purse and pulled out the smooth black pebble The Russian had given me. I rubbed it until my craving subsided then threw it back in my purse.

I finally found Matilda's driveway and pulled my BMW Z3 close to the barn. A figure in a hooded sweat suit was squatting in a vegetable patch next to the house, tying tomato plants to sticks in the ground. I revved the engine, and the figure stood up, waving me in with one hand and pulling the hood tighter with the other to cover her face.

"Matilda?" I called.

She opened the kitchen door and skulked in, hunched over like a girl with new breasts. She motioned for me to follow.

"Stay here," I told my dachshund, Devil Dog. "The top's down, see? You'll be okay." I wrapped his leash around the door handle for good measure. Matilda seemed skittish and I didn't want to spook her. Dogs scare some people, although I never understood why. I've always found people far spookier than animals. And less keen judges of character.

The house was low and modern and ambled back for several wings. Through the morning mist, I could see a pond, an old barn and a carriage house—vestiges of a farm that was originally on the property. It was a nice place, but not as spectacular as I'd imagined the Stubbs' country retreat to be. Actually, I would have thought they'd have a house on the north shore like most of my other wealthy clients. But one thing I've found out about wealthy people is that they are as varied in their eccentricities as those of us who aren't rich enough to showcase them.

I walked into the kitchen, letting the screen door slam behind me, when a voice called from another room: "I'm in here, Swanson."

I inched down a few steps into a dark living room. The air was stuffy. The place had to have central air, but it wasn't on. I wouldn't last ten minutes in here. The curtains were drawn, but I could make out the paintings on the walls, wild faces that looked like screaming vampires. There were only three paintings, but the faces were so large in relation to the canvases and the pain in the faces was so intense, that they filled the room. I felt as if I had stumbled onto a stage set of a nightmare, or the remains of an all-night *X-Files* and pizza binge.

Matilda huddled in a rocking chair in the shadows. Her hood still covered most of her face. She looked like the specter of Death grieving the loss of its scythe.

"Can I turn on a light?" I asked, searching for a switch. "It's awfully dark in here."

"No!" She started rocking fast then slowed down. "Yes. Okay. What's the difference?"

She got up herself and pulled open a curtain, sat back down and began crying.

I let her get it out of her system. "Matilda, I've already seen your surgery. They can fix that. We'll sue the bastard who did it to you. We'll run him out of town. He'll never operate again."

To be perfectly honest, I've never understood the urge to undergo plastic surgery. More than one person has suggested that I am twenty pounds away from being pretty and that liposuction would make my life more worth living. And maybe I will, if I ever see a piece of chocolate capable of giving me less pleasure than slender thighs. But not now.

"He told me it would look better in a few months." Matilda stood up suddenly and pulled off her hood.

I grabbed onto the back of a chair and squeezed to stifle a scream. Her face was more frightening than the paintings on the wall. Skin was stretched so tight over her bones she no longer looked human, but like one of those monkeys with red pillbox hats who collect money for street musicians.

"Sweet Jesus," I said, involuntarily.

My reaction, oddly, seemed to calm her. She crossed her arms and let me get my fill of looking at her.

"We'll bring him down," I said, quietly.

Matilda let out a chirp. She was trying not to disturb her scars. "Bring him down?" she asked.

"God, name your price. What's his is yours. Look at you! No offense, but no jury in the world would let that doctor walk the streets again, let alone operate for money unless he's building a new Frankenstein."

"That's enough," Matilda said, sharply.

I sat down on the sofa and opened my brief case. "Let's talk strategy," I said, pulling out a legal pad and pencil. "Who is this butcher?"

There were maybe a handful of good plastic surgeons in Boston. I was mentally reviewing the list when Matilda said, "Dr. Witherspoon only did what I asked him to do."

I put my pencil down. "I don't understand."

Matilda sat down next to me. I shivered seeing the blue veins under her taut skin, and examined my pad as if I had written something there.

"It's not Dr. Witherspoon's fault." She grabbed my hand. "I made him do this. Can you imagine? I made him go further and further, thinking my youth was just a millimeter away. One more cut. Just a little tighter." She started to cry. "I wanted so much to please him, and now I'm scared to even see him."

I looked down at my hands. God, give me a good piece of chocolate over a man any day.

"Mrs. Stubbs, if you're not suing Dr. Witherspoon, what did you call me for?"

She looked up, startled. "You're a divorce lawyer, aren't you?"

I nodded.

"Well, I want a divorce."

"You did this for Mr. Stubbs, and now you want to divorce him?"

"I did it for Mr. Stone Stubbs, not Mr. Carlton Stubbs."

I dropped my pencil. "I don't understand."

Matilda got up and paced. "Stone and I were always in love. But the timing was wrong. We were an item in all the papers. You're probably too young to remember that." She wrung her hands. "At the time, we were too young. He had a lot to get out of his system. But he's ready now."

"I see."

"Stone's father was anxious for us to marry. I had a lot of money, you know, before Carlton went through it. But that's another story. Anyway, when Stone decided he had to….go away." Her voice got so low I had to lean in to hear her. "His father pushed Carlton and me together. They're identical twins you know." She said it as though it justified her actions. Then she sat down and slumped. "But they're nothing alike. They couldn't be more unalike if they had come from different planets."

"I see."

"Do you?"

"Well, it doesn't matter if I do or not, I'm here to represent your interests."

"That's so cold," Matilda said. "I thought a woman lawyer would be more understanding. Haven't you ever been in love?"

I scowled. "That's irrelevant to whether I can represent your interests."

She put her hand in mine and I patted it absently.

"Who's his lawyer?" I asked.

"Milton Baum."

I moaned silently. Milton Baum was the lawyer of choice for all the city's rich sonsofbitches. This would be the biggest case I'd ever handled, with the promise of some sizable fees at the end, but Milton Baum on the other side of the aisle meant that I would have to work twice as hard just to hold my ground.

"I need a financial disclosure from your accountant. What's his name?"

She told me and I wrote it down. "Ballpark, what is your combined net worth?"

Matilda shrugged. "Carlton went through the 25 million his father gave him years ago. Then he went through mine. He's a horrible businessman. Or just unlucky. His trust is coming due in a couple of weeks. That's 125 million. Thank God! I would like to recoup my losses."

"Do you think he's hiding any money?"

"No one could go through that much money in twenty-five years."

"Any clues you want to give me?"

"I'll mail you a retainer tomorrow."

"How much are you hoping to recoup?"

"I just want enough to live on," she said.

"You have a pretty lavish lifestyle."

The place where her lower lip used to be quivered a little. She fought to control it so her scars wouldn't burst. A tear hovered in the corner of her eye, but because she couldn't blink, it stayed there until I took out a tissue, got up and brushed it away.

I wondered if they could take some fat from her fanny and plump her face back up. But even in that bulky sweat suit her butt looked meager. I couldn't imagine the logistics of repairing the damage that had been done to her. Anyway, sitting around wasn't doing my client any good. I closed my briefcase and got up to leave.

"Can I ask you a question, Mrs. Stubbs?"

She nodded.

"Why now? Why did you wait 25 years to agree to marry Stone?"

Matilda giggled girlishly. "He just asked me."

Massachusetts has a no-fault divorce law, which means that, regardless of who wants out of the marriage and the wrongs inflicted, both parties get half of the wealth that was accumulated during their marriage. Of course, it's the natural tendency to hide some of that wealth. It was my job now to see if Carlton was hiding anything.

But, looking for hidden money is harder than looking for a dead body, which will eventually stink and lead you to it. Hidden money acquires a perfume with age that lulls people into thinking its root was divine enterprise, and not the out and out thievery (both legal and illegal) that constitutes the basis for most fortunes.

I checked Carlton's financial records on the Internet. Massachusetts has some of the toughest privacy laws in the country, so it was tedious, checking county by county, coming up only with the fact that he was doing business as at least ten different entities, none of which seemed to have any liquid assets. This seemed to confirm Matilda's assessment of Carlton's business acumen. But I've been involved in other cases in which the husband played the fool and hid the money. It would eventually come out, but sometimes not for years after the divorce was finalized.

Most of Matilda's assets on the other hand were still in her name. Despite her claim that Carlton had squandered her money, she had key properties on the waterfront, lots of cash, and art—the famous Bates Collection. All of which Matilda's father had deeded to her before her marriage. "Enough to live on" was a relative amount.

Matilda and Carlton had two grown children, so I decided to visit them. If Papa Stubbs was hiding money with his kids, their lifestyle would reflect it. Inherited wealth is a lot more tempting to spend than the type you personally schemed to get.

Dick, the private detective I keep on retainer for contested cases, told me that Tucker, the 24-year-old son, was an artist living in Vermont. On the drive up, I juggled steering wheel, MapQuest directions and Tucker's photo, taken at graduation from the School of the Museum of Fine Arts in Boston. The photo was shot with a telephoto lens, a white circle around Tucker's head. Although the photo was grainy, I could make out his features: long blond curly hair that escaped from either side of his mortarboard, movie star cheekbones, and a sneer that curled his full lips downward, keeping him from being handsome. While the other graduates in line were frozen in laughter and conversation, Tucker stared stonily ahead, his arms crossed over his chest. His partner in line was a tall blond woman with angular features who fixed a cold stare on him. Something about her made me shudder.

"Poor little rich boy," I said aloud, flipping the photo on the pile of other papers on the passenger's seat before consulting the MapQuest directions. I must've missed a turn while looking at the photo because the directions now made no sense.

"Damn." I pulled to the side of the road, got the road atlas from the trunk and spread it open over the steering wheel. I was way off. I threw the atlas in the back seat, hitting Devil Dog. He yelped indignantly. "Sorry." He kept crying. I caught his eye in the rear view mirror. "I said, I'm sorry." I had forgotten he was back there. My Uncle Stevie had given him to me a few months ago, and I still hadn't gotten used to having the dog with me.

I reached in my purse and pulled out some Doggie Yum Yums. He snatched them eagerly from my palm, forgiving me. Dogs were easy.

I oriented myself to the map, turned the car around and headed west. I picked up some more papers from Tucker's file. Dick had included a few snap shots of his paintings. You couldn't make out much, except that they were obviously done by the same tormented soul who had done the paintings at Matilda's house. Dick had told me that Tucker's stuff was too derivative of Francis Bacon.

"But it's powerful," Dick admitted. "He might turn into something."

"Is that your opinion or what?" I had asked him, surprised that Dick would have anything to say regarding modern art.

I turned into Tucker's driveway and was overwhelmed by huge plaster casts of faces, lining the dirt road leading to the house. It was as if they were meant to scare off intruders. Devil Dog, that fearless dachshund, growled at them, confident, I'm sure, that the statues were harmless. He snorted at me when we pulled up to the front door, proud to have kept the menace at bay.

"Good boy." I hooked the leash to his collar and looked around. Several small buildings dotted the property, probably studios, I thought. The main building was an old farmhouse. Curtains billowed out of the windows on the second floor, the last flap giving a snap like a flag in the wind. The screen door to the kitchen was partially open, swollen from the humidity.

I knocked on the screen door, then shielded my eyes and peered in.

"Hello?" I shouted.

No one answered, but I could hear a rhythmic crack, almost like a shutter banging in the wind, coming from somewhere in the house. I opened the door and went in. Devil Dog followed willingly, so I figured it was okay.

Another half-open door in the kitchen led to the basement. The cracking noise grew louder as I neared it, so I knocked again on the doorjamb, debated whether or not to descend, then started down the darkened stairs. The pungent smell of damp and moldy earth burned my nostrils. The noise grew louder as I passed dusty shelves of peach preserves and through a room of wine racks to a lower cellar. In the angular shadows of a dim, unshaded bulb, I made out a man and a woman, each at least six feet tall. The man hung, chained to a beam, like a shank of pale and scrappy meat. His outstretched arms and dangling legs made his potbelly protrude. Except for a baseball cap with a dirty blond ponytail poking out the back, he was completely bare. Even from his contorted position, I recognized Tucker's sneer from the photographs. The woman wore a frilly white bustier with white garters and hose and stiletto heels. Her arm rose and fell with hypnotic regularity, her ping pong paddle spreading an angry blush across his butt.

So engrossed were they in their enterprise, they didn't see me. I hid behind the wine racks, watching the movement of the paddle, like a spectator at a tennis match. I felt shocked, but was unable to turn around and leave.

A phone rang. The sound was muffled as if it were buried in the wall. Without breaking cadence, the woman reached into her bustier and pulled out a cell phone.

"*Hallo? Ja, ja. Ja..*" She paused. "*Aber natürlich.*" She snapped the phone shut and put it back.

She continued to spank Tucker, rhythmically, with a lack of passion I found astonishing. Even Devil Dog's little head and tail were synched into the beat, like a metronome. Finally she stopped. She opened up a black leather doctor's bag, put the paddle in, retrieved a key and released Tucker. He rubbed his wrists while she threw a white trench coat over herself, picked up her bag and shook his hand.

I panicked. There was no way to get up the stairs without them seeing me. Deciding a good offense was the best defense I stepped out of the shadows and called out a cheery, "Hello! Anybody down here?"

The woman's eyes drilled through me. She looked vaguely familiar. I narrowed my gaze. Her hair was now raven, but she was the blond in Tucker's graduation picture.

She turned to Tucker suddenly, as if I weren't there. *"Bis später, Liebling.* Five o'clock on Friday. *Ja?"*

We watched her go up the stairs, teetering in those shoes. When we heard her heels click across the floor above, he turned to me. We looked each other over. He was smaller than I originally thought, maybe 5'10". His eyes had the shifty quality of a mood ring, changing color in the bulb's sallow glow. Gray, green, blue. The tantalizing color trick almost hid their cornered look. His baseball hat had the New York Yankees logo embroidered on it. I didn't like him.

He stuck out his hand, not bothering to clothe himself. "Tucker Stubbs."

Maintaining fierce eye contact, I shook his hand, which was sweaty from his workout. "Swanson Herbinko."

"Like Gloria Swanson, the actress?"

"Only incidentally," I said. "I was named for a TV dinner. Fish sticks and mashed potatoes. It was a very romantic night for my parents."

Tucker let the difference in our social status sink in before he said, "And what can I do for you, Miss Swanson?"

"Miss Herbinko," I corrected him. "I'm representing your mother. She's suing your father for divorce." I handed him my card.

"Mother is divorcing Dad?" He seemed surprised, but laughed derisively. "Do lawyers make house calls now? Or are you what they call an ambulance chaser?"

"Ambulance chasers practice personal injury law," I said sweetly. "I practice family law."

"Family law sounds like a misnomer doesn't it? I mean, what you're doing is practicing ex-family law. Am I right?" He crossed his arms, waiting for me to take the bait.

When I didn't answer, he laughed. "Death, taxes and divorce: the three fates. Divorce law's a recession proof gig, isn't it?"

I winced. That's the same thing my Uncle Joe said to encourage me to go into divorce law, although truthfully it didn't take much to convince me to abandon corporate law. I found CEOs on the ropes even more ruthless than scorned spouses.

"Nevertheless. Mrs. Stubbs is my client and I'm trying to verify your mother's assessment of your father's financial position. For a rich man, he doesn't seem to have a lot of cash."

Tucker laughed. "Daddy's dying. What's the difference?" His eyes narrowed.

"What do you mean, 'Daddy's dying'?"

"She didn't tell you?"

I shook my head.

"Well, it looked like he was dying. He has a rare form of kidney cancer. But, just our luck, an experimental drug seems to be working on him." He looked pointedly at my full hips, tiny waist, finally settling on my breasts. "We'll probably die before him."

I sucked in my cheeks to look healthier.

"Have you ever modeled?" he asked suddenly.

"Are you crazy?"

"Not for a fashion magazine, but for a painter. A real artist."

I shook my head. He took my hand and pulled my arm overhead, twirling me around. "You're a type," he said. "An odalisque." He looked me in the eye, seducing me with my odalisqueness. I tried to look knowledgeable, but I had no idea what he was talking about.

He dropped my hand.

I rearranged my dress modestly. "So your father's not dying?" I asked

"He's closer than most of us, but it's no longer imminent."

If I looked too closely at the morals of my clients, I probably couldn't defend any of them. But there was something distasteful about Matilda leaving Carlton to die alone.

Tucker put on a threadbare terrycloth bathrobe and led me up the stairs to the living room, which he had converted into an art studio. The smell of turpentine and linseed oil made my head ache. The place was so dusty, you could see mites dancing in the sunbeam that pierced the room. A half-finished painting was clamped in the easel. Other paintings, brothers of those in his mother's house, lined the walls.

"Your paintings bring a substantial income?" I asked.

He shrugged. "Art goes in cycles."

"Who buys your stuff? Individuals? Corporations?"

"I have a collector in Chicago who is very interested in my work," he said. "He has an associate come by and selects pieces. Writes me a check on the spot."

"Lucky for you to have a rich supporter."

"It's a tough time for art, but quality always asserts itself. I count on the proceeds from my art for living expenses and luxuries. Look at this." He pulled out a dusty album full of clips—sidebars mostly—of reviews of his work.

I scanned them. He wasn't the main event in any of the shows he participated in, but he was still young, and I assumed it was the way all artists start out. I closed the book and handed it back to him.

"Let me ask you this. If you needed say, ten thousand dollars to hold you over a dry spell, could you ask your father for it?"

"I'm not sure why you think that's any of your business."

I smiled winningly.

"You think a man like Carlton Stubbs encouraged his son to be an artist?" he asked.

The Stubbs' name was connected to almost all the blockbuster shows that came to the Boston Fine Arts Museum: Fleet Bank and The Stubbs Charitable Trust presents Matisse, Monet and Mondrian. "He's a big contributor to the arts," I said.

"It's a lot different when your son's an artist. He's tried to starve me out, but I have no choice. If you're born an artist, you have to follow your destiny." He went over to one of his paintings and stroked the screaming face affectionately. "Dad's a Tom cat, the kind of man who eats his sons. If I needed money, and I don't, I would ask Uncle Stone."

"Why him?"

"He's sole trustee of $125 million. He's back in town, too. You might want to talk to him about my parents' financial situation. He's a little more savvy than either of them about art and money."

"How's that?"

"He actually *has* some." He laughed, dismissively. "I have my talent. The market has its ups and downs, but talent always supports itself. Nothing takes that away."

I waited, half-hoping he would mention my odalisque-like figure again. Then I nodded, tried to look agreeable, and yanked Devil Dog's chain to leave.

I had found Sarah Stubbs address and directions to her house in Virginia on the Internet, which pissed off Dick, as he grumpily verified that the information on the Net was correct. Although he took some solace from the fact that one of the streets was wrong. Alexander Haig Highway had been renamed Little Rocky Road after Clinton's re-election, and that information hadn't yet found its way to the database. Dick was on a one-man crusade to demonstrate that man was smarter than machine. He would take tasks I asked him to perform, which could be done in a few minutes on-line, and insist on taking a full day to follow a physical trail. It was no use pointing out to him that the machine was a creation of man and so only as good as man and, by the way, a lot less moody.

"I hope you're not charging me a full day for that information, buster," I said.

He crumpled a piece of paper and chucked it into the wastepaper basket. "I was doing this stuff before you were born."

"It shows," I said.

"I have more." He sat down in the visitor's chair and pulled a small, leather bound notebook from his breast pocket. "Do you want to know about *l'amour de Sarah Stubbs*?"

"No French, Dick. I'm not in the mood."

Dick was an anomaly for an ex-police officer. He never dressed in ratty clothes, but always appeared in well-cut Armanis. Last year's Armanis, to be sure, that he bought at seventy-five percent markdowns at Filene's Basement. But they fit him like paper on a wall, as my mother used to say. At 55, he kept himself fit, another anomaly for a cop. Never smoked, never saw him drink, and worked out four times a week according to the gym rats who kept me posted on who was pumping iron. Give me a list of rich middle-aged guys at the gym, and I can tally my workload for the next month. There is no better way to gauge who is having an affair than a middle-aged man's anxiety about pleasing a young woman.

"Do you want to know about the affair or don't you?" he asked.

"Just not in French."

"Sexual liaisons sound more tasteful in French."

I sighed and pulled out my pebble, rubbing it vigorously.

He flipped a few pages in his book, reading down his notes. He looked up at me suddenly. "And I didn't get any of this from the Internet."

"Okay!"

"She has a lover."

"Big deal."

"Her lover is a six-foot tall, black, Army drill sergeant."

I sat up. The Stubbses would have strong opinions about that. "Where did they meet?"

"In basic training, of course."

"Our girl Sarah was in the Army?"

"Ft. Jackson, South Carolina. She got a general discharge for lack of suitability to military life."

"That would say more positive about her than not," I said.

"I'm not making a value judgment," Dick said.

"Neither am I."

"It sounded like one to me."

"So, go on," I said, irritably. I put the pebble in my mouth then spit it out when it almost choked me. "Where does she live now?"

"They. You mean, where do they live?"

"Okay, they. Where do they live?"

"Carlton bought them a house in Alexandria, Virginia. To keep them out of his hair, I suppose. Although, they are now in Boston living with Stubbs and they seem to be making no attempt to leave."

"Have you seen this guy? Sarah's lover?" Seeing the daughter was as good an excuse as I was going to have to see the Stubbs place on Beacon Hill. I nudged Devil Dog, who was dozing in the corner, and snapped on his leash, ready to go.

"It's not a guy," Dick said, pleased with himself. "It's a woman."

"The six-foot tall drill sergeant is a woman?"

"There was an incident in the drill sergeant's basic training. She accidentally killed a recruit on the firing range. The Army investigated, of course, but she was acquitted. Struck it from her record. I only found out because of my contacts," he added pointedly. He didn't expound on who those contacts were. Dick's history would probably fill a couple of file cabinets. He rechecked his notes to see if he had forgotten anything before snapping the folder shut. "Her name is LePage."

    I had attended a society luncheon last December in Louisburg Square, the swank part of an already swank Beacon Hill. Then, however, a bevy of valets had stood by, ready to whisk my car to a safe haven, away from meter maids and other vandals. No such luck today. I parked in a place that plainly warned me to stay out. In the glove compartment, under a stash of melting Mounds Bars, I kept official-looking signs that kept the timid away. I flipped through them until I found one that might deter a Beacon Hill meter maid: Her Majesty's Secret Service. A couple of eagles clutched something that appeared to be a sheaf of wheat, but on second look proved to be carrion. The seal was overlaid with Latin. I stuck it in the windshield and grabbed Devil Dog.

    "Behave yourself," I commanded as I rang the bell at 23 Louisburg Square. Devil Dog and I were examining each other critically, sure that the other was not up to the social demands of the visit, when a young Hispanic woman opened the door. Her curly black hair was pulled back into a severe braid. She wore not the expected maid's uniform, but a nurse's outfit. Her posture was that of the lady of the house and her eyes blazed with exaggerated dignity. While she was technically a servant, there was nothing servile about her.

    "Good morning," I said, handing her my card, "I'm here to see Miss Sarah Stubbs. Is she available?"

    The woman looked at the card with disdain, then incomprehension. Perhaps she couldn't read English.

    "She's not expecting me," I continued, "but I'll only take a moment, tell her. I'm here for her mother."

    "Wait here," she said.

    I wedged a foot into the door before she could close it. "Can't I come in?"

    She tsked, eyeing the dog.

    "He's clean," I said in Devil Dog's defense, although truthfully, I suspect Devil Dog lives a filthy life when I'm not around to police him.

    She opened the door allowing us to slip in, leaving barely enough room for me. A wicked smile twisted her thin, overly lipsticked lips, revealing an overbite that gave her a snake-like look.

She disappeared and I looked around the foyer, decorated in typical Beacon Hill High Wasp. Nothing quite matched, as heirlooms are accumulated in different eras, along with fortunes. It's the essence of High Wasp charm.

I wandered down the hallway and peeked into the dining room. Several old oil paintings graced the walls. Despite my Survey of Art History undergraduate course, I found them indistinguishable from the art on the walls of my other clients' homes. Several picture hooks had nothing on them. The clean, unbleached wallpaper around them indicated that paintings had hung there previously. They were probably being cleaned or on loan.

But if the visuals were what I expected, the smell of the place was not. I had anticipated the lavender smell that comes with high-class housekeeping. Instead, the place reeked of medicine and decay. Not furniture and drapery decay, but human decay. Someone in 23 Louisburg Square was dying.

The nurse, who I learned later was named Ines, startled me when she returned. She smirked when I jumped then pointed to the parlor. "Wait in there," she commanded.

I didn't have to wait long. A six-foot tall black woman stepped immediately into the room. Slender, light-skinned with fine features, she was not the Amazon I had expected. She looked like the picture of Queen Nefertiti that was plastered on billboards around the city, advertising a show at the Museum of Fine Arts. She waved me down as I rose to greet her, and sat on an ornate gilded chair, throwing a nervously pumping leg over the arm.

"Sarah's sick," she said.

Her voice was low so it made her Southern accent less irritating to my Yankee ears.

"Sick?"

"*Ennui*. Wouldn't you get it here?" She waved her arm around the room. "The girl is prostrate with boredom. It's like living in a mausoleum."

I leaned in towards her and whispered. "Why stay then?"

Queen Nefertiti's face narrowed. "The family needs me."

"So the nurse is for Sarah?"

"Sarah? Oh, no, of course not. She's bored, honey, not diseased. Ines is for the old man."

"Carlton?"

"Of course, Carlton. Now what can I do for you?"

"I'm representing Matilda Stubbs. She's suing Carlton Stubbs for divorce." I handed her my card.

She tossed it on the end table without looking at it. "So what?"

"I just want to meet Sarah. Get her take on her parents' marriage. I like to see firsthand if the separation is warranted, or if there is hope for reconciliation. You know, if it's just a stage of life some people go through or if there's something a little more...."

"Calculating?" LePage interrupted me.

I thought of the drastic rearrangement of Matilda's features done for Carlton's twin's benefit. "Perhaps."

LePage didn't answer for a while. "I don't know why she's even bothering. Carlton's dying. Why go to the trouble?"

"I thought he had a reprieve."

"What?"

"I thought they were giving him a drug that appears to be working."

"Sarah didn't tell me anything about that."

"You're assuming Sarah tells you everything."

"Don't you tell your husband everything?" she countered.

"I don't have a…" I stopped myself. "You're Sarah's husband?" I asked.

She threw her head back in disgust. "We don't have husband and wife titles like breeders. She's my committed partner. Are you going to ask me how we do it, too?"

"Have you ever met Matilda Stubbs?" I asked as nicely as I could.

"Of course I met her," LePage said. "She was at our wedding."

"You and Sarah?"

"Of course, me and Sarah. Her parents bought us our house in Norfolk."

"Same sex marriages aren't legal in Virginia."

She looked at me coolly. "So?"

I felt a chill, remembering that she had killed a person. I reminded myself it had been an accident.

Still, we were getting nowhere fast with this conversation. Devil Dog, previously asleep by my feet, sat up, his attention fixed on the stairs. He started thumping his tail and whimpering. I reached down and petted him, wondering what he sensed that I, with my foggy human wit, couldn't.

"How long have you lived here?" I craned my neck to get a look up the stairs.

"We're not living here, we're just staying here until the old man dies, we get our share of the trust and live happily ever after...."

Just then there was a sudden crash upstairs, then a second crash with broken glass. LePage, Devil Dog and I were on our feet when Ines came running down the steps.

"Señora LePage, please!" she yelled and ran back up the stairs.

We followed her to a second floor room that was redone into a studio. A huge canvas was on the easel, a portrait in progress of Carlton Stubbs, dressed in a suit and tie, one hand lightly grazing a globe. The Boston Harbor was the in the background, but it depicted futuristic looking development, not the way it really was: much like the man in the foreground. Carlton Stubbs on the canvas looked trim, confident and athletic. The flesh and blood Carlton Stubbs lay on the floor clutching a broken lamp, emitting a septic odor.

The artist coolly cleaned her brushes, making no move to help him. Neither was Ines who was screaming to God in English to take her if she were remiss in her duties in any way.

LePage stooped, took Carlton's pulse, then called an ambulance. I racked my brain trying to recall some rudimentary first-aid from summer camp, but all that I could remember was "loosen the victim's clothing" because loosening each other's clothing was all we were interested in at summer camp. That piece of advice didn't apply to Carlton who was, as I said, naked.

The ambulance arrived in five minutes. All services come quickly to the rich.

"I thought he was on a new drug," I said to no one in particular. Even if the guy were a huge sonofabitch, I feel sympathy for anyone who is losing the final round.

A dour woman wearing a too-large maid uniform appeared, tucking strands of dirty blond hair under her lace cap. She seemed annoyed that Carlton collapsed on her shift.

"Don't be knocking things over," she said in a thick brogue, bossing the ambulance drivers as they struggled with Carlton's girth.

A fragile young woman who looked a lot like Tucker came into the room and watched them strap Carlton onto the stretcher. She took LePage's hand and looked up at her with huge navy blue eyes and asked, "Is he?" Then she laughed.

LePage shook her head and indicated to me that I should go. I turned to look at the portrait again. The artist was in the way. She wore her long black hair in a demure bun, a painter's smock that had no paint smears on it, and white stiletto heels. I caught the artist's eye. It was Tucker's ping pong partner, the Dominatrix! Her artistry, it seemed, found expression in several venues. I waited for a sign that she recognized me, but if she did, she didn't want to exchange pleasantries.

Ines, still crying, saw me to the door. I was glad to be out of there, even though I hadn't yet made sense of what I had seen. But I wasn't happy when I saw the empty space at the curb where my car had been parked. It had been towed.

Chapter 2

Food For Thought

I finally located my BMW in the tow lot at Dudley Station, which is like searching for your car in the Six Flags parking lot after a day of too much sun and beer. The attendant, a lethargic kid with "Dead Wrong" tattooed on his shaven head, wore a leather vest over his bare scrawny chest. He took his time checking and rechecking the license plate against the number on my receipt.

"It's my car. I should know my own car," I said, irritably, rubbing the pebble, which seemed to be out of order. The Russian had given me a phrase to repeat when the pebble didn't work, but his English was so bad, I couldn't understand him, and I was too embarrassed to ask him to repeat it. I'd have to pay him the fifty bucks I owed him to get a booster.

"I have to make sure it's your car." He pointed to a digit on the license number block of the receipt then studied the license plate for a long while. "You wouldn't want me giving your car away to someone else would you?"

I paid the ransom and left in a foul mood.

As usual, when I need nurturing, I drove home to South Boston to visit my mother's brothers who raised me: Uncle Stevie and Uncle Joe. Although they are fraternal twins, like the Stubbs' brothers they couldn't be more different from one another if they purposely tried. Uncle Joe is a conservative man who wears his balding hair clipped close and pastes flag decals on everything as if to disown his conscientious objector status in the Vietnam War, which he spent as a chaplain's assistant. He supports the underdog in political elections, which, in Massachusetts, means he votes Republican.

Uncle Stevie, on the other hand, drunk on patriotism, joined the Army and went to Vietnam. He came home quietly, grew his hair long, started smoking pot and became active in local politics, running, unsuccessfully, for city councilor in 1982 as a Democrat.

They each own a hot dog stand on Broadway across from one another, small aluminum and glass affairs erected in haste. Both are called Swanson's Hot Dog Emporium, after me, of course. They haven't spoken to one another since I can remember. Each claims the other stole the secret sauce for the dogs, which have made them famous in Southie. It's a flimsy reason for a feud, but what other kind is there?

Regardless of the source of their feud, both enterprises are slowly going out of business, because no matter how delicious the sauce, there are only so many hot dogs the people in Southie can eat.

I am sort of an emissary, going to Uncle Joe's, grabbing a dog and the messages he wants delivered to Uncle Stevie. Then I relay the messages to Uncle Stevie munching a few more dogs. The arrangement is even more absurd when you know that they live in the same house, which has been divided, not by floors, like regular feuding people who are chained to each other by financial considerations, but in halfsies. Uncle Stevie gets the front of the single-family frame house, which includes the spare bedroom, and Uncle Joe has the back, which has the kitchen. After I moved out to attend college, they were either too lazy or too tired to redesign. At night, they sit on the second floor watching their separate televisions, one in the living room, the other in the dining room, divided by ill-will and one of those expandable fences people stretch across doorways to keep babies from wandering out of the room.

I visited Joe first. The door was open and an old industrial fan, way too powerful for the twelve-seater counter, almost blew me back out the door. I ducked my head and forged in. One customer was at the counter, holding down his paper plate with one hand while he ate with the other. The little American flags taped to the sides of the napkin holders blew fiercely.

"For God's sake," I said, "Turn that thing off."

"It's hot," Joe said. "Aren't you hot?"

"Yeah, I'm hot." I squinted at the fan. "Turn it down at least."

Joe sullenly turned it off. He dished up a couple of dogs and leaned over the counter to talk. Sweat beaded up on his forehead and rolled down his nose. "Guess who came around looking to get an option on this shack?"

"Somebody wants to buy this place?"

"Carlton Stubbs."

"What did you tell him?"

"Not him. His assistant. I told her that his brother already took an option on it."

"Stone?"

"Five years ago. I'm just waiting for the deal to go through."

"Stone wants to develop the waterfront, too?"

"He just bought a luxury condo on the wharf."

It was news to me that Stone was interested in developing the waterfront. As I said, the redevelopment project had stalled when Carlton and the city wrangled over who was responsible for cleaning up the notoriously dirty harbor. The city said that Carlton was responsible because he would profit from any development there. Carlton said that the city and state were responsible because they made the mess in the first place. Carlton finally dropped out, claiming he couldn't afford to clean it up and develop it, too. Also, Stone wouldn't release the money from The Trust to do it. Anyway, after intense pressure from the local citizens, the city and state eventually ponied up and now the Boston Harbor is a poster child for big environmental clean-ups.

"Maybe you can get a concession stand in the new ballpark," I said, inhaling the aroma of Swanson's Secret Sauce.

"Eh! It's all crooked. It's all who you know. Who do I know?"

"Probably nobody."

He looked at me uncertainly as he wiped down the counter. "You don't think I know anybody? I know people!"

"I'm sure you know people," I agreed, reaching for the onions.

"You think it needs more onions?" he asked, looking nervously across the street as if Stevie could see our transaction.

I tapped a tablespoonful of onion across the saucy dog. "I think they fucked up my drive train when they towed me."

"Watch your mouth! Who's going to marry a girl with a dirty mouth?"

I sighed. "You think Mikey can take me today?"

His answer was to pick up the phone and speed dial Mikey's Overnight Repair. He put his hand over the mouthpiece. "You're better off taking it to the dealer. You're still under warranty. Hello? Mikey? Okay. Hey, the girl needs her drive train looked at. They fucked it up when they goddamned towed it. Yeah, probably. Yeah." He hung up without saying goodbye. "Tomorrow afternoon."

"Watch your language," I said. "No one's going to marry a boy with a dirty mouth."

"It's not my mouth that the problem. It's my goddamned dirty mind."

We laughed. It was a mystery what women found attractive about my uncles, who were out shape and going out of business. But they couldn't keep up with the women who wanted to date them. My theory was that the residual smell of garlic and onions on their hands attracted them. The primal mating call of food.

"But I got to tell you," he said. "Some of these babes can out-dirty me. Jesus, are they filthy. *Nymphogeriatriacs*."

"That's not a word," I said.

"It is if someone uses it. I'm using it."

"It's not in the dictionary."

"I'm sending it to Houghton Mifflin. They can put it in their next dictionary. No charge," he said magnanimously. "Here." He shoved a crossword puzzle magazine towards me. "Sixty-eight across," he said. "Seven letters. 'Green-eyed Ethiopian'."

"Othello."

He wrote it in. "Hah! Fits."

"Anything else?"

"That was the last one." He looked at the puzzle and frowned, erasing a few entries. "That changes everything."

I left him there, pondering the pleasures of dirty babes, jargonauts and how one new word in a puzzle changes everything. I stepped out into the wavy heat of traffic. I crossed the street, dodging the Broadway bus. The bus driver laid on his horn as his vehicle nipped my briefcase. When it was a safe distance away, Devil Dog barked his disapproval. We got faces full of black exhaust for our irritation.

I dragged Devil Dog by the leash to Uncle Stevie's, which was pretty much a replica of Uncle Joe's—minus the fan and flags. An autographed picture of Ted Williams, Stevie's prize possession, hung on the wall over the register.

Two men sat at the counter reading the sports pages, eating dogs and swilling root beer. I sat between them.

Uncle Stevie smothered me and Devil Dog in kisses, then smothered a couple of dogs in sauce and onions and set them in front of me.

"How's business?" I asked.

"I got first dibs on a concession stand in the ballpark." He patted Devil Dog, his present to me, then cut up a couple of wieners and put them in a bowl on the floor.

"Put some stuff on them," I commanded.

"Dogs don't eat that stuff. You'll make him sick," Uncle Stevie said. "What do you know about dogs?"

"I have one, don't I? Put some stuff on them. He eats everything I do."

"Yeah, well, who got him for you? If it weren't for me, you'd be alone and vulnerable." He turned his attention to Devil Dog. "You doing a good job protecting your mistress? Good boy!"

"Who do you know?" I asked between bites. "Who do you know to get a concession stand? Why can't Uncle Joe get one?"

Uncle Stevie stood up. "He isn't trying hard enough." He looked irritated and turned his attention to his customers. "What about that Pedro, eh?" he said.

"They shouldn't have pitched him last night," one of the men said. "They should have saved him for New York."

The other man sitting at the counter laughed. He had a wild mane of hair, graying sideburns and a barrel chest. "It doesn't matter who you throw at us," he said. "You're doomed."

"What do you mean, 'us'?" I asked.

"You can't beat the Yankees. You're just an annoying gnat that we have to flick away."

"What do you mean, 'we'?" I repeated.

"Anyway, all the best Boston players come to New York. Wade Boggs, Clemens," he said, pausing dramatically. *"The Babe."*

We sulked. Everyone in Boston knows that the curse of the Bambino is responsible for our unhappiness during baseball season. Or maybe, our perverse happiness. Roger Kahn said you glory in a winning team, you fall in love with a losing team.

"If Ted Williams didn't lose five years in the war, he would have been the greatest player ever. He didn't go to New York," I said, testily. "He stayed in Boston."

"Yeah, well, that was his mistake," the Yankee said.

"It doesn't matter," I said. "Clemens is injured. They might as well use Pedro against Seattle.

The Yankee fan held up a finger. "Give me another dog."

Stevie nodded.

"What do I owe you?"

Stevie added the bill in his head. "Seven fifty-six."

"Four championship rings in the last 6 years. How about that?" He laughed.

I took a swig of root beer. Nothing is more satisfying than an original Swanson Hot Dog washed down with root beer. I went behind the counter, grabbed a bowl and poured some for Devil Dog. Life is too short not to enjoy its pleasures. Even dogs know this.

"You're not going to give that to the dog, I hope," Uncle Stevie said. "He'll explode from the carbonation."

"Why can't you help Joe get a stand?" I asked. "In fact, why can't you just go in together?"

"It's too late for that."

The Yankee fan swiveled off the stool, picked up his crutches, grunted good-bye and swung out the door. The bell on the door jingled with his departure.

"Friend of yours?" I asked, accusingly.

Uncle Stevie frowned. "Marty Simon. Says he was in Nam. He's head of the public relations team for a company that's bidding on the new ballpark."

I snorted. "You don't care if they move Fenway out here? Where's your sense of tradition?"

"You gotta move on in life, Swanson."

"Did you know Uncle Joe sold his place? He said Stone Stubbs took an option on it five years ago."

"Yeh, I know." Uncle Stevie rolled the dogs on the grill with a bandaged finger. "Damn! I burned it again. I can't believe we're brothers sometimes. Stone Stubbs just wants to tie up his property. He has no interest in Southie."

Uncle Stevie wrapped two hot dogs to go and gave the customer his change, then got out a new pack of hot dogs and put them on the grill. "Jesus, I hope he didn't option his half of the house, too." He licked his finger and got out a bun when another customer walked in. I hoped the Board of Health never caught his act. I got up to leave.

"Come over for dinner, Swanson. We never see you anymore. Are you dating someone?" He looked hopeful. "Or are you still on that sabbatical?"

I had told my uncles about six months ago that I was taking a sabbatical from men. I was tired of men thinking that because I had a sensuous figure, I wanted sex all the time. Well, maybe I did, but not necessarily with *them*.

"I'll be over soon," I promised.

"Tomorrow night," he persisted.

"Soon."

"Tomorrow."

"Okay, tomorrow."

The next afternoon, I took my car into Mikey's shop. It was a typical South Boston garage. No money wasted on frills. Mikey's secretary/bookkeeper, Trish, had attempted to fashion a few seats into a reception area. The result was Early Garage: two gray army surplus chairs; a giant wooden cable spool serving as the coffee table; back issues of Popular Mechanics, Soldier of Fortune, and Fly Fisherman.

Trish's desk was less than a foot away. Trish ran on chemicals, not calories. She chained-smoked and a sign over her typewriter said, "Thank You For Not Telling Me to Quit Smoking." She kept a pot of fresh coffee for customers, or as she said, "kustamahs," but went across the street to the Dunkin Donuts for her dose of caffeine. The wastepaper basket was filled with three giant Styrofoam cups, and it was only one in the afternoon.

I inhaled some of her second-hand smoke then reached for my pebble. When I told her I had to make a call, she offered to let me use her dinosaur two-button phone set, but I held up my cell-phone and dialed Matilda.

"What does Stone have to do with the redevelopment project?" I asked.

"Stone?"

"Your fiancé, remember?"

She didn't answer.

"Is Stone taking out options on waterfront property?"

She paused. "Is he?"

"Is he working with Carlton?"

"They're twins, you know."

"Fine. By the way, why didn't you tell me Carlton is dying? You might not actually need a divorce."

She laughed. "Carlton's not dying. He's on some new drug. He'll be around long after we're gone." She sounded just like Tucker.

"I just saw him, Matilda. He collapsed and was taken to the hospital."

Hidalgo Gomez, one of the men working for Mikey, stood in the doorway motioning to me. He had taken off his shirt, revealing, even if the temperature weren't near 100 degrees, a good enough reason for not wearing a shirt.

"Look, Matilda, I gotta go. Get your accountant to finish your financial disclosure," I said. I would get a copy of The Trust agreement later. I scribbled some notes about our conversation on a piece of paper and followed Hidalgo into the garage. Finally, I was getting somewhere.

Hidalgo had the hood of my car open and we stood over the engine examining the tangle of parts. His arm was stretched up, holding the hood. He looked over at me until I was forced to meet his stare. He said, "You had onions for lunch."

He didn't say it in a way that I felt compelled to reach in my purse for a breath mint. I have never found the smell of onion or garlic offensive. I find it delicious. Apparently, Hidalgo did too.

"You had a Swanson hot dog," he continued.

"Several," I admitted.

He smiled. His teeth were small and white and even, like young corn. I smiled back.

"I can make a simple baked potato taste like heaven," he said. "I bake it in the oven. A little chive. A little cheese. And bacon. I make it in a restaurant where I used to work. An American restaurant, Ruby Tuesdays. Have you ever had?"

We stared at each other, the image of the baked potato between us.

"No," I said. "I never had."

"I will make you sometime."

He let the hood of the car drop closed. "There's nothing wrong with your car." He handed me an invoice. The amount due was zero. I smiled at him. I knew there was nothing wrong with my car. I had only used it as an excuse to see Hidalgo who I had seen every week when my Chevy Cavalier was dying a few months ago. Since I bought the BMW, I had missed the pleasure of his seducing me with recipes.

He was going to come to my apartment to cook for me a week ago, but he cancelled. Something had come up, he said, family problems. Immigrant types always have family problems.

I was getting ready to ask him again when a small woman in high heels came into the garage. She looked at me, then Hidalgo, and sneered. It took me a minute to put her in context. It was Ines, Carlton Stubbs' nurse.

She started talking rapidly to Hidalgo in Spanish. He tinkered with a few parts of a 1968 Volvo engine, not answering, as she got louder and shriller. Finally, he slammed a wrench on the table, said a few words and buried his head under the hood. Ines stamped her foot, obviously frustrated with his reply.

"How's your boss?" I called to her.

Ines threw back her head. "They sent him home."

"You're kidding!"

"No I am not kidding," she snarled. "Rich men like Carlton Stubbs get new drugs and medicine right away. Poor Mexicans like us only get them if we are part of an experiment they can't do on animals. He's back in his home, bossing everyone around."

She said something again to Hidalgo in Spanish. Something about *leche* and *pan*. He couldn't be interested in her, too. She was so damned skinny. Maybe they were related.

Finally, after giving me one last dirty look, she turned and left.

"See you later, Hidalgo," I said.

He gave me a half-hearted wink, and put his head back under the hood of the car.

Uncle Stevie cooked dinner, mostly because he had the kitchen. I insisted he include Uncle Joe, but neither would agree to it. Uncle Joe did, however, turn down the volume of his television and sat close to the dining room while we ate. While they could agree on nothing else, they agreed that I should get married. It was unnatural for a woman to be alone and childless. They were nervous, because I didn't have any prospects. When, they asked, was the last time I had a date?

"What do you know about dates?" I asked testily. "Calling up some floozy for a nightcap after the bar closes? Is that a date?"

"It's different for guys," Uncle Joe said.

"Yeah," Uncle Stevie agreed, not looking at his brother.

"Since I'd probably be dating a guy, you've made my case for solitude," I said.

They nodded without looking at each other, as if they had won the argument. They were maddening. It was my turn to nag them.

"And what about your doggie shacks? Why are you selling options on them?"

"I didn't," Stevie said. He jerked a thumb at Joe. "He did."

"You want to inherit a lousy 250 square feet with a grill and 12 stools in Southie?"

"I want you to be happy," I said.

"I'd be plenty happy to sell to the highest bidder."

"Stone is going to screw him," Stevie said to me.

"We'll see," Joe said. "When they take his place by eminent domain, he'll be lucky to get what he paid for it."

"I hope he didn't sell an option on his portion of the house."

We waited for Joe to answer, but he didn't.

"Fer chrissake," Stevie said.

I looked around the house. It was shabby and as I was the only female (to my knowledge) who had ever lived there, it lacked the quality that said "home." Still, it was familiar and all that tied us to one another.

We ate in silence. It was a good meal, chicken marinated in green olives and baked slowly in white wine, followed by strawberry shortcake, made with biscuits instead of angel food. But the image of the baked potato with a little chive, a little cheese, a little bacon, prepared by a lovely brown shirtless man wouldn't leave me. At the end of the evening, I had to admit that maybe my uncles were right: I was lonely.

I walked Devil Dog before going into my apartment on Beals St. in Brookline. It was past midnight, but it was a safe neighborhood, and I had every intention of sleeping late the next day.

The concierge nodded when I entered then went back to dozing. I scowled. A hefty portion of my condo fees supported concierges, none of whom I have ever seen awake. I would bring it up at the next condo meeting. Maybe we could just prop up a dummy at the concierge desk and save some money.

I emptied the mailbox directly into the wastepaper basket. It was all junk. I climbed the steps to my fourth floor condo instead of taking the elevator. Everyone was right; I should try to get some exercise. I made it to my landing without the usual gasping for air. Not smoking for 3 weeks had made breathing a little easier. That was something.

Dick was waiting outside my door. I blinked, thinking the oxygen from the climb had made me hallucinate. He was sitting with his legs crossed, yoga-style, oblivious to the wrinkles this was putting in his Italian silk pants.

"This better be good," I said, stepping over him to open the door.

"It's better than good." He unwrapped himself and got up from the floor, smoothing his clothing.

"I suppose you know that old Carlton made another run from death's door," I said. "That new drug they gave him seems to be working. God, everyone's got to be so disappointed. They already had the money spent."

Dick smiled and followed me into my apartment. I made some coffee, aware that if I drank it I would want a cigarette. But Dick didn't seem to be in a hurry to tell me his news. I had been working with Dick for only a few months, and I was already accustomed to his maddening personality ticks. One of which was not getting to the point.

I held up the sugar bowl. Dick shook his head, and I helped myself. I put in one demure teaspoonful, then two more. What the heck, tension would burn it off.

"When did you hear about Carlton?" Dick finally asked.

"I saw his nurse at the garage. Oh, maybe, four o'clock this afternoon."

Dick smiled. "Mikey's Garage? Isn't your car still under warranty?"

He probably knew I had a thing for Hidalgo. I was too tired to care. "Am I under suspicion here for something?"

"It just seems odd that Ines would be away from her patient when he has just had a close call with death."

"Ines said he was home. That guy has some will to live. I called the hospital. He's home. Resting, probably."

Dick smirked. "He's resting all right."

I put down my coffee cup. Down the hall, a door slammed.

"What do you mean?"
"Someone shot him right in the head."

Chapter 3

Is That Your Gun?

At 2 a.m., I followed Dick to Louisburg Square. The square, in fact the entire Hill, was quiet and dark. The feeble glow from the gaslights barely illuminated the brick sidewalks heaved up by the roots of ancient ash trees. I stepped carefully on the cobblestones and shivered in anticipation of the grisly scene inside.

Two squad cars parked in front of number 23 were the only indication a man had been murdered that evening. I thought of a similar situation I'd seen in Mattapan, the poorest section of the city, when I was doing a *pro bono*. I helped a woman divorce her husband who beat her then stalked her, despite repeated restraining orders. She finally shot him when it was clear he wouldn't stay divorced. The street was in turmoil for days.

On the front steps of the Dodge's, across the street, stragglers from a dinner party lingered, oblivious to the violence in their midst. Lowell Dodge, scion to the Dodge fortune, stood in the doorway with his wife, Titi, saying goodbye to the last of their guests. I recognized Titi from my lunch circuit, but she didn't return my wave.

Police hate clutter at a crime scene, but one of the cops knew Dick and grudgingly let us both in. The house was quiet. I'm not sure what I expected. The grieving Stubbs family? Those people existed only in my fantasy.

We went up to Carlton's bedroom on the third floor, where he had been shot. A strip of yellow tape barred our entrance. We peered into the room. The body had been removed to the morgue, presumably after the police photographers had taken pictures and collected evidence.

The bloody bedclothes still had the impression of Carlton's body, and thousands of goose feathers lay scattered around the room.

"Someone shot him through a pillow," Dick said.

The image of someone being shot in the head and feathers flying out made me laugh.

Dick looked at me disapprovingly.

"I'm tired," I said, defensively, fondling my pebble.

"Why don't you just try willpower? That stone isn't doing you any good."

"What stone are you talking about?"

"You think I don't know you grab that ridiculous pebble every time you want a cigarette?"

I let the pebble drop from my fingers into my pocket. "Do you want to investigate me or this murder?" I asked.

We stared at the murder scene. A carafe of water with a glass was on the nightstand. Next to the carafe was a tape player. The top was popped and no tape was inside.

"Dick!" I pointed to the machine.

"I saw."

"You think someone would tape a murder?"

Dick shrugged. "I've seen more bizarre things."

I inhaled deeply. The place smelled of blood.

"'Who would have thought the old man to have had so much blood in him?'" Dick arched an eyebrow at me. "Lady Macbeth."

"I know," I said. "I went to college. Where is everyone? The place was crawling with leeches yesterday afternoon."

"One of the theories is that he committed suicide."

"Give me a break. Where was the murder weapon?"

"In his hand. They're checking the registration now. No usable prints. The place was lousy with prints and DNA. You'd think Barnum and Bailey performed here. No burn marks, either. They're looking for latex gloves with burn marks on them."

"You think that Hispanic nurse?" I asked, although she had as little reason to kill Stubbs as I did. She was the hired help whose job ended with Stubbs' life. I just didn't like her.

"She wasn't here. She gets off work at six after she feeds him his dinner. She left with the maid. He was killed about 8:30. The night nurse was on duty then. She went out for a break and must have panicked when she saw the police cars because she never came back."

"Does she have a reason to lie?" I asked.

"She's probably illegal."

"Ah." The third question on a deposition is your citizenship status. Illegal immigrants were rightfully leery of having their status on a document that could find its way to immigration.

"Why don't they contact the agency that hired her?'

"The Stubbs' used referrals, not agencies. They didn't want to pay taxes on their help."

"That other nurse, Ines, could have stuck around," I said.

"Could've."

We stood in Carlton's doorway, thinking about the dead man. Somebody obviously didn't like it that his new, experimental drug was working. They wanted him dead.

"The question is," Dick said, reading my mind, "Who benefits?"

"None of his heirs, that's for sure," I said. "A murder investigation is going to tie up Carlton's money forever."

"The spouse is always the prime suspect, no matter what," Dick said. "There's money, and then there's passion. She was pretty frustrated. He took advantage of her, then the mistress."

"What mistress?"

Before he could answer, a uniformed cop, a big red-head, came up behind us. He looked like the brother of someone who went to Boston Latin with me. Of course, Southie is a pretty small gene pool. He ignored the radio that squawked on his hip. "You done here?" he asked Dick.

Dick nodded.

"Any suspects?" I asked.

"Well, we didn't have to look far. The perp confessed," the cop said.

"To you?" Dick asked, surprised.

The cop pulled himself up. "Yup." He looked as if he were imagining the promotion this would bring.

"Who?' I asked.

"The daughter." He brought out a little notebook and flipped it open and read the name. "Sarah. The daughter." He looked up. "Turns out her lover was having an affair with the old man. Sarah got pissed and popped him."

"She said that?" Dick asked, his color high.

"Yup. Right away. Well, folks, I have to write up my report. You want to get going?"

Dick walked me to my car. The sky was brightening. I felt depressed for having pulled a pointless all-nighter.

"I guess that's the end of that," I said, yawning. "Passion. Just like you said."

"Are you kidding? You think Sarah did it?" Dick asked, incredulous.

"Well, there is the small matter of the confession," I reminded him. "I can't believe that old Carlton was screwing LePage. For God's sake, he was half-dead." I tried to shake the mental image of Carlton engaged in the intimate act.

"A crime scene confession is the worst thing you can get," Dick said. "If she doesn't recant, and my guess is she will, it'll never hold up in court. That butthead probably didn't even read her her rights. Or can't prove that he did. Which is just as bad."

I put my car into gear and pulled out of the space. I lowered the window and yelled out at him, "Go to sleep, Dick!"

He bent down so he could see into the car. "That butthead let everyone onto the crime scene. It's polluted beyond hope now. They'll never find the killer on evidence. And that's the only sure way."

I inched the car forward so I wouldn't damage Dick's head and left him there yammering about polluted crime scenes, rookie cops, and how the police confessor would be lucky to stay on the force.

I slept a few restless hours, before awaking to something soft and moist on my hand. It took a sleepy minute to realize it was Devil Dog, wanting to be walked.

"Didn't we do this last night?" I asked, as he led me out into our Brookline neighborhood. I tried to remember why last night I thought exercise would make me happy. It was a mystery this morning.

We stopped for chocolate bagels and coffee at Max's Deli on Beacon Street. Max Oppenheimer was a transplanted Jew from Brooklyn. He wore long sleeves, even in the hottest weather, which I attributed to old world formality, though he had left Czechoslovakia as a child. Once, when he was leaning on the counter in front of me, I saw blurry blue numbers on his wrist. When he saw me staring, he tugged down his cuffs and left hurriedly to get something from the kitchen.

Twenty years ago, he and his wife Connie had come to Boston for a simpler life. It was tough going at first because everyone was eating doughnuts and Max was a bagel baker. Two separate arts, he had told me. Two separate philosophies. But then the health craze kicked in and the bagel was heralded as a health food. Max rejoiced to me repeatedly at the renaissance of the bagel. He couldn't believe his good fortune to be alive to see the whole world in love with bagels.

"I always said bagels had potential," he said. "Who couldn't see that they had potential? Look, chocolate bagels. Who would have thought?"

He threw in an extra bagel out of professional courtesy to my uncles, whom he met on a foray into their neighborhood looking for food ideas.

"Try this one," he said. "It's a peanut butter and chocolate. The inspiration was a Reese's Cup. It's just an idea. I'm still doing market research. Tell me what you think. Be honest." He wagged a finger at me as if he would find out if I weren't telling the truth.

I put a couple of tubs of cream and some logs of raw sugar in my coffee and took a polite chew out of the Reese's Cup bagel. Max was leaning over the corner watching me from narrowed eyes. I held it up in salute.

"Not bad," I said.

"Do you think too much salt? Connie thinks it may have too much salt."

"It may have too much salt," I said, agreeing with his wife who was, as he always said, "my best friend and my best food critic."

I picked politely at the bagel, but I couldn't get the picture of Carlton's bloody death out of my mind. I kept seeing his face with a big hole where part of his head used to be.

I paid Max.

"The chocolate was primo," I said, giving him a thumbs-up.

"What about the Reeses?" he asked, pretending nonchalance as he counted up some change.

"Devil Dog liked it," I said.

Max put another one in a waxed bakery bag and handed it to me as I left. "For the dog," he said.

"Here, let me pay you." I reached into my purse, but Max cut me off, holding up his arm and closing his eyes.

"On the house. For the dog. I'm a big dog lover. Although I don't have one myself. Connie doesn't like them."

I left. If I had to choose between a man and Devil Dog, who would get the boot? Uncle Stevie had given me Devil Dog only a few months ago, and I could no longer imagine life without him. Uncle Stevie hadn't considered that having a dog would actually deter me from attaining his goal for me: marriage. That's the thing about presents, they acquire a life of their own.

I was thinking about the presents family members bequeath one another as I drove out to Harvard to see Matilda Stubbs, and find out how she wanted me to proceed now that she no longer needed a divorce. I wondered if Tucker would be there. He seemed to despise Matilda as much as he despised Carlton. But murder is the kind of thing that brings families together.

It had started to rain and the house looked dark and closed. I knocked anyway. No one answered. I went to a window and looked in, but couldn't see a thing. I knocked again and this time Matilda answered. She was dressed in a black suit and hat with a thick black veil, which immensely improved her appearance. She seemed to have survived the shock of Carlton's murder pretty well.

"I'm sorry about your loss, Matilda," I said.

"Oh that." She waved her gloved hand, fanning a dose of Joy and gin towards me. It was ten in the morning.

"Did I catch you at a bad time?" I craned my neck to see into the house. "Are you just going out? I could drive you." She didn't need a DUI to complicate her affairs.

"I have a ton of things to attend to." She sounded girlish. Hopeful. She didn't seem sad that what she had to attend to was the disposal of her husband's remains. "But, yes, of course. Come in."

She led me into the living room. It was stuffy and as dark as before, maybe darker because it was an overcast day, but there was no mistaking what was on the walls. Or rather, what wasn't on the walls: Tucker's paintings were gone. In their place were demure Indian miniatures. Ivory carvings of ships. A few family photographs. I couldn't have imagined those frightening paintings, but it was as if they never existed.

"Is Tucker here?" I asked.

"Why do you ask? He was here last night. He wanted to pick up some of his things."

"The paintings?"

"Well, yes. It gave him great delight to hang them here for a while. I guess it no longer gives him great delight. He just swooshed in and took them all." She waved her hands dramatically.

Tucker's delight. I wondered if Matilda knew what else gave her son delight.

"Anyway, I'm glad to see you, Swanson. Now that Carlton is gone, all we have to confront is paperwork."

Pink lipstick shone like neon beneath her thick veil, which encased her and her delusions like a suit of armor. "I know it's not a divorce anymore. But I'd like you to stay on retainer. Look out for my interests. All of the family's lawyers are really Stubb's family lawyers. I am a Bates, not a Stubbs."

"You might be better off finding someone who handles estates and trusts, Matilda. I can recommend someone for you."

"Nonsense. I need someone who doesn't run in the same social circles as us. Someone who isn't privy to vicious gossip. There'll be a little something extra in it for you." She got a little mirror out of her purse and checked her face. "It's funny how things work out, isn't it?"

"Yeah," I nodded. "Funny."

Suddenly a loud noise echoed up the hall, like someone was moving furniture.

Matilda tensed. "That damned girl."

"Is someone here?" I asked.

"Yes. Bunny. Excuse me for a minute."

I amused myself by examining the walls until she returned. They were still tacky. The paint must have been applied just hours ago. It would never dry in this humidity.

Devil Dog was aware of Bunny's entrance before me. He tugged on his chain and started a low growl in the back of his throat, ears pinned back. A tall slender woman with straight platinum hair stood in the doorway, an amused half-smile on her full lips. She wore no make-up and the bareness contributed to her fragile look. She was in her thirties; beautiful. And she looked eerily like pictures I had seen of Matilda when she was younger. I patted Devil Dog. "It's okay, boy. Easy."

She held out a hand. "Bunny O'Reilly."

Bunny O'Reilly was the name of Tommy O'Reilly's older sister.

She was a senior at Monsignor O'Brien High School when Tommy and I were sophomores at Boston Latin. Tommy O'Reilly's sister, however, weighed 200 pounds. It couldn't be the same woman. I squinted.

"You're no relation to Tommy..."

"Sister." She cut me off.

"What is your relationship to Mrs. Stubbs?" I asked.

"To her? Nothing. I was Carlton's personal assistant for three years."

"Where did you meet him?"

"You're not a cop or anything are you?"

"Hell no! I'm Mrs. Stubbs' attorney. Her divorce attorney, actually. Of course, that need has been superseded by other events." She looked confused, so I said, " Like his death."

"Oh." She started winding strands of her gorgeous hair around a finger. A platinum Rolex encircled her dainty wrist.

"What are you doing here?" I asked. "Don't you have to help dispose of Mr. Stubbs' affairs? He must have left quite a mess."

"On the contrary," Bunny said. "I'm his office manager. I organized all his affairs. I did all his paperwork, took care of all his obligations. Everything is neat as a pin."

"And you're here for what again?" I pressed.

"Carlton left this house to me."

"You want to kick Mrs. Stubbs out?"

"It's not hers," Bunny said firmly.

"You think it's yours?"

She held up her index finger then left the room. She came back with a stack of papers and dropped them into my arms. "The codicil. This house is payment in lieu of wages. I am owed wages for three years."

"The codicil gives you this house in lieu of wages?"

She thwacked her middle finger on the papers in my arms. "It's all in there. Take it. I have copies."

I nodded numbly and put the papers on the floor.

"I was advised to physically take possession or I would never get it," she said.

She was right. It was a lot easier to give someone something they already possessed. If she didn't occupy the house, she would be lucky to come out of all this with two weeks severance pay—if she were extremely polite to the judge.

"Who advised you? Your attorney?"

"My brother. You know, Tommy."

"What's he doing now?"

"Time."

"Excuse me?"

"He's in jail for running an illegal tour boat from Boston to Columbia. He didn't have a permit. Can you believe they put him in jail for that? Anyway, he has a lot of time to read law books and he told me to move in and not budge."

I searched her face for cynicism and found none. "Tell him I said hello."

She smiled.

"So you knew Carlton well?"

"Three years, like I said." She brightened, glad to talk about her love and loyalty to Carlton. "I met him at a party he arranged for some Japanese businessmen. They were trying to get him to buy into some rental car business. Nixon-Rent-A-Car. Carlton wanted them to change the name and they wouldn't. It must mean something in Japanese."

"What do you think it means in English?"

"Does it mean something in English?" She looked slightly panic-stricken then recovered. "Anyway, I was the only girl at the party. I could carry an entire party because I have a college degree."

"A party?" I asked—stupidly—before realizing what kind of party Bunny was talking about. Bunny had obviously been an escort who had been hired to entertain the businessmen. But she was one of those escort girls who instantly transform themselves into tea-drinking Presbyterians when powerful men marry them. "I mean, did Carlton go into business with them?"

"No. It was the night he got sick. He was playing squash with Shuyo. I was watching in the visitor's gallery. I could tell something was wrong with him, even though I had just met him. When he was playing, he kind of grabbed his side at one point and dropped the racket. Just like that. He was a good player, so it seemed kind of weird, although he picked the racket right back up, smiled and bowed to Shuyo. Kept right on playing."

She looked like she was going to cry. I was flabbergasted. I wished I had seen Carlton before he had become a beached whale.

Maybe then I could fathom his appeal. I had always been interested in sex as a purely sensual experience. I had no understanding of people who were turned on by power, which was surely the aphrodisiac Carlton used to such good advantage.

Matilda came into the room. She had been standing in the doorway, listening. "That's just so touching," she said. "I'm touched. Bunny, are you finished? Did you find what you were looking for?"

Bunny stood up and pressed her pants with her hands. "I contacted the sheriff. You have to leave. This isn't your property anymore. Carlton let you stay out of the goodness of his heart."

Matilda opened her handbag, looking for something, hopefully a breath mint to mask the gin fumes then snapped it shut. "The goodness of Carlton's heart. My word! I have to see to Carlton's funeral arrangements. I hope they're up to his innate goodness. Such a good man would be appalled that his widow was being evicted before his body was even cold." She turned her veiled head towards Bunny. "The sheriff will have to decide, I suppose, whether I'm worth the trouble of evicting. And worth the publicity. The publicity will be terrible, throwing a widow out on the street. The sheriff has to think about these things in an election year."

Matilda left us in living room. Bunny clenched the back of the chair, watching through the window as Matilda got in her Lincoln Town Car. "She is such a bitch. Carlton was a saint to put up with her for as long as he did. She should be grateful for anything we decide to give her."

"We?"

"Carlton and me. We were going to make sure she was provided for, but he died so suddenly. That drug was working. He seemed so much better yesterday." She started to cry again.

"To say 'he died' is rather euphemistic, don't you think? It appears he was murdered."

Bunny looked startled. "The police said it was suicide."

It was my turn to be surprised. News of Sarah's confession must not have gotten out yet. "Did he ever talk about suicide?"

She shook her head.

"Did he even own a gun? Did you ever see one?" Dick had told me last night that Carlton hadn't registered for a gun permit, and a man like Carlton was too smart to overlook a detail that could needlessly get him in trouble.

"I can't see what that has to do with anything. He was obviously desperate. The man was in a lot of pain. But," she leaned in conspiratorially. "You're right. He wouldn't commit suicide. He wanted to live and marry me. We were going to honeymoon in Isla Mujeres."

I looked at her blankly.

"It's in Mexico. We wanted to start a family. With *normal* children..." She looked around furtively. "I think....Matilda."

"You think Matilda what?"

"She was so jealous. He never loved her. He told me that." She made a face like a pickle, obliterating the physical resemblance between her and Matilda. "If his father hadn't forced him, he would have never married her in the first place. He regretted that. He told me. She was pregnant with Tucker, you know."

I didn't. "Lots of women are pregnant when they get married," I said.

"She was in love with Stone when Carlton married her. Didn't you know?" she smiled evilly.

I nodded dumbly. Even if Tucker were Stone's child, it would be impossible to prove. Identical twins have identical DNA. "Well, anyway, they haven't discounted suicide. He was in a lot of pain. He could have killed himself to be free of it."

"That new drug was making him better. He was going to get better." Bunny slumped then pulled herself together. "I don't know how he bore it as long as he did. He never complained either. He wouldn't burden anyone with his pain."

I yanked Devil Dog's chain. "So, are you staying here, or what?"

"It is my house," Bunny said. "The place is mine. Carlton said I could have it. It's in the will. Or the codicil. And Tommy said to stay."

"Do you have legal representation?" I cleared my throat. "Besides Tommy, I mean."

"Do you think I need it?"

Devil Dog gave Bunny a short bark as we left. I snapped him back. I thought of a dozen law school classmates who would be happy to accept a case as ripe with billable hours as Bunny's promised to be. "Yeah, I think you need it."

I parked my car at home and walked the two blocks to my office at the Arcade. The first floor of the Arcade was rented to businesses that seemed quaintly out-of-date in the cyber-age: a used record shop (and I do mean records, not CDs); a second hand clothing consignment shop, my Russian hypnotist, and an outlet devoted to fishnet stockings. The proprietor of the later, a thick-set man in his mid-forties, wearing a yarmulke, snapped the pages of the *Herald* as I walked by.

"*Zaftig,*" he said.

I nodded coolly.

Mostly Jews lived in Brookline. Or single women, like me, who liked the protection an intelligent, homogenous group seemed to give.

I climbed the worn marble stairs to the second floor. On one side of my office was a one-chair hair salon, with the waiting room—two wrought iron chairs with plastic cushions and a stack of ten-year-old Cosmopolitans—in the hallway. I never saw anyone waiting, or anyone inside for that matter. The sign on the door said, "Back in ten." On the other side was a new store, *Grand Opening*, which catered to "women's sexuality." The curtains were drawn across the windows. By the time it dawned on me which grand opening they were talking about, I had already signed the lease.

A Russian Countess who did facials and depilatories was the previous tenant of my office. Her sign said "by appointment only" and since the phone company had to install a phone jack for me, I guessed she hadn't been over-booked. The landlord, an ancient Hasidic Jew, gave me a break on the rent for leaving her lettering on the door. "In case she comes back," he told me. "I think she will come back." I fantasized that he was in love with her, and agreed to keep Madame Kabalevsky's name on the glass. What the heck, a hundred bucks a month is a hundred bucks. That would almost make the car payments on my BMW affordable.

The place was old, but the locks were strong, so naturally I was surprised to see Dick pacing inside my office. I hadn't bothered to get a secretary because I found I could do the work faster than I could explain it and besides, it was an expense that I was willing to forego at least until I paid off my law school debts. Of course, at the slow rate I was building my business, I might be secretary-less well into middle age.

Regardless, I didn't have a secretary, so when I'm not there, the office is locked. I had never given Dick a key. He was showing off.

I strode past him and slid my briefcase onto the desk, causing a whirlwind of papers to float up and glide gracefully to the floor at his feet, where I left them.

"What do you have?" I asked.

He pursed his lips. "Why didn't you call?"

"Why should I call?"

"I've been beeping you all morning. Your phone was turned off."

I felt myself turn red and reached in my briefcase to check my beeper. I had turned it off and had forgotten to turn it back on. Surreptitiously, I pushed the button.

"And you think I'm a technophobe," he sounded pleased to have caught me in a Luddite act.

"Okay, okay, so you got me. I'm here now. What is it?" I pointed to a seat and indicated that he should sit down. His nervous energy was annoying me.

He sat down and pulled a leather mini-notebook out of his breast pocket. It was a miracle that he maintained such a sleek line with all the junk he carried in his pockets. "Stone Stubbs has been taking options on waterfront property," he said.

"Old news." I pulled the bagel out of my briefcase and held it up in the air. "Want to try a peanut butter and chocolate bagel? You can be part of a test group."

He looked at me disdainfully. "I've already eaten breakfast."

"So have I." I broke the bagel into bite-size pieces and started feeding them to Devil Dog.

Dick looked away in disgust. "Stone has called a press conference for this afternoon. I think it has something to do with the waterfront development."

"Why is that so important to everyone?"

"Legacy to the family name. Money, of course."

I snorted. "Legacy." The idea sounded funny to me. My family's idea of a legacy was hot dog sauce. "Did they find that tape?"

Dick shook his head. "Fingerprints on the tape deck weren't useable. Ines said the night nurse used the tape player to try to get a feel for real English."

"So she got scared enough to run away, but remembered to take her English tape with her? Puhlease."

"So where is this nurse? Who hired her?"

"Friend of Ines. Apparently she moved, and even Ines can't find her."

"Why don't the cops just try to find her themselves," I said, disgruntled.

"This might interest you," Dick said. "LePage was having an affair with Carlton to insure that he wouldn't do anything to jeopardize Sarah's inheritance."

"I thought LePage liked girls."

He shrugged. "She was using him. Same as he was using her."

I munched on a piece of the sweet dough. The chocolate and peanut butter had jelled into more distinctive flavors. I would tell Max tomorrow. "And?"

He got up. "I told her we would see her in," he looked at his watch. "An hour."

I gathered up my things and led him out the door. "Where is she living now?"

"Where do you think? In *their* house."

"Not 23 Louisburg Square," I said. "They don't think that belongs to them, I hope."

"They do. She said Carlton promised it to her."

"Is that true? Does she have it in writing?"

"Afraid so."

I was sorry to hear that. I was starting to like LePage. Being the beneficiary of a large bequest makes you an automatic suspect, when the death is a murder. Dick preceded me to the door.

"What about Sarah? She confessed to the murder. As LePage's wife, or whatever, she can't benefit from the murder. Even if technically their marriage is illegal because they're the same sex."

"Sarah recanted. I told you she would. She said she thought LePage did it to get out of the affair with her father. In the heat of the moment she confessed to save LePage."

I groaned. "Where does that leave us?"

I closed the door behind us and stepped out of the way of a young woman heading into the *Grand Opening*. She was slightly built, had curly black hair gathered in elastic, and wore black-rimmed metal glasses. I craned my neck to see around her into the store, but the door slammed behind her before I could get a good look.

"You should just go in sometime," Dick said.

"What? Oh, I was just curious. So, oh yes. Where does that leave us?" I mused aloud. I couldn't figure out what this all meant for Matilda until I got a copy of the Trust agreement.

"You want a copy of the Trust agreement?"

Sheepishly, I held out my hand.

We walked a few feet and I turned around. "Oh," I said, smiling sweetly. "Be a dear and lock the door."

A tour bus, engine idling, blocked the entrance to Louisburg Square. The driver sat at the wheel while a crowd of German tourists wandered around the square, taking photographs of the historic neighborhood and reading about the points of interest in their guidebooks. They all seemed to be wearing green suede.

"Excuse me," a middle aged woman asked in tortured English, "where does Robin Cook *wohnen*?

"*Nichts 'wohnen*', 'live'!" a younger man interrupted her.

"Yes, I mean *lif*."

The woman looked pleased to have gotten the question out and even more pleased when Dick gave her the directions in German. The group followed her like baby ducks after their mother as they went to gawk at the Robin Cook residence. They politely stepped over the yellow police tape that was torn and thrown into the shrubbery at the foot of the stairs of number 23.

"Since when do you speak German?" I asked Dick.

"I was stationed in Heidelberg in the seventies," he said, while stepping over a few plastic bins and into the open door. He didn't elaborate. I followed him in.

Stacks of plastic Rubber Maid containers filled with stuff wrapped in disposable diapers and bubble wrap lined the hall.

"Hello!" I yelled. The house had an echo-y empty sound. Our heels resounded like hammers on the parquet floor. Off in another room, I could hear K.D. Laing on a tinny boom box.

No one answered so we walked around the first floor until we heard voices in the dining room. We entered in time to see Sarah and Ines pulling on a silver samovar which had griffin wings for handles. The spout came out of the griffin's mouth. The griffin looked on indifferently as the two women tussled for control in a swirl of black and red hair.

"Give it to me, you little bitch!" Sarah said, trying to overpower the smaller woman. She was breathless with the effort. "I should call the cops on you. Thief!"

"Who's the thief?" Ines screamed. "I earned this. I clean up the old man's poop. What right do you have?"

"I'm family."

"A family of dykes and sickos," Ines said.

They gripped the monstrosity between them, like partners in an exotic dance. Sarah suddenly let go and Ines went flying into the wall still clutching the hunk of metal. I winced. She lay on the floor, stunned. Sarah wasn't finished yet. She grabbed a candlestick and brandished it over Ines' crouching figure, when Dick intervened. He wrested the candlestick from Sarah's fist.

"That's enough, ladies," he said, emphasizing the last word.

Ines was still dressed in a nurse's uniform, even though her patient was dead and even though Dick had discovered through a records check that she had no nursing training whatsoever. At least she wasn't certified in the United States. She held the samovar close, looked at us through suspicious, black eyes then scurried away with her loot.

Sarah started to follow her then gave us a sheepish squint. "Oh, fuck it!"

"You should wait until the estate's been through probate," I said. "Until they rule it's yours."

"It's mine all right," Sarah said, carefully bubble wrapping the candlestick she was about to hammer Ines with. "You saw the letter Daddy gave LePage," she nodded at Dick. "Anyway, I'm the only one around here who knows what this stuff is worth. That little bitch will just trade it for spare change. Who should have something? Someone who knows the worth of a beautiful object or someone whose tastes are so crude they would melt it for its metal content?"

"Ownership has nothing to do with either of those," I said. "It's about legal possession."

LePage stepped in front of Sarah, who ran from the room. "And possession is nine-tenths of the law. You think I'm a fucking idiot? If I don't have this stuff in my grubby paws, you think some pink judge is going to hand it to *moi*? Right! And it is mine. Carlton gave it to me. We had a deal. Believe me, I earned every fucking square inch of this house. That bastard was a p-i-g."

I caught a look of self-righteousness. The house alone was worth more than four million in the current real estate market.

"Have the police been here this morning?" I asked, suddenly curious that the place wasn't crawling with them.

"Of course they were here. They put that fucking yellow tape across the door. What kind of idiots would think that plastic tape would keep anybody out. Give me a break."

I had known tough babes like LePage. Getting through to them was a royal pain in the ass. You either had to disarm them with kindness or bully them with legal muscle. I decided to try a little tenderness.

I sat down on a metal folding chair, the Empire dining room chairs having been taped together and stacked in a corner. "When did they release Sarah?" I asked.

"About six this morning. They had her at the station all night, rubber hosing her. They wouldn't even tell her I was in the station, wanting to tell her I didn't do it, so she could just tell the truth and get her butt home. I didn't think to call a lawyer. I never think of lawyers. No offense." She nodded to me and continued, "They were just so damned pleased to have their little murderess all wrapped up in a neat little package, they didn't even check the evidence. Assholes."

Dick nodded.

"What are you going to do with this stuff?" I asked.

"Get it out of here. Try to sell it. Sarah's going to get screwed so she's trying to grab what she can."

"Doesn't she trust her mother to do the right thing?"

LePage snorted. "Would you? This whole family is too cold for me. Especially her own father. He treated her as if she didn't exist. You know what I think? I think she was jealous of my affair with Carlton because it seemed to her that I was just one more person he loved more than her." She looked down at her hands, as if ashamed of her involvement with Carlton. "Sometimes, I think he wanted me just because he knew it would hurt Sarah. He never had any intention of making good on his promise."

"He gave you a note."

"A fucking piece of paper. You said so yourself. What a bastard.

I haven't seen one person come in this house who wasn't as needy as a flea on a dog. Look, no one came here to chat about the Red Sox. They were all after his money."

"Including you?"

"I'm after his daughter," she laughed. "But if she comes with a dowry I'd be a damned fool to throw it away."

"You think love is different in this part of town?" I asked, almost as a joke.

"Damned straight it's different. For all their money, no one cares around here. No one's come over with a casserole or condolences or any other damned thing since Carlton died. They think it don't mean nothing to lose a father, even if he was the prick of the fucking universe. They think we aren't human or something. Well, they're the ones who aren't human."

She wasn't going to get an argument from me on that one.

"But," she continued. "I don't think anyone in the family killed old Carlton. Every one of them hated him, yes. But he cast a hypnotic spell over them. It's hard to explain. It would be hard to kill someone you're in awe of."

"You think he committed suicide?"

"I can't see it. But despite everything, I didn't know him that well."

"How did you meet Sarah?" I asked.

"At Fort Jackson. She was a recruit. I was a DI."

"Drill Instructor?"

"That's right."

"But you're not anymore?"

"Right again. Someone asked and I told." She laughed. "Threw away thirteen years for that girl."

"What was she doing in the army anyway? It's kind of unusual, isn't it, for a girl like Sarah to join the Army?"

LePage nodded. "Every now and then you meet one like Sarah. A rich bitch who wants to try it on her own."

"There are easier ways," I said, thinking of glamorous jobs in auction houses or jewelry stores that always needed women with the breeding of a Sarah Stubbs.

"But none as definite." She leaned forward and told me that Sarah was just another raw, unformed recruit to her when she met her. "I didn't think much about her one way or another," she said.

"She was cute, sure, but all nineteen year old girls are cute. I never lost sleep over any of them, even if I am the way I am. I'm cool."

She told me she didn't think about her until one night she was in a bar in Columbia, having a drink, when she heard a rumble in the pool room: furniture cracking, raised voices. LePage wandered in to check out the trouble and saw some brothers giving a female recruit a hard time. The recruit was Sarah. She wasn't supposed to be off base, and LePage was about to call the MPs when she heard enough of the argument to figure out what was happening. Sarah had bet on her pool game. "She would bet on anything, even if the sun would come up. And if you gave her good odds," LePage said, ruefully, "she would bet against the fucking sun." She had run out of money and had promised sex to the boys to pay off her gambling debts. She was having second thoughts, however, at pay-off time.

"I inserted myself," LePage said, pulling up her impressive torso, showing off her overwhelming six-foot stature. In some ways, a magnificently large woman is even more intimidating than a man, because of her sheer unexpectedness. The taboo against women in combat always seemed shortsighted to me. There were some women I would welcome at crunch time, and some men I wouldn't trust to pull their weight in a mosquito attack.

LePage continued. "I knocked a few heads together and got Sarah out of there before the MPs came. It was the first time I knew her name was Sarah. I'd always known her as Stubbs. When I called her Sarah, something just clicked in me. I felt myself going soft on her, even though I knew it was against every reg in the book. Especially against my better judgment. Anyway, I got us out of there and we went to my apartment to have some coffee and a little chat. I knew I should have called the MPs. But I didn't. I was in over my head. I could only go one way once I invited her back for coffee."

"So," I said, "You send her back to post, get someone to tuck her in and that's the end of it."

"Life ain't that simple. Maybe yours is, but mine sure ain't."

I looked down at Devil Dog who even for an animal was predictable. It was true, my life was simple. My biggest complication was whether to go with peanuts or walnuts on that chocolate sundae. I had the sudden, unwelcome insight that my love-affair with food was a substitute for the real thing. Real life is messy and full of uncontrollables. I never met a man who acted the way I wanted, who never made any demands. One of the big reasons I became a lawyer was I wanted a sense of control in life. Of course, it soon became apparent that the law was every bit as unreliable as a man—or a woman for that matter.

"You didn't know she was rich?" I asked.

"Oh, I figured she had something. That's not why I fell for her, though, don't think it was."

"But now you have it all. Or so you think," I said.

"There's no thinking involved. We have this place. Signed, sealed and dee-livered." She got up. "And now, unless there's something pressing you want to talk about, I have work to do."

"You crossed a police line," I said, "And you're basically pillaging a murdered man's house. Are you prepared to take responsibility for the consequences?" I would be responsible myself if I didn't warn her of the legal morass she was stepping into.

"I'll tell you what," LePage said, showing me and Dick to the door, "Tell me how much that bitch Matilda is paying you and I'll double your fee to represent me."

I paused for a minute, thinking that, even if it were unethical, it would enable me to get a secretary. I recovered from my reverie, but it was too late. LePage had seen the moment of hesitation on my face. She threw her head back and laughed, a big throaty laugh.

"Watch that yellow tape, you don't trip on it," she called at us, right before she slammed the door.

Dick's tan Taurus was illegally parked by the entrance of the L Street Gym where Stone Stubbs' press conference was taking place. I tucked in behind him, rummaged through the Mounds Bars in the glove compartment to find a sign that enthusiastically endorsed the local fire department, stuck it on the dashboard and followed the crowd inside.

The gym is a former South Boston bathhouse that now houses weight rooms, saunas and steam baths. One side for men and a separate side for women. It's on the beach and instructors occasionally move a yoga or aerobics class outside to enjoy the weather and the view.

The gymnasium was humid with sweating bodies on aluminum folding chairs. Thankfully, there was no smoking allowed, or I would have lit up immediately. I scanned the room and found my uncles. Dick was sitting between them. I climbed over legs, saying "Hi there!" to the many people who knew me and finally plopped in an empty seat in the row in front of my men.

"Quite a turnout," I said.

"It's not every day that you get a say in forces greater than yourself," Uncle Joe said.

Uncle Stevie rolled his eyes. "What makes him think this is going to be any different than before is beyond me. He still won't be able to get along with anybody." He leaned forward and whispered loud enough for Joe to hear. "He doesn't understand that he has to get along with people."

"I can get along with Stone. It was that prick Carlton I couldn't stand. It's different now that Stone is involved. It takes a lot of guts to come back to a place that has nothing but unhappy memories. A lot of guts."

I wanted to tell him that Stone was the one who walked out on Matilda, but attorney-client confidentiality sealed my lips.

"There's money here. Of course he's going to come back." Uncle Stevie looked at me and pointed at Joe. "He thinks Stone's going to give away the store because of a few unhappy memories? That's why he ain't successful."

They sat back in their chairs, arms folded over their chests. Dick nodded at me. Someone was tapping on the microphone, and everyone's attention turned to the front. There were an extravagant number of American flags stuck on the podium and in the rafters, too, for that matter. But since 9/11 that didn't seem unusual. Everything was draped in the flag, even a private redevelopment project. Camera crews from the local television stations trained their equipment on the speaker. A reporter from the *Boston Herald* was chatting up a pretty local woman with a really big butt.

Solly O'Brien, owner of three bars in the neighborhood, was at the podium. "Let's get started, ladies and gentlemen. It's a pleasure to see you all today," he said. "We'd like to thank Stone Stubbs for being here tonight." He turned to the back door where Stone and a man in a dark suit had slid in. Matilda, dressed in a navy blue suit, fushia blouse and a matching, veiled hat, walked in behind them.

"Carlton's wife?!" Uncle Joe said.

Stone nodded to the crowd, to Matilda, and took a seat next to the podium. The bodyguard stood by the door. Like Stone, he was expensively dressed, but had the air of a secret service agent.

Solly said a few words, but no one was really listening. Everyone was examining Matilda and Stone, whom no one had seen since he left Boston 23 years ago. He looked at the crowd, smiled and nodded when he saw a familiar face. Goosebumps rose on my arm when I thought that this was exactly what Carlton would have looked like.

Stone went to the podium. He grasped it on either side and looked at the audience for a long while. Finally he spoke. "It's good to be back in Boston," he said. "Although I wish the circumstances of my return were more pleasant."

A sympathetic murmur went through the crowd.

"Thank you. Well, let's get down to business. The time is right to do something with the harbor. My brother thought so. And with the exception of a few Fenway fans, you all think so, too."

Laughter went through the crowd. Probably most of the people here were promised concessions or something, like Uncle Stevie. Or had sold options on their property, like Uncle Joe.

"But friends, it's time we did a lot of things in Massachusetts. We are known for doing things the same old way, but I'm here to suggest to you that it's time for a change. Why, for instance, do we need a Senate and a House in State government? We aren't the federal government. We aren't big government. The time has come to question everything."

Dick poked me in the back and whispered in my ear. "I can't believe it! He's going to announce for Governor!"

Stone went on for a few minutes in the same vein. The reporter from the Boston Herald snapped out his cell phone, talking excitedly. The television crews moved in closer. People stood to get a better look. While it was common for politicians to change locale to increase their chances of success, usually they left Massachusetts to do it, not the other way around.

Stone turned to Matilda, who joined him at the podium. He kissed her cheek and they raised their clasped hands overhead. After a beat, the crowd applauded, then were on their feet cheering. Stone kissed Matilda again and she looked up at him with adoration. I felt a hollow, gnawing sensation in my gut.

I got up to leave, gave a thumbs up to Uncle Stevie and Uncle Joe and tapped Dick on the shoulder. He turned in his seat and scanned the room. "The timing is kind of funny."

"Lots of stuff here is funny. I got to run, I have an appointment."

"You mean a date."

I scowled, not wanting to admit that I did not. "Let me know what happens."

Chapter 4

Just Because I'm Wearing Garters and Carrying a Whip, Doesn't Mean I'm a Dominatrix

I felt like I had been asleep for five minutes when the ringing telephone woke me up. It was Matilda.

"She's a barracuda," Matilda said. "And probably not the last one we're going to see either."

"Who's a barracuda, Mrs. Stubbs?" I forced an eye open and looked at my clock radio. It was midnight.

"She claims that Tucker owes her a lot of money. It's probably the other way around."

"Mrs. Stubbs, *who*?"

"Ulrike."

"Ulrike Meiner?" I was fully awake now. "What do you want me to do?"

"Find out what the bitch knows."

I sighed. "This isn't exactly my field."

"There'll be a little something extra in it for you."

I mumbled something about her having a nice evening and hung up. I had the awful feeling I was in way over my head with the Stubbs family. But when I told Dick about it the next morning, he was elated.

"The police have totally botched the investigation, this is our entrée to find out what she knows."

"Dick, we're protecting Matilda's financial assets," I reminded him. "Not investigating Carlton's murder."

"Same thing," Dick said. "Until the police find the murderer, Matilda doesn't get her hands on the Trust money. And you don't get paid."

We hung up and agreed that we would drive to the North Shore later to check on Ulrike, a prospect that didn't thrill me. I paced then forced myself to sit down. I rubbed my stone furiously, but still craved a cigarette. Devil Dog sat at my feet and I absently stroked his head so hard he yelped and ran away. Since Dick couldn't meet me for an hour, I grabbed my car keys to do what all stressed-out Americans do: go shopping.

Everybody has at least one vanity, and despite appearances, I do too. I'm vain about my feet: delicate size six and a halves, perfect instep—high enough for a graceful arch, low enough to fit into any shoe. I have no corns, bunions, calluses or other blemishes that would result from a normal life of walking, because I never walk anywhere. I drive. For a 30 year old woman, I have astoundingly low mileage on my soles. Just last year, I was approached by a scout, looking for foot models, in Prada's in New York City.

"The shape of the toes, the nail beds are," he looked at me reverently, "exquisite. They make any shoe even more beautiful. They are the reason we make beautiful shoes."

We sighed with admiration at the altar of my feet, but, while vain, I am easily bored, and couldn't imagine a career with people rouging and grooming my dogs for a photograph. In the end, the purpose of feet, no matter how resplendent, is to transport the rest of the body to interesting experiences. I passed.

But seeing the painter/Dominatrix wearing strappy stilettos reawakened the passion in me. I headed blindly to Neiman Marcus' shoe department, like an alien receiving a call from the mother ship to head home. In a white heat, I tried on every limousine shoe in inventory. I made up some story to the snooty clerk about why none of them were quite what I had in mind, before driving to the Discount Shoe Warehouse, to find something similar in my price range.

I wore them out of the store and sneaked admiring glances at the gas pedal, my foot nestling in its new shoe: black suede mules with cut black crystals edging the pointed toe.

"Watch where you're going," Dick said. "You almost hit that truck."

"Yeah, well, I didn't." I swerved widely into the left lane, and smiled calmly. I waved at the man driving the Poland Spring truck, who was shaking a fist at me.

We were driving up the coast along old Route One to the Dominatrix's house. As I said, we weren't exactly invited. Ulrike told me she could spare 15 minutes, and I could tell from the tone of her voice that she had a tight schedule.

While I drove, Dick filled me in on Ulrike Meiner's background. She came from Hamburg, Germany and her father was a rich banker, descended from a long line of merchants and financiers. Her specialty was whipping some of the biggest names in Boston black and blue. She graduated from the School of the Museum of Fine Arts the same year as Tucker.

"She was next to him in the graduation photo," I said. "Did you see? I guess the art thing didn't work out. Although the portrait she was painting of Carlton was pretty good."

"She was obviously painting from a photo," Dick pronounced. "Even you could do that."

"How do you know I don't have hidden artistic talent?" I asked.

"Do you?"

"No," I admitted and geared down as we neared her house in Manchester. "Hey, Dick," I said, trying to be nonchalant, "What's an odalisque?"

Dick looked at me a long moment, then burst out laughing. "That would be you, my dear. What kind of circles are you traveling in these days?"

I mumbled something about having read the word in a magazine and got out of the car.

"You stay here," I commanded Devil Dog. I was about to tie him to the door handle, then decided against it. He barked once at the ocean, then, satisfied that he had subdued that force of nature, lay down for a snooze.

Dick and I got out of the car, stretched and looked around. The house was a Gothic monstrosity on top of a cliff, which plunged straight into the sea.

"Looks like the Addams Family homestead," I said, as we stepped onto the front porch. "Think whipping those boys into shape is a profitable business?"

But before Dick could answer or I even had a chance to pull the handle of an old-fashioned doorbell, *Fräulein* Meiner herself yanked open the door. She wore a black chiffon dressing gown, concealing nothing. Her only other accouterment was a whiff of Paul Gaultier perfume and black heeled mules, suede with cut black crystals rimming the pointed toe. She looked down at my feet, a knowing smile curling the sides of her mouth.

"You're late," she said.

I blinked at my watch. We were 30 seconds late. She was certainly strict about time. She swept away from the door, gesturing that we should follow her into the surprisingly austere house. Despite the Gothic, forbidding appearance of the exterior, the effect inside was sterile and clean: white furniture against white walls. Amazingly clean. The floors shined, the mirrors, and there were lots of them, sparkled with reflected sea light. There wasn't even an hour's accumulation of dust on the glass coffee table. She must have a full-time cleaning staff, I decided. Why didn't my guidance councilor suggest this lucrative career path?

She went to the bar and pushed a button, opening the liquor cabinet. "A *trink*?" she asked.

Dick, I saw, was mesmerized. "Vodka," he said, as if in a trance. I had never seen him take a drink before. I snapped my fingers in front of his eyes to break the spell.

"And you?" she asked.

"The same. With Kahlua and Baily's," I added hastily, not seeing the point of alcohol without sugar coating. I saw a cigarette box on the bar. Since she was offering hospitality, I asked, "May I?"

She followed my stare. "A cigarette?"

I nodded.

"They are very bad for you," she said. "They are so *ungesund*. How do you say?"

"Unhealthy," Dick said, being helpful. "*Lassen Sie ihr nicht ein haben.*"

"*Sie sprechen sehr gutes Deutsch.*" She smiled at Dick and put the cigarette box into a drawer and locked it. I scowled and clutched my pebble.

"I cannot join you," she said, apologetically. "I *verk* today. I *verk* this morning. This afternoon. This evening. All the time *verking*." Her dyed raven hair fell to her shoulders. Her eyes shone the color of icebergs. She sprawled on a white leather chair, looking like a sleek black spider in the center of her gossamer web. "*Und* so now. What? You are a friend of Tucker's? And Carlton and his *vife* as well I think?"

"We appreciate your time, *Fräulein* Meiner," Dick said.

"'Ulrike,' please. This is America. Nobody calls me *Fräulein* Meiner except my clients. And they do it for their pleasure, not mine."

Dick smiled, and I had the ghastly thought that perhaps Dick was into this S&M stuff. Although Uncle Stevie had recommended Dick to me, I didn't know Dick at all.

"My client, Matilda Stubbs, was surprised to get your phone call," I said. "She wasn't aware that Tucker had any outstanding debts."

"Yes, Tucker owes me quite a bit of money," Ulrike said, spreading the wisps of her garment over the chair, gesturing for us to sit down.

"Do you have documentation?"

"*Nein*. We have a, how do you say it? A handshake."

"Handshakes don't hold up in court, Ms. Meiner," I said.

"I don't think I will see him in court. I think finally he will be pleased to pay me the money he owes me. But if he can't I'm sure his *Mutti* will have no problem giving me what her son owes me."

"Unless you have something in writing, Mrs. Stubbs has asked me to tell you not to contact her again."

"What is between me and her son is not in writing. She will pay, I *tink*, to have it stay between us. She is a public figure now, no? And she has a very naughty boy."

I gulped, remembering what I had seen at Tucker's Vermont farmhouse. "You're talking blackmail, Ms. Meiner?"

"I do not know this *wort*."

"How much do you think Tucker owes you, Ms. Meiner?" I asked.

"Forty two million dollars," she said, in un-accented English.

Dick and I looked at each other. It was Tucker's share of The Trust.

"You know," I said, "that the police aren't sure that Carlton's death was a suicide. Until that matter is cleared up, nobody is going to get any of Mr. Stubbs' money."

"The police," Ulrike smiled and waved an arm around. "They were here this morning. Two detectives. They were very interested in my work."

She had this look as though more than police business was conducted during their visit. The thought that our men in blue could want to add black to their blue was repulsive, like picturing your parents having sex.

"And so you...talked...to them?"

"*Ja*, we talk. We talk and walk. I show them the house. Would you like to see the house?" She got up suddenly. I could see she was getting bored with the meter turned off, watching us sip our drinks and wasting time when she could be *verking*.

Dick was up before the sentence was out of her mouth, and we practically ran after her as she pointed out room after room: each one whitewashed, all furniture polished and cleaned. It didn't seem like a den of sordid sex fantasies. It was more like an advertisement for a house cleaning service. I was vaguely disappointed.

When I thought the tour was over, however, we walked through the kitchen where she yanked open a door, revealing a dark abyss. A gamey smell wafted up. "*Und* the basement." She didn't snap on a light, but took a kerosene lantern from a hook and snapping a Bic (from God knows where, there was no place to hide anything in her clothing) lit it, held it slightly above her head, and descended, on moaning stairs, into the belly of the beast.

I thought it would be like the basement of Tucker's house, where he was tied to a hook on the ceiling. But this basement was divided into what looked like storage bins with wooden bars. Padlocks and chains were wrapped around each gate. Hay was strewn around the floor as if animals lived there. The place stunk.

"What on earth..."

"My clients have special needs," Ulrike said. "They stay here overnight to atone for their sins."

"People stay here?"

I looked at Dick to see if he were as shocked as I was, but he looked interested, not amazed.

"Their sins," Ulrike repeated. "Something must be done."

"What sins?"

Devil Dog had somehow found his way into the house and to the basement door. He scratched at the doorpost, sniffed at the top of the stairs then jumped down, his elongated body lurching comically, to join us. Ulrike, forgetting her position as Mistress of the Domain, smiled and picked him up.

"*Kleiner, süsser Hund!*" She laughed, hugging the dog to her. She went to one of the cells and took a dog dish that contained water, washed it carefully and refilled it with fresh water before setting it on the floor for Devil Dog to drink.

Devil Dog lapped the water happily, occasionally licking the Mistress's hand. Jealousy stabbed my heart. Hey, I thought, I'm your mistress! Well, not that kind of mistress. Maybe dogs couldn't tell the difference.

"So, what kind of 'sins' do your clients think they've committed?" I asked. "I mean, aren't they mostly CEOs of major Boston corporations?"

"Yes, Chief Executive Officers," Ulrike tsked. "But I am not their confessor. I only help them with penance."

She got out some dog treats from a big bag in the corner of the cellar and fed them to Devil Dog affectionately. Since I didn't see evidence that she owned a dog, I had to assume the doggie yum yums were for her clients.

"So, they come here to pay for their lifestyles? Is that what you're saying?"

"They come here to clear their consciences then go back to another day of 'business-as-usual'," Ulrike said.

I bent down and joined her in petting Devil Dog, who suddenly seemed blameless if only because he was an animal. I was about to say something, when I noticed a pegboard on the wall in the shadows. At first it looked like a tool board in any basement, where men hung power drills and hammers. But this one was lined with instruments of a different kind. A collection of cat-o-'nine- tails hung in brackets next to a ball with spikes, like I had seen in pictures of medieval torture. Two revolvers with ornately carved handles faced each other as if in a ghostly shoot-out. They framed a bare-spot with brackets where a pistol would fit perfectly.

"You're quite a handyman," I told her, getting up to take a closer look. "Some of these guys like rough stuff, huh? Guns too?'

Dick had noticed the missing gun as well. I could tell by the way his eyebrows raised and lowered.

Ulrike shrugged. "I try to bring my clients to the next level of pleasure."

"And pain?"

"Same thing." She pulled up a corner of the peignoir, which had slipped off her shoulder.

"Carlton Stubbs," I asked. "Was he at that level? The gun level?"

"He was an important man."

"That doesn't answer the question."

"Important men have higher levels."

Ulrike put the dog biscuits back in the bag and led us up the stairs, blowing out the lamp and closing the door firmly behind her.

"So they stay here and you…." I was trying to wrap up the whole sick scene.

"I lock them up, humiliate them, tell them what I think of their life. Then a little rough stuff, then…" Ulrike paused.

"Sex?" I prodded.

"No. Never that." Ulrike stalked through the dining room, the sparkling glass doors of the hutch reflecting the sailboats in the ocean. "Clean. I make them clean the house."

Dick stopped in his tracks, his eyebrows frozen halfway up his forehead.

We were almost at the door, when I asked, "When was the last time you saw Carlton? As a client, I mean."

"Long time. Now I just paint his portrait. I get the same fee for both. I support my poor mother in Stuttgart with the money."

The clock on the mantle chimed the hour, and Ulrike tensed, moving us politely, but firmly, towards the door.

"I have no more business with that family. Thank *Gott*."

"Not even Tucker?" I asked.

"Where is your little *Hund*?" she asked suddenly, looking around.

Devil Dog wasn't much of an explorer, but I didn't see him. "Devil Dog," I called. I heard a little yelp upstairs and I ran to get him. "He must have wandered upstairs," I said.

"Don't worry, I will find him," Ulrike said, pushing me out of the way and running up the stairs. We clumped up the steps in our twin mules, Ulrike turning once to give me a phony smile. "You can stay there. I will find him."

But I followed, simply because she didn't want me to. She headed to a door that appeared closed when we had made the tour. Behind the door was a red velvet curtain, heavy enough to keep smells and sounds inside. I pushed the curtain aside and followed her in. The wall was lined with three canvases, the smell of oil and turpentine telling me they were still wet. But they weren't portraits of CEOs. They were old-fashioned portraits and landscapes. They had a familiar look. Devil Dog yapped at a landscape.

"It's a hobby of mine," Ulrike said, picking up Devil Dog and wagging a finger at him. "Bad boy."

I smiled wide-eyed at her. "I don't know anything about art."

She handed me Devil Dog, pouring his long body into my arms. He licked my face, and I was reassured that he did indeed know who his mistress was.

"They aren't very good," she said.

We smiled blandly at each other. She wanted to believe I was as ignorant as I claimed, but then she looked down at my shoes. A frown formed on her face. The clock downstairs chimed the quarter hour, and she firmly pressed me down the stairs and out the front door.

"I have to *verk*. You're a *verking* girl, too," she smiled solidarity with me from the front door and waved to Dick who was waiting in the car.

I deposited Devil Dog in the back seat, where he immediately went to sleep, put the car into gear and drove off. We stopped at the end of the driveway to turn onto the road. I was about to tell Dick about the paintings, when a silver Lexus pulled in and tentatively drove up the long path to the house. I quickly donned sunglasses to hide while getting a look at the next victim. I couldn't imagine the executives I knew submitting to the punishment Ulrike prescribed for their crimes. The driver of the Lexus wasn't interested in me, and I got a good long look as he drove by. My mouth went dry.

"This is like Pandora's Box," Dick said.

We looked at each other and silently mouthed the name of the driver: Stone Stubbs!

I dropped Dick off near Coolidge Corner where his car was illegally parked. He drove a new tan Ford Taurus, the rear window plastered with Patrolmen's Benevolent Association and Mason decals like an undercover cop, so he was never ticketed or towed. He told me to buy one, so I could park unmolested. But driving a boring car was too high a price, in my opinion, for a safe parking space. Besides I had my glove compartment full of permits.

We agreed to cross-pollinate later in the day. Dick wanted to do a more extensive background check to see if any more skeletons populated Carlton Stubbs' over-crowded closet. Also, he wanted to check on the missing gun in Ulrike's collection. See if the cops had traced the registration of the gun tucked in Carlton's fist and if they found any usable prints on it.

And I needed to catch up on some other cases and clear my brain with some good old nasty divorces.

I called a young web-page designer, Marissa Thwaite, who was trying to create an amicable divorce with her soon-to-be-ex, Donald. Both of them had come to my office while I explained the necessary paperwork and coached them on the questions the judge would ask them if they were representing themselves *pro se*. They laughed a little and put their heads together while they completed the paperwork. Marissa had given me a four thousand dollar retainer, but I only used up half. Their lack of passion during the divorce convinced me they were doing the right thing. I found it sadder than the tales of plate throwing that were routine in my business.

I made that call then reviewed the financial disclosure papers for the non-contested divorce of the Humbolds. In a burst of stupidity, and despite his attorney, Milton Baum's, strenuous protests, Mr. Humbold, majority owner of the Marshfield nuclear power plant, was giving his wife of 35 years just about everything to fulfill his fantasy of eternal youth with a lover a third his age. The haste with which he wanted to rid himself of his wife deepened the insult of pronouncing his lust and renewed vigor "love."

"What about 35 years of devotion?" Mrs. Humbold had cried delicately into her linen handkerchief. "What about two children and a lifetime of memories? This wasn't love?" On my first visit to her house, she had photo albums on the sofa next to her, evidence that she had known love. By the second visit, she had ditched the albums and answered the door in a black leotard and ballet slippers. She had discovered therapeutic dance, other women just like herself, and was beginning to imagine a new life. She added several items to the list of things she wanted: boat, house, summer house, stock in the nuclear power plant.

"If it wasn't love, then I was a whore, right?" she asked, pliéing nicely on her toe shoes. "And whores get paid."

I finished up a letter to Milton Baum detailing Mrs. Humbolt's new requests, and thought about the Stubbses.

The afternoon dragged on, and I was no closer to the truth about who murdered Carlton Stubbs. But I was honing in on a truth about myself: I was lonely. Scrounging around the Stubbs' lives made me realize that my own consisted of walks with a chocolate-colored dachshund, double-headers at Fenway sitting between Uncle Joe and Uncle Stevie, and curling up in bed with a hunk of Nestlés bittersweet.

I left Dick a voice mail telling him I wouldn't be back. I fought my way through the hot wavy air thick with traffic exhalations and driver obscenities, across town to Mikey's garage. The reception area was deserted. Trish was across the street at Dunkin Donuts. I squinted and could see her through the big plate glass chatting to one of the women in pink behind the counter, sharing a cigarette and the gossip that fuels tiny neighborhoods.

Relieved that I wouldn't have to deal with her scrutiny, I stuck my head around the doorway leading into the garage. A Porsche 911 was on the lift. A tinny boom-box played Latino jazz, bass button turned way up. I couldn't see the head of the mechanic beneath the Porsche, but I could see his shirtless torso.

I coughed so I wouldn't startle him, and waited until he finished tightening a bolt before I approached. His head emerged from the bottom of the car and when he recognized me, his eyes became soft then concerned. He turned down the volume on his boom box.

"*Querida*," he asked, "What's wrong?"

"That's a beautiful car," I said, pointing to the Porsche. Tears filled my eyes then spilled over. The dam holding back my emotions gave way, even though I had no logical reason to cry. "It's beautiful that you can fix it, too."

He seemed at a loss as to how to cheer me up. His tongue flicked around his perfect white teeth then he smiled. "Tonight, I make a *pollo*, you know? A *pollo* with rosemary and lemon grass, like the Chinese. They make very good lemon grass *pollo*."

"I love *pollo*," I said, hoping it was chicken.

"And *arroz*. Delicious." He put his forefinger and thumb to this lips and made a kiss.

I wished he were kissing me and I could tell he was wishing the same thing. But he didn't move. He was probably too much of a gentleman and anyway didn't know how the *gringa* would take his advances. It wasn't unnecessary caution on his part. The dockets were full of assault cases in which the defendant (an immigrant) was sure the woman was saying "yes." And in his own culture, she may have been, but not in the U.S.A, where women had more options than "yes" or "no." Even though Hidalgo should have known by now what I thought of him, perhaps he was too shrewd to get involved with a *gringa*.

He looked as if he were struggling with himself, then suddenly hit the table that held his tools with his fist. They jumped and the resounding clang startled me.

"You come eat with me," he said. "Tonight."

"With you?" I looked down at the scribbled address he put into my hand. His greasy fingerprints were on it.

He held out his hands apologetically. "Please come. We are simple people, but I want to cook for you."

"We?" I asked, as he led me to the door and past the smirking Trish who had come back and had probably heard everything.

"Car on the fritz?" Trish asked. She tapped ash from her cigarette with a glued-on white frosted fingernail.

"No." I paused to inhale some of her smoke. "Everything's working just fine."

I rummaged in my closet for an hour, trying things on, throwing them on the bed. Nothing seemed right. It had been so long since I had a date, I didn't know what was appropriate. I pulled a red dress from the back of the closet and held my breath as I slipped it over my head. It still had the tags on. It fit, but I thought the red looked like too blatant an invitation. I finally put on a pair of black jeans, black sweater and my new mules, topping it off with red lipstick. It didn't matter how inviting my lips looked. I bent over and shook out my dyed dark hair until it achieved a suitably tousled look. I smiled at myself in the mirror, smacked my lips together, put some doggie treats in a dish for Devil Dog, and stopped at the liquor store for a bottle of red before heading to Dorchester.

Melville Avenue was a row of old wooden frame structures that was Irish a few decades ago. Before that the neighborhood was Jewish. Now mostly Haitians and Hispanics lived there, sometimes crowding three families into a unit that was meant for one.

I parked my car, activated the anti-theft device, clubbed the steering wheel, and pulled the FBI sign, gooey with melted chocolate, from my glove compartment and stuck it on the dashboard. Kids were playing stickball in the empty lot across the way. I watched for a minute. You never know where the next savior of the Red Sox will come from.

A group of men were gathered around a card table across the street, playing dominoes. I found the house, number 81, and as I checked my lipstick in the glass door, one of them let out a long wolf whistle. I smiled as I rang the buzzer and pouted my lips to greet Hidalgo when the door flew open and there was...Ines!

I stared, speechless. I looked down at the piece of paper with Hidalgo's address. I scootched my head around to recheck the number. It was 81. "I was looking for Hidalgo Gomez."

"Come in," she said, impatiently, "We are waiting for you." She flung open the door. The fire that had illuminated her face the last time I saw her at Louisburg Square was gone. Her hair, which she had previously worn in a tight braid, was loose and soft around her face. She was the "we" Hidalgo had referred to. My heart felt sick.

I followed her up the wooden steps. The paint had worn off revealing layers of different colored paint. The center of each step was bare wood. They creaked in a familiar way that made me feel oddly at home. The stairway was filled with the spices of foreign cooking; sweet and tart and sensual.

"I didn't know you and Hidalgo were..." I started to say, 'living together,' but I thought that might be insulting. Maybe she was his wife. Hidalgo was probably just being hospitable and kind when I obviously needed a friend. I was glad I hadn't worn anything more alluring. I would have felt even more foolish.

"Hidalgo is my brother," Ines said, opening the door at the top of the landing, revealing a table set for six, the loud chatter of Spanish, and delicious smells coming out of the kitchen. "He's in the kitchen." She shrugged then disappeared.

I stood in the doorway, blinking. Two older, heavy-set women sat on the sofa, smiling at me approvingly. They were twins. Only their dresses—same cut, different material--allowed me to tell them apart.

"*Un placer de encontrarle*," one said.

I smiled back. "Same here, I think."

They conferred, then one of them got up and said, "*Bonita! Muy bonita!*"

I blushed. I did know that word. "You too. You are very bonita too." I pointed at both their chests so they would get the idea.

They looked at each other, trying to decide what they thought of this, then laughed, showing their perfect teeth.

Hidalgo, wiping his hands on the bottom of an apron which read, "Please kiss the cook" came into the living room to see what was so funny.

"You are finally here!" he said, giving me a chaste kiss on the check, which sent the women into paroxysms of hilarity. "I see you met them," he said, indicating the women and leading me out of the room. He steered me into a screened-in front porch filled with mismatched garden furniture. An expensive 32-inch screen television was tuned to a soccer game on the Hispanic channel. An older man wearing a straw Panama, white shirt and suspenders sat on a squeaking glider, watching the game. He tipped his hat when I entered.

"*Bienvenido*" he said then went back to the game, frowning because he'd missed a goal.

"My father," Hidalgo said. "I'm sorry, he doesn't speak English."

"I don't speak Spanish." A deficiency I was determined to remedy as soon as possible. Already, I saw a life (my life!) taking shape: learning Spanish, dinners at the Gomez *hacienda*. Maybe going shopping with Ines. She might be a good ally. I hoped they liked dogs, because this vision included Devil Dog sprawling under the table, catching scraps beneath the embroidered tablecloth.

We went into the kitchen. Intoxicating aromas swirled over me. Hidalgo took the wine out of my hands, put it on the counter and circled me with his arms. He looked deep into my eyes then kissed me on the forehead. I sighed.

"Thank you for coming," he said, going back to work at the stove.

He sprinkled exotic spices on the two chickens, which were stuffed with lemon grass and roasting in the oven. He'd prepared rice and black beans and *ensalada* especially for me, because he said that Americans were crazy for *ensalada*. Maybe I wasn't the first *gringa* he had asked over for dinner. I let myself worry about this for a minute then forced myself to forget it. I decided to be happy to have a nice healthy start on my new life, which now included a diet and some rigorous exercise and another visit to the Russian. No one in the family smoked.

I helped Hidalgo place the food around the table. His father said a prayer in Spanish and we ate. The woman who pronounced me "*bonita*" was Hidalgo's mother. Ines and Hidalgo took care to translate everything for me, but after a while it didn't seem to matter. I was awash in the good feeling of their home. Everyone tasted the wine, politely, and thought it was not sweet enough. They didn't say it as a criticism, Hidalgo assured me, but so that I wouldn't waste my money on inferior wine. I swallowed the information that this inferior wine cost twenty dollars.

Dessert was a chocolate mousse and coffee—artfully poured from the mouth of the griffin on the Stubbs' samovar. I had a hearty serving of the mousse and demurred on the coffee out of respect for my client.

After dinner, Hidalgo's mother and aunt cleared the table, making a big fuss that I was not to help them, while his father went back to the television. I sat on the sofa with Hidalgo and Ines, who didn't find it strange that she was cutting in on my date. Maybe she was the chaperone.

Anyway, I wanted to know more about their family, but I didn't know what rules of etiquette to follow. Not knowing what constituted a personal question in Mexican culture, I thought I would stick to work.

"Now that Carlton Stubbs is dead, what will you do? I guess there are lots of sick people who need someone to care for them?" People always hired cheap labor under the table, even if they weren't certified or licensed, like Ines.

Ines snorted and pulled herself up proudly. "Sick people disgust me. I am a school teacher."

"I didn't know." And I had thought Ines was illiterate. I glanced at Hidalgo for support, but he was peering around the corner to see the soccer game. There wasn't much difference between cultures after all. "I didn't mean to insult you, but you were taking care of Carlton Stubbs and…"

"I couldn't get a job in the school district last year, so that was all I could find. I am not certified to teach in Massachusetts. The Teacher's Union. Bah."

"There are private schools," I said.

"I don't want to teach in private schools. I want to teach my own people. I want to tell them the truth."

"The truth about what?"

"The history of this country. The history you teach in schools is all lies."

Hidalgo looked over from the soccer game and groaned. "Oh, no. Don't get her started."

"You think everything is fun in this country," she hissed at her brother. "You think because you have big job and big car and Anglo girlfriend everything is fun. You find it easy to forget that the Anglos stole from us and now we have to start again with nothing."

"Ines, we are here now. We work hard and make a life. What else can you want? You are just a silly woman." Hidalgo rolled his eyes and went back to the game, suddenly yelling with his father when their team scored a goal.

He hadn't contradicted the "Anglo girlfriend" part. That was hopeful. In Latin households, you have to be approved by the entire family before you can be friends with one member. I held out my hand to her. "Maybe we can get together sometime. Do something. Do you like to shop?" She was wearing Sigrid Olsen jeans. Everyone has a vanity.

"Yes, of course. Copley Square Mall. I love it."

Sisters under the skin.

Ines narrowed her eyes. "Have they decided who gets the Stubbs' money?"

Her question surprised me. "The Stubbs' money is tied up in a Trust. They can't distribute any of his assets until they find out who killed him."

"What's the difference, eh? He's dead." She looked at me slyly. "I cleaned his poop. I should get something. A lot, I think. You're a lawyer. You can make that happen."

Ines looked at her watch and, before I could answer, she stood up. She said she had a date and hurriedly left the apartment. I exhaled.

Hidalgo and I talked a little more then I got up. I had an early reveille.

I waved good-bye to the "Bonita Twins" and Hidalgo walked me to my car. Slowly, obviously not wanting the evening to end any more than I did, he played with my hand. Not quite holding it, but teasing me. I could feel the heat radiating from him.

"My sister," he said, "she is very political, you know. A little crazy." He laughed. "She's going to a fund raiser for Señor Stone Stubbs tonight at the Sheraton."

"Ines...to a fund raiser?" Maybe she was going to try a get a job with Stone.

"She acts like we are royalty. Our family had money once, yes." He shrugged as if it meant nothing. "But life changes. Nothing stays the same forever. My sister does not understand this. She thinks because our family was rich once, that now we are owed something. I do not think we are owed anything."

He picked up my hand and kissed the palm. "You are very beautiful." He released my hand and opened the door. "Your little dog," he asked, "where is he? Next time, you bring him here. My father loves dogs."

I smiled. There would be a next time. I took the club off my steering wheel, put the FBI sign back in the glove compartment, and waved once out the window like a glamorous woman in a foreign movie. I gunned the engine and watched him in the rear-view mirror watching me drive down the street.

He called after me. "Next time, I make crowned *cordero*. Next time, *Querida*! Hey, do you like *cordero*?"

"Yes, of course," I shouted back, not knowing what it was.

The concierge was asleep, so he missed my surplus good humor. A pale blue envelope was stuck in my mail box slot. With a stupid smile still plastered on my face, I pulled it out and opened it. Cut-out letters from the newspaper were glued on the same blue paper as the envelope. The message read: "I'M WAITING FOR YOU."

Chapter 5

When the Going Gets Tough....The Tough Go Shoe Shopping!

The day was typical Boston Summer: high 90's, humidity high enough to grow mildew on an oyster cracker. My pantyhose kept me from sticking to the chair, but I felt like a kielbasa steaming at a cookout. I could go to the beach at Revere, but the thought of sand, sticky with discarded Creamsicle wrappers, sunk that idea. The only cool place would be on a boat about twenty-five miles out at sea. I closed my eyes and pretended I was on a whale watch, the cool air tangling my hair, huge whale flukes slapping the water, splashing my face with a refreshing mist.

"Swanson, are you even listening?" Dick asked.

I opened one eye just in time to see a drop of perspiration roll down my nose and splat on the notes that he'd placed in front of me.

"Jeez, Dick, you know how to ruin a good daydream."

"That's already more than I want to know, Swanson."

I gathered up the notes, giving him an evil look. It annoyed me that he managed to look cool in a sport coat and tie when the meteorological conditions were like a rain forest. Granted, the jacket was silk. "Breathable," he informed me, sneering at my polyester shirt-dress. "It's not a snob thing. Don't you want something that breathes on your body?"

I most certainly did not want things breathing on my body. Also, I didn't like feeling inferior to an ex-cop. When somebody disclaims the snob thing, you can be sure that's exactly what they are.

I threw his report back on the desk and sighed. It explained The Trust in greater detail. As I already knew, Stone was trustee for $125 million, to be given to Carlton when he demonstrated "business acumen" or after 25 years had passed. Carlton had repeatedly petitioned to have his inheritance released, and Stone had relentlessly refused. Carlton claimed he was operating at a disadvantage until he had some real money to invest. Stone countered that Carlton had run through the $25 million that their father had given to him outright, as well as going through a substantial amount of Matilda's money. All on questionable business deals. Just like Matilda had told me.

"There's something I didn't put in the report," Dick said.

I leaned back in the chair. "Are you going to tell me, or make me guess?"

Dick sneaked a quick look at the wire mesh glass on the door to make sure no one was standing outside. "This is pretty confidential."

"Aren't you on my dime?"

Dick considered this then said, "Stone filed a paternity suit, claiming that Tucker is his son."

I sat up. "Wow! When was this?"

"A week before Carlton was murdered."

"Oh my God. Who told you this?"

"Bunny O'Reilly."

"Right." I hadn't told Dick much about Bunny, so it surprised me that he had taken the initiative to talk to her. I fingered the file. "Why now? Why not when he was born?"

"I guess Stone needs a nuclear family for his political career. Funny he didn't pick up one of his own somewhere along the line."

"Yeah, funny."

Dick nodded at me. "You can't prove paternity with identical twin fathers."

"Well, then it's a moot point."

"Not exactly. Bunny found letters that Matilda sent to Stone from when they were having their affair. Bunny claims they're pretty explicit."

"About Matilda being pregnant with Tucker?"

"No, about them being in love. They don't actually say Stone is the father."

"How did Bunny get ahold of them?"

"They were in Carlton's safe. He probably had a private dick investigate Matilda somewhere along the line. Don't know why I didn't hear about it. Milton Baum probably hired an out-of-state pro." He smiled admiringly.

Anyway, it had been five days since Carlton was shot, and the police still didn't have enough evidence to make an arrest. The tape hadn't been found. They were still floating the suicide theory. This enraged Matilda, the beneficiary of a multi-million dollar life-insurance policy that contained a big ugly suicide clause. It didn't amuse me either. Matilda had promised me "a little something extra" to expedite the insurance matter.

"Well," I said, "Our concern is Matilda. She is our client. We just babysit this murder investigation and see that she gets her share of The Trust money…"

"There's more, Swanson."

"What?"

"There's no money in The Trust. Stone drained it."

I gulped. "Stone stole 125 million dollars?"

"All of it."

"For what?"

"He's a compulsive gambler."

"Like Sarah?"

"He plays in a different arena. He threw in with George Soros when Soros invested in Russia. He lost the 50 million he borrowed to invest in that. To cover that loss, he borrowed 50 million and sold short on a series of tech stocks."

"That was a good decision," I said. "Everyone I know lost money in tech stocks."

"Yeah, but he was a year too early. He lost that. He borrowed the remainder to buy tech stocks, but then he was too late."

"How does he think he's going to cover it?"

"Well," Dick said, "He's probably investing in something else right now to cover it."

"Like what? Everything's losing money right now. Except real estate." I blinked. "You think the waterfront?"

"Exactly."

"You sure about this?"

He nodded.

Dick could go places an attorney couldn't. I knew from contested divorces we had worked on before that he had a network of moles in the various financial institutions around town. I sighed. Matilda would have to be told.

As if reading my mind, Dick said, "I say we wait, Swanson. If we let on how much we know, whoever killed Carlton will start blowing smoke in our faces."

"You think Stone?"

"I don't *not* think Stone, let's put it that way."

I watched him leave the office, his silk blazer and trousers unwrinkled, revealing nothing.

"We'll cross-pollinate later," I yelled after him. I reached for the pebble then remembered it had lost its power. I had kept it together, but now I began to hyperventilate.

The Russian said when I needed nicotine, to visualize myself someplace beautiful. I closed my eyes, tried to catch a breeze from the fan and recapture my whale watch fantasy. I saw myself quite clearly on the whale watch boat—smoking.

I opened my eyes and saw the picture, left on the wall by Madame Kabalevsky, of Twiggy, a fashion model from the late sixties. Twiggy was tied to a tree with an apple on her head. I don't know why I never took it down. It was faded to a ghostly blue and magenta. Dick, who was actually sentient in the sixties, claimed that Twiggy started the craze for skinny women. "Hips," he said, "have never been popular since." I got up, took it off the wall, and threw it in the trash basket. In its place I put my law degree from Boston University. I admired it, then took the picture of Twiggy out of the trash and stuck it in my bottom desk drawer. "Just in case Madame Kabalevsky comes back," I said aloud.

I hung around, waiting for the mail. A few checks were overdue. The box was stuffed with junk: a Pottery Barn catalogue, Stop and Shop circular. I was relieved as I almost expected to see a sister note to the one I found the previous night at home. I hadn't told Dick about the note. I didn't want him to see my fear.

I dropped Devil Dog at Max's Deli, which was air-conditioned, then took the Green Line to Fenway to wait for Uncle Stevie. I was glad to be going to a game. My brain was about to explode. The Sox were playing the Yankees in a double header. I was early, so I ducked into Jack's Sport Shop on Yawkee Way. Jack was talking to a middle-aged man. A shoebox of old baseball cards lay on the counter between them.

"Roger Maris just doesn't bring much. I don't know why he wasn't as popular as Mantle. Do you have a Mantle?" He handed the card back to the man.

"But Maris broke the Babe's record."

"Look, I don't determine who's popular. I just know what I can sell, and I can't sell Maris. Look, try eBay. Or Becketts."

The man filed the Roger Maris card back in the shoebox and left in a huff. Jack shrugged and looked at me. "Still have that Mantle,

Swanson?"

I nodded. I owned a signed, rookie Mantle baseball card in mint condition. It was my prized possession, part of the baseball card collection I inherited from Uncle Stevie. The collection was intact, not because Stevie had foresight, but because my uncles lacked a resident female to police their packrat tendencies.

"Ready to sell?" Jack asked.

"I'm waiting for a rainy day," I said.

"I hear ya," Jack said. He turned to help another customer.

I met Uncle Stevie at the gate and we took our seats in the bleachers. A hapless Yankee fan was being heckled because he had the nerve to wear a New York hat. We bought root beers and hot dogs, then settled down to watch the Sox beat the Yankees 3-1. The Yankees were up one zip at the end of the seventh inning, but in the eighth, with two outs, Boston put 2 men on base and Manny Ramirez brought them home with a long double to the wall. That's what I love about baseball: the way one stroke can change everything. I had to leave before the second game. Uncle Stevie clucked disapprovingly. Pedro was pitching the second game. The Yankees were doomed.

I left Fenway reluctantly, thinking this might be one of the last times I got to enjoy a game in the ballpark, stepped back into reality and retrieved my phone messages. Matilda Stubbs had called and asked me to meet her in Harvard. I put the top down on my car and drove up.

I could hear the screaming before I turned off my car engine. High pitched female voices spewed ugly words above the sound of breaking dishes.

I ran through the vegetable garden (sprinkled with an elaborate three-hose system, despite the four-county water ban) and into the kitchen. Matilda brandished a knife with a three-inch wide blade. Bunny, in a bikini, was standing in front of her, trembling. A broken chair lay splintered on the floor between them.

"She's crazy," Bunny hissed in my direction. "Make her put that damned thing down."

I flipped my briefcase on the counter. "Put that thing down, Mrs. Stubbs," I said, coolly. "I would think you'd had your fill of knives."

Matilda snorted through her truncated nose. "That's why I pay you the big bucks, Swanson. You make me laugh."

"So far," I reminded her, "No one's paid me any bucks, big or otherwise." I had expected her retainer in the mail today, but it wasn't there. Not to mention "the little something extras" she used to tantalize me into doing her bidding. The biggest problem with rich clients was their blindness to the fact that some people lived for the check in the mail.

"Can't you call the police or something," Bunny said. "This woman wants to kill me."

"Not kill. Just rearrange. If you're going after what's mine, you should know what it feels like to be me." She lunged at Bunny with the knife.

Bunny screamed and ran from the room. Matilda sighed and threw the knife in the sink, where it clanged harmlessly.

"Where does that little bitch get off thinking she can waltz away with my home?"

I nodded, dreading her reaction when she found out Stone had waltzed away with the money in The Trust.

"What was she, a secretary? It was one of those do-it-yourself-will kits, too, that she downloaded from the Internet. Jesus. She could have had some class about it."

"Do you want me to call the police? She's trespassing," I said.

"No, no. It's not necessary." Matilda looked around nervously. "The publicity would be horrible." She put her head in her hands. "I have nothing against her really. In thirty years she's going to be in my shoes. We all end up in the same place. Except you working girls. You don't have time for men."

I swallowed hard. The thought of being alone and working in thirty years was dreary. "Are you scheduling a memorial service?" I asked.

"In a month. When the investigation is over."

Matilda was being pretty optimistic about police efficiency.

"Stone and I are planning it."

"Stone?"

"Why not? He's Carlton's brother." Matilda shrugged. "We're getting married as soon as the memorial service is over. We don't want a lot of publicity."

The scars around her face were beginning to fade, and if I squinted, I could see her as she wanted to be seen. "Matilda, probate can't proceed until we get this matter of possible suicide out of the way. Or find the murderer."

"I'm in no hurry," she said. "I have the houses. And my own money. Enough to live on until I am officially entitled to the insurance money and my share of Carlton's Trust. Some jewels." She twiddled with an intricate necklace.

"How much is that thing worth?" I asked, thinking she might have to pawn it eventually.

"About a hundred dollars. The original is in the safe. That's worth about 200 times this," she said absently. "But it wasn't suicide, Swanson. Carlton was too hateful to commit suicide. His last act was throwing broken glass in the street for me to walk on. I'm glad he's dead." She stuck her chin out defiantly and twirled her reproduction necklace.

"In the meantime..." I looked around the kitchen. The broken chair was part of a barricade between two halves of the kitchen. A coffee table and other chairs snaked through the dining room and living room, blocking things off. Curtains had been taken from the windows and tacked to the ceiling, partitioning the family room. Matilda and Bunny had divided the house just like Uncle Stevie and Uncle Joe.

"In the meantime?" Matilda asked.

I kicked the broken chair. "How long are you people going to live like this?"

The next day was another swelter. I walked Devil Dog, retrieved my phone messages and drove myself to one of the true class-blind events in Boston: the semi-annual Filene's Basement Bridal sale. Society scions and daughters of postal workers push against the doors waiting for the eight o'clock opening when thousands of bridal dresses go on sale. A bell rings, the doors unlock, and hundreds of women elbow their way past security guards to racks of famous designer gowns, grabbing armloads to try on over leotards. It's a great sporting event. Occasionally I would go as a friend of a bride. On this August day, I had no friends who were getting married. Yet I found myself in the size 12 aisle.

"That's too yellow for you," I advised a young woman as I grabbed a beautiful dress from her pile.

Her mother came out of nowhere and snatched it back, glaring at me. "It is not." She moved her daughter's pile of dresses to a safer location.

I tried on a simple ballerina dress with seed pearls accenting the skirt like water bubbling over a fountain. Breathtaking. I preened in front of the mirror and twisted to see the back. I felt someone watching me in the mirror. The hair raised on the back of my neck, but when I turned to get a better look, they were gone.

I peeled off the dress and looked at the price tag: one thousand dollars marked down from three. It was all silk and genuine pearls. Dick couldn't accuse me of polyester taste in wedding gowns. I put it back and wandered the aisles stepping over jeans and discarded bridal gowns. Everyone was engrossed in bridal gown frenzy. A finger poked me sharply in the back. I jumped.

It was Ines.

"What are you doing here?" I asked, relieved it was only her.

She sniggered. "What are *you* doing here?"

I blushed. "I was looking for shoes."

"Over there." She motioned to the other side of the basement, a sneer accentuating her overbite.

"Thanks."

I left quickly then drove to Brookline to pick up Devil Dog from Max, who encouraged me to stay for lunch.

"I have chili today. Not the wimpy chili they make over there," he pointed with disgust across the street to the Hammer and Pickle, the only bastion of communist vegetarianism on the planet. That they stayed in business was a tribute to Massachusett's liberal leanings. You had to plow through a lot of worn propaganda on the walls to locate the menus. But, it was worth it to get to their vegetarian chili.

"Let's see what you got," I said, taking a seat at the counter.

Max put a bowl in front of me, with a huge glass of ice water, and started banding bills at the register, while he waited for my pronouncement.

"Well, what do you think?" he asked, impatiently.

I took a spoon and plunged in. It was hot. Not too hot, but spicy enough to bring tears to my eyes. I resisted taking a drink of water, because I wanted to give the aftertaste a chance to kick in.

"Cumin?" I asked.

Max smiled. "Yeah. Cumin."

I closed my eyes. "Something else. Anise?"

He laughed. "Oy! What a palette!" He came over and leaned on the counter in front of me. "What do you think?"

"I think it tastes just like theirs."

He slammed the counter. "It's not just like theirs!"

"What's the difference?" I asked.

He hit his forehead with the palm of his hand. "Can't you tell? It has meat! Good All-American ground beef."

I picked through the beans, surprised. "Really? It's so spicy I couldn't taste the meat." I took another bite. "It's good though. Great. The meat angle is good. Lots of people are eating meat again."

"But it's like theirs?"

"Why don't you throw in a bagel?"

"You think I should?"

"I think you should. Absorb some of the spice."

Max looked thoughtful. "Stone Stubbs is coming to Brookline this week to give a speech. I thought I should have something special prepared in case he stops in. Do you think this is good enough? Maybe I should ask Connie."

"Yeah, ask Connie. How much do I owe you?"

"It's on the house. I liked having the dog here."

"No, really." I got up to leave and put a five on the counter, grabbed Devil Dog by the leash and headed for the door. "Tell me what Connie thinks about the bagel."

"Yeah." He smiled at me and looked at my bowl on the counter. "Hey, Swanson, you didn't finish it! You didn't like it!"

"I'm on a diet, Max. I loved it." The size 12 wedding gown had barely fit.

"Not you too," I heard him groan as Devil Dog and I jumped in the car and headed for South Boston to visit Uncle Joe. I wanted to give him equal time since I spend yesterday afternoon at the ballgame with Uncle Stevie.

As we drove up Broadway, I could see that the doors of both establishments were open. My Uncles claimed it was to entice customers with the smell of sauce and onions. I knew it was because they couldn't afford air-conditioning. I was sorry now I had pulled

Devil Dog from his comfy lair.

I gave Uncle Stevie a wave then popped into Uncle Joe's. I fought the blast from the fan and wedged myself onto a stool between two construction workers. Uncle Joe was rolling dogs on the grill with his bandaged fingers.

"I hear you had a date last night." He smiled and pulled a root beer out of the fridge.

"Better make that diet," I said.

He pulled out another bottle and set it in front of me with a straw. "It's true then."

"So I had a date. It's no big deal. Dinner with his family. A zillion chaperones."

"He's a nice boy, Mikey tells me."

I took a sip of the diet root beer. The taste of saccharine made my mouth pucker. "What's going to happen now that Stone is running for Governor?" I asked.

"Dinner with the family is not a small thing in that culture," Uncle Joe said. "It means he likes you a lot."

"Stone Stubbs? The Stubbs Pier project?" I persisted. "He has an option on this place. What's going on with that?"

Uncle Joe dished out a couple of dogs, which I put on the floor for Devil Dog.

"You have to eat something. You're going to starve yourself."

"I ate at Max's," I said.

Uncle Joe shrugged. "I got the money for the option. I should be happy with that. I was hoping to sell and get out of here, but I guess that's not to be."

I was dying to tell Uncle Joe that Stone had raided his brother's Trust, and there was no money to go ahead with the plans. "You don't think Stone is going ahead and developing Southie?"

"Why would a politician want to get his hands dirty with development? Especially before a big election?"

"What else did Mikey say about Hidalgo?" I asked, patting Devil Dog. He seemed thicker in the middle, a dangerous thing for a dachshund whose belly already skimmed the ground. "This is the last Swanson Dog for you, pal," I said stroking him on the head.

"He acted like he was doing us a big favor, coming in here, throwing his money around. Saying he would make us all profitable, if we could just hold out until the ground was prepared. Give us air-conditioning, a fancy new place. Those were his exact words, 'hold out until the ground was prepared.'" Uncle Joe got some more dogs out of the refrigerator and put them on the grill. He laughed. "It was a scheme to stop his brother. It had nothing to do with us. Men like Stone Stubbs don't do something for nothing."

"Why should they?" I asked.

"Why should I help them?"

I sucked the last of the diet root beer through the straw. "There doesn't seem to be much you can do about it."

Uncle Joe waited on a customer then wiped a rag over the counter in front of me. "Hidalgo comes in here for Swanson Dogs all the time."

"Does he?"

"Then he goes across the street and buys a couple more from Stevie. I don't think he wants to offend either one of us, in case..."

"In case what?" I asked.

Uncle Joe stopped wiping the counter. "Mikey told me he doesn't have papers, Swanson. You should know that."

The straw dropped out of my mouth. "He's illegal?"

"Yeah, Swanson. He's a *sansdocuworker*."

"That's not a word."

"It should be. I'm sending it to Houghton Mifflin." He wrote it on the back of a check. "No charge."

I got up to leave.

The next morning, Dick called with news that the police had cleared Ines in the Stubbs investigation. She had no motive.

"What about fingerprints?" I asked.

"Her fingerprints were everywhere. Her DNA probably too. She worked there. Anyway, I don't know why people have this fascination with fingerprints. You know how hard it is to get a really good fingerprint?" He explained that most murderers don't have the courtesy to leave a nice juicy thumbprint at eye level. It was a sore point with him.

"What about the night nurse?"

"They still can't find her."

I was relieved for Hidalgo's sake that Ines was cleared. And mine. Now I could continue my campaign to win over the whole family in good conscience. I called Ines to meet me at Copley Square the next day to go shoe shopping.

"Shoes are the only thing I can try on and feel fashionable," I confided to Ines, hoping to ingratiate myself with her. "I guess that's why I have so many."

"In my country you are fashionable," Ines said. "Women are supposed to have curves."

I steered us into Nieman Marcus, not knowing if Ines could afford to splurge on such extravagant brands as Prado or Walter Steiger. But her eyes lit up when she saw the displays of rhinestone and feathered evening shoes and exuberantly colored pumps. She charged ahead, picking up an armful of slippers from the displays. A salesman was quickly at our side, complimenting us on our taste and delicately-sized feet then going into the stockroom to retrieve our selections, snapping his fingers overhead for another salesperson to assist him.

"This is fun, huh?" I asked, tentatively, settling into a plush chair.

"Yes, it's fun." She looked haughtily at the salesman who was kneeling in front of her, slipping a shoe on her size five foot.

The salesman brought out box after box of impossible-to-wear-but equally impossible-to-resist shoes.

"The first thing I noticed when I came to the United States was the size of the women's feet. Anglo women have such big feet," Ines said, laughing for the first time since I'd met her.

"See," she said, picking up a pair of strappy sandals that stabbed the eye with their brilliance: fuchsia, lime, parrot blue. "These are my colors! Colors that belong in my country. These have no place in Boston." She clicked her tongue in disapproval.

"You're lucky," the salesman gushed. "It's the only five in stock. We only order one five in each style because no one has such tiny feet."

Ines gave the salesman a gracious smile and put the shoes on her "yes" pile.

We snickered when a blond bobbed woman on the chair across from us bared her size 10 extremities to the salesmen. We laughed out loud when she tried to stuff them into a mesh bootie fringed with ostrich feathers. She looked like Cinderella's stepsister trying to force her foot into the glass slipper.

I felt queasy as we paid for our purchases. "How are we going to pay for all this stuff?" Each pair of shoes had cost at least two hundred dollars, and we had each bought three, completely unnecessary, possibly unwearable, shoes. At the rate I was flashing plastic, not only would I never be able to afford a secretary, I might have to cash in my Mickey Mantle baseball card. But Ines didn't flinch.

We entered Louis Vuitton and browsed the luggage. A young Asian woman smiled vaguely, but left us alone, correctly assuming that a two thousand-dollar travel case was not in our budget.

"Who wants to have someone else's name all over your suitcase?" Ines said, loudly.

"I think we've spent too much anyway," I said, glad that no one had challenged my will power.

We schlepped our booty into the Marriot Hotel lounge for a drink. I faked a laugh and plopped into a burgundy leather lounge chair.

Ines ordered an iced tea, and, remembering my diet, I ordered a diet soda.

"I hope you're not on a diet," Ines said. "Hispanic men don't like skinny women. Hidalgo hates skinny women," she added in case I didn't understand the implication.

"You're skinny," I said. Her feet weren't the only size 5s she wore.

"I don't want a Hispanic man."

"Oh!"

"I don't want any man," she said with defiance, then jerked her head towards me suddenly. "I don't want a woman, either, if that's what you think. I'm not like LePage."

I wiped the soda that had come involuntarily out of my nose. "What's LePage like? Is she a gold digger?"

"What's a gold digger? She's taking back what's hers."

"I don't understand."

"The Anglos stole the labor of her parents. She is taking back what's rightfully hers from the people who stole from her. Is that a gold digger? I think maybe the Anglos were the first gold diggers."

"That's an unusual way of looking at it."

Ines smiled and raised her glass in a toast. "To fresh perspectives!"

"Think LePage killed Carlton?"

Ines shrugged. "She hated him."

"Didn't you?"

She smiled and held up her glass again. "I hated cleaning up his poop." She leaned in to me. "I don't want a man until I find my place in this country. Then I will know what kind of a man I want. Same as you, I think. When you find your place, then you will know. No?"

I thought of Hidalgo. He was close to the kind of man I wanted. Straightforward. Hardworking. Handsome. And such a good cook. I smiled thinking about my evening at their house.

Ines looked at me cynically. "You're using Hidalgo. But women have used him before. And he wants you, I know. My mother, my aunt, they want you too. They think an American lawyer can help them. None of them have papers."

I felt myself blush.

"Don't worry," she said. "They think you are very *bonita*, too."

"Immigration law isn't my specialty."

"They don't know that. Anyway, what does it matter? You will get tired of Hidalgo soon. When you find what you really want."

She sighed and got up, leaving me to pick up the tab. If I wasn't trying to ingratiate myself with the Gomez family, I would have confronted her.

I heard a buzz that sounded far away and muffled. I stared blankly, trying to place the sound, finally realizing it came from my purse. "Oh, it's my beeper."

I dialed the unfamiliar number on my cell phone. Le Page, talking between sobs and hiccups, answered.

"Sarah's on a binge somewhere. I know it. She had that look in her eyes. I shouldn't have left her alone. Help me look for her."

"I don't know anything about gambling," I said.

There was silence. Then a hiccup. "If I were home, I could call my Mama or Gerard."

"Gerard?"

"My brother. I don't know anyone in this town."

I sighed. "I'll be right over."

She didn't thank me. The click and the dial tone told me she had hung up. "Are you ready?" I asked Ines. "I'll give you a lift."

"Yeah, I'll take a ride, thanks," Ines said. "By the way, Hidalgo wants you to come to dinner."

It was a command, more than a request. She seemed sure that I was available. So, I was happy to say I had other plans.

"Work," I said.

She tilted her head, obviously believing that it could be nothing else. "*Mañana* then?"

"*Mañana*. Hey, how are you going to pay for all this stuff without a job," I finally asked as we rode down the elevator to the underground garage.

She smiled as if she were royalty. "Don't worry, I'm taking it all back tomorrow. Maybe I'll wear them once, first. I don't know. Anyway, I have a job with Señor Stubbs."

"Teaching?"

"No, he needs a cleaning lady."

As I drove, Ines pestered me with questions about Stone Stubbs. She said she didn't know until recently that Carlton even had a brother.

"He came to see LePage once," Ines volunteered, intruding on my reverie. "That's when I found out."

"Who did?"

"Stone. He came to see Sarah when Carlton was dying. Stone is the same as his brother, I think," she added. "They act like it is a big privilege to clean up their poop."

She asked me some more questions, and I answered absentmindedly, dropping her in Dorchester, looking too long at the windows to see if Hidalgo was looking out. He wasn't. He probably wasn't even home.

I plunged into rush hour traffic on Storrow Drive on my way to Beacon Hill. Sitting in the stagnant lines of idling vehicles, I had plenty of time to think about gold diggers and using people and if anything between two human beings could ever be completely honest.

Chapter 6

Double Dog Dare

"It's like a disease, you know," LePage said as we parked the car at Suffolk Downs race track. "She can't help herself." She looked at me defensively.

I wondered if a weakness for gambling was hereditary. Stone's bad investments seemed like the same disease.

Bachelor buttons grew in the cracks of the blacktop parking lot. A shuttle bus from the Blue Line subway stopped at the entrance and disgorged ten passengers: retirees in powder blue, immigrants in baggy pants and the latest model sneakers. No one moved too fast because of the oppressive heat. The bus driver shut the door laconically and headed back to fetch another load of gamblers. I saw an ad in the subway a few months ago for the Mohegan gambling casino in Connecticut. The ad said, "Do you know there are no words for having a bad time in the Mohegan language?" Underneath, a cynic had written: "But there are dozens of words for sucker."

We kicked our way through a carpet of discarded green racing forms and cigarette butts. About a hundred people, numbed by dollar beers, sat immobile in front of monitors. The bizarre thing was that there was a track but no actual horses. The only action was on the monitors, showing horse races in different parts of the country. Between races, the monitors would flash upcoming races and show the odds, which changed constantly, for each horse. TV trumpets heralded the starts of races and the spectators perked up long enough to see the results then drop their losing tickets on the floor. Occasionally, a gold-toothed smile went to the betting window for a payout.

We asked person after person if they had seen a woman fitting Sarah's description: slightly built, strawberry blond hair.

"She smells like honeysuckle," LePage volunteered.

Those who spoke English looked bored and shook their heads. Others shrugged apologetically. Finally, an older Haitian man wearing a straw Panama and a creamy embroidered shirt, said he saw a red-haired girl wearing a plaid dress leave an hour before.

"Is she your sister?" the man asked me.

"She's my lover," LePage said, daring the man to make an issue of it.

"Well, you'd better catch up with her while you still have a house to go home to," he said. "She was throwing money around like it wasn't hers."

"It isn't," LePage said under her breath, leading me through the litter to the parking lot. "What I'd like to know is, where the hell did she get the money? Let's go to the dog track. She's probably there."

We got in the car and drove the short distance to the Wonderland dog races. LePage guided me around the parking lot. "There! No. Quick, there's a spot, over there."

She was a worse navigator than I was a driver. I swerved into a spot between two jalopies. Mine was the only car in the lot less than ten years old.

I left the top down. Devil Dog was already growling, smelling the other dogs. Maybe smelling their mistreatment. It was no secret that racing dogs were abused. Many people thought dog racing was as inhumane as cock fighting.

"It's okay, Devil Dog," I said, slipping him a peanut butter doggie biscuit, guilty about his diet. I got an umbrella from the trunk and opened it in the back seat, making a canopy. "If you get hot, go in there," I commanded. "Don't worry. This is high-strung dog land. No one's gonna touch you. You're not nearly neurotic enough." Devil Dog barked at nothing in particular then settled down in the shade of the umbrella for a snooze.

LePage ran ahead of me. I lost sight of her, as I struggled across the parking lot in my high heels and sank into a pothole. By the time I made it to the entrance, I was soaked with perspiration.

I scanned the restaurant off the entrance. A bored waiter was smoking by his station. He mashed out the cigarette with one stroke of his thumb and wandered towards me with an oversized menu. I turned and fled.

I hobbled to the betting windows, then the cafeteria, and finally made my way to the bleachers, which were sprinkled with old men:

white guys in powder blue polo shirts, black socks pulled halfway up their calves, and cloth hats protecting their fair Celtic skin from the sun. LePage's sculpted presence was immediately visible. She sat with an arm wrapped around a small figure so immobile it was as if rigor mortis had set in. But when she tried to pry the racing form from her hands, Sarah resisted and started shouting at her.

Just then the bell rang and the greyhounds sprang from the gates. Sarah and LePage rose as one and stared at the track. I walked down the bleachers and stood behind them. The dogs raced around the track chasing a hunk of fur they thought was a rabbit. One of the dogs had a black ring painted around his left eye, like Petey in Our Gang.

"What's the name of the dog with the fake monocle?" I asked. "Number 2?"

They didn't answer, clenching their hands into fists as the dogs made the loop. The dog with the monocle was in the lead, nipping at the rabbit.

"Jesus, shouldn't they speed up that rabbit a little?" I asked. When a dog caught the rabbit, his racing days were over, because he knew the rabbit was a fake.

"Come on, you dumb bunny!" I shouted. I didn't want to think what would happen to Number 2 if he caught it. "Come on! Come on! Come on!" It seemed as if the rabbit were slowing down. The metal arm holding it lurched and stalled.

Number 2 caught the ball of fur between his teeth. He tore into it, growling and banging it against the ground. Balls of stuffing flew around his face. The other dogs circled him, trying to get a piece of the action.

One lone dog, who trailed the pack, strolled past the feeding frenzy, as politely disinterested as if he were witnessing a domestic squabble on a walk through the park. The people in the stands booed him, and he looked up, happy to have their attention. He trotted towards the stands, but when all he got were angry snarls, he wandered back to the track, paused to get his bearings, sniffed the finish line and, despite discouragement from the bleachers, stepped over it.

Trainers and owners dragged the dogs away from the melee and off the track. A voice on the loud speaker announced a delay as they replaced the rabbit and announced the name of the winner: "Pipe Dream."

LePage and Sarah stared at the track.

"How much did you lose?" I asked.

Sarah laughed suddenly. "I'm sorry. If that stupid dog hadn't caught the rabbit, I would have broke even."

LePage looked as if she were going to cry. "Stop trying to do me favors. Where did you get the money?"

"I sold one of Mommy's paintings."

LePage grabbed Sarah's hand and dragged her up the bleachers. "Let's go," she commanded me.

I watched the trainers and owners retrieve their dogs from the field. An Asian man wearing a white linen suit came for monocle. He took off the dog's racing number and snapped his fingers, ordering the dog up. The dog looked away. His sense of reality had been shattered. He probably wondered why he had to listen to this guy. Maybe if he bit him only stuffing would come out.

"Are you coming?" LePage asked me.

"I have to see something," I said, not taking my eyes off the pair in the middle of the track.

"For God's sake," LePage said, testily. "We're already losing stuff that isn't ours. You got to help me, Swanson. This girl is out of control."

"You can handle her," I said.

The owner called to somebody off the track and a man in jeans and tee shirt ran out, grabbed the dog by the collar and pulled him away.

I ran down the steps and asked an attendant to point me to the dog pens. I got there before the Asian man and his dog. When they arrived, the Asian man said something in the trainer's ear and instead of locking the dog back in the pen the trainer led the dog away.

"Excuse me, sir, please," I tugged on the owner's sleeve. "What are you going to do with that dog?"

I half expected him to speak in Chinese, but he answered in perfect English.

"Are you with the press?"

"No."

"Animal Rights group?"

"No."

"What then?"

"I just like dogs."

"So do I. I like them when they win. When they don't, then I don't like them so much."

I breathed heavily. The excitement and the heat made me woozy. "I mean, what's that dog's name?" I pointed at the dog being led away by the trainer.

"In this race, his name was Howie Carr."

"What do you mean 'in this race?'"

He ignored the question, but I knew the answer. The owners would add a little paint and change the names in order to run dogs in more than their allowed number of races.

"Isn't that illegal?" I persisted.

"What are you, a cop? I give to the policeman's fund every year. Isn't that enough?"

He reached for his wallet, but I stopped him.

"Oh, no, no, no. I just. Well, what you going to do with the dog? With, uh, Howie?"

"What do you do with any piece of machinery that doesn't work anymore?" he asked. "You get it fixed or get rid of it."

"And Howie can't be fixed?"

"What do you want me to do? I don't run an old dog home. I'm a businessman."

It took only a few minutes of negotiation before the trainer was handing me a leash with Howie Carr on the other end and I was walking through the parking lot, stepping in pot holes and giving Howie Carr instructions on how to relate to Devil Dog.

"He's a male, but don't let that intimidate you," I advised Howie, who the trainer had told me was a female.

LePage and Sarah were waiting by the car. LePage squinted at Howie Carr, and said, "For God's sake, Swanson. You're too soft. How the hell are you going to amount to anything if you got a soft fucking heart?"

I looked at Sarah nestling into LePage's shoulder. "I'm not the only one with a thing for wounded animals."

LePage groaned and the women piled into the passenger's seat—Sarah on LePage's lap.

I smiled into the rear-view mirror and caught a glimpse of Devil Dog and Howie on the back seat having a mad sniffing party, deciding whether to co-exist.

I raced to Beacon Hill to drop off LePage and Sarah. Whoever said your problems go with you was right. The Stubbs' stuck to me like glue. But as I checked on the dogs in the rear-view mirror, their presence, for the moment at least, made everything seem okay.

Despite protests that Connie didn't like dogs, Max accepted Howie Carr when I dropped him off later.

"He'll make a good watch dog, I can tell," Max said delightedly. He carefully folded a blanket in the corner and set out two pasta bowls: one for water, one for food.

"It's a she," I told him.

"Even better! Females are vicious!" Max winked at me. He put out a bowl of chili for Howie.

"You're going to blow out her insides with that stuff," I said, sounding just like my uncles. I was turning into my uncles, like normal women turn into their mothers.

"Dogs want to enjoy life too, don't you, Howie?" Max squatted and stroked her head while she ate. "She loves it. Do you want a little sparkling cider with that, Howie?"

I left, not wanting to see the results of that combination on the insides of a skittish racing dog. Also, Connie had come in from the kitchen, thwapping a wooden spoon in her palm. Connie was not a dog person.

It was late afternoon when I drove back to my office to check messages and to work on some pending cases.

As I walked down the hall, I saw that my office door was ajar. I had visitors. Dick was sitting behind my desk, his elbows on the arms of the chair, talking to two men, one sitting in the visitor chair and the other leaning against the file cabinets. The men were paying the price of cheap "nonbreathable" suits: sweat poured down their overheated faces. No one had bothered to turn on the fan, a choice I didn't rectify. The more uncomfortable they were, the faster they would leave.

I transmitted Dick a look that conveyed my displeasure, but he wasn't receiving.

The men introduced themselves, flashed their police badges then slipped them back into their breast pockets without giving me a chance to read them. Their names were slightly ridiculous, like "Tom and Jerry" or "Larry and Mo."

"Friends of yours?" I asked Dick.

"Colleagues."

"And we are discussing what?"

"Stolen art," the man sitting down said.

"Forged art," the other man said.

"Whichever it was, we think it's been going on for a few years."

"The owner of the original paintings just found out when she lent them to the Museum for a show. The Museum Director broke the news to her that they were fakes. She called the police right away."

"The owner didn't realize she didn't have the real paintings?" I asked.

"The forger is very talented."

"So, how does this involve me?" I asked.

The cop I decided was named Tom cleared his throat. "Well, no one on our staff is actually an art expert. Except Dick here. Since he left we have nobody who knows this stuff."

I arched an eyebrow at Dick. So Dick was an art expert. That explained a lot.

"Also," Tom said, "Dick tells us you may have actually seen the forgeries. Or some of them."

"I did?"

"Manchester by the Sea," Dick said.

It took a second to sink in. "Ulrike Meiner?"

Tom nodded. After I had gotten over the shock of seeing Stone drive up Ulrike's driveway as we were leaving, I told Dick that Ulrike had a lot of wet canvases around. Not knowing anything about art, I didn't know what, if anything, it meant. But I did know a guilty demeanor when I saw one. "You were there, too," I said, guessing they were the cops that Ulrike had entertained before we arrived.

"But we didn't see anything." Tom looked at Jerry for verification. "Nothing of that nature."

"So what makes you think she's a forger?"

"Ms. Meiner has access to the art that was forged."

"So does the cleaning lady," I said.

"She's a trained artist. And the owner of some of the paintings that were stolen was suspicious of her. We've been watching her, but we can't seem to nail her with the goods."

"And yet, you were right there in her house," I said. "You must have been distracted."

Jerry's face got redder. "It's really hot in here. May I?" He pointed at the fan and looked at Dick for permission as if it were Dick's office. "That lady's into some weird stuff," Jerry said, laughing nervously.

"Not illegal though," Dick said, "In Massachusetts."

"I thought your specialty was art," I said.

"Art covers a lot of territory."

"Watch you don't reveal yourself," I told him. "Well, anyway, what if I did see something. I'm not an expert. How do I know what I'm looking at? I don't know if she's just a hobbiest," I nodded to Dick, "or a professional. Maybe she gives them away as Christmas presents."

Jerry leaned towards me. "We just need enough to get a warrant. Dick says that you saw some paintings. Were they good enough to pass for originals? We can't get a warrant based on second-hand information, which is what Dick's evidence is right now. He never got a chance to eyeball them. You did."

I sighed. I didn't have anything against the police busting up Ulrike's cottage industry. But I didn't want them to spook Ulrike before the police disproved the suicide theory. As Dick told me, repeatedly, police often mangled and distorted evidence in their quest to obtain a conviction.

"I saw some paintings," I admitted. "She has a studio upstairs. But to my admittedly inexpert eyes," I bowed to Dick, "I have no idea if they were intended as professional forgeries."

"But they looked like old paintings?" Jerry asked.

"Yes, I guess. Okay. They looked like they could have been old except the place reeked of turpentine and oil paint."

The policemen smiled at one another. I went behind my desk and opened the top drawer, forcing Dick to get up. I plopped down in my chair. "Is that all? Or is there something else I can help you gentlemen with?"

"That's all, ma'm." They said good-bye and almost knocked each other over retreating from my hot tiny office.

I picked up a file and opened it. A pair of French cuffs poking out of a silk blazer planted themselves on the desk in front of me. I looked up.

"Yes, Dick." I tapped the desk with my pencil.

He cleared his throat.

"Those are Matilda's paintings that Ulrike was copying."

"Matilda's? The Bates Collection?"

"The show was *Boston Collects*."

"You know, Dick, Sarah took a painting to sell on the black market."

"How do you know?'

"She lost a lot of money at the track. A lot of money she didn't actually have."

"That would have been nice to know before."

I arranged some papers. "How many did Ulrike copy? Do you know?"

Dick shrugged. "Hard to say until an expert has a look at them."

"Which Matilda will never agree to."

"Right. They aren't any closer on the Stubbs homicide," Dick said, reading my mind.

"They've decided it's a homicide?" I asked, hopefully.

"No, that's just what I think. They're still trying to make the suicide theory stick."

"Did they check out the gun?"

"Ulrike's. But she wasn't there when it was used. Air-tight alibi."

I nodded.

"Ines said she saw the gun in Ulrike's paint box when she was wheeling the old man in. Anybody could have taken it, really. Ulrike admits it's hers, but claims it was there for self-defense."

"Yeah, against the marauders who frequent Beacon Hill. Crooks would need more than guns if they came up against her. Who found the body? Did they find that out?"

"Ines Gomez. Said he was dead when she got there."

I sat up, surprised. "I thought Ines went home at six?"

"Apparently a neighbor recognized her and said he saw her going into the house around 8 o'clock. The DA questioned her again, and she admitted she forgot her purse and came back to get it. LePage and Sarah were at a movie. Ines told the DA that the night nurse walked down to the Seven-Eleven on Charles Street for a pack of cigarettes. An informer told me she was at The Sevens having a few pops. But, it's like she disappeared off the face of the earth. No one can find her. Or that tape."

"The DA should subpoena Ines for that tape."

Dick made a note.

I frowned. "Why did Ines go into Carlton's bedroom?"

"It's natural for a nurse to check on her patient, even if she's not on duty."

"She's not much of a nurse," I ventured.

Ines certainly had no reason to kill Carlton, except that she hated sick people. And that wasn't a compelling reason. I don't like vegetarians and people who are able to stick to low-fat diets but I don't go around killing them.

"Who was the last person to see him alive?"

"LePage."

I didn't say anything.

"Don't you want to know why LePage went in his bedroom?" he asked.

"She was supposedly having an affair with Carlton."

"Not a happy one, apparently. She said she was going in there that night to break it off. For good. She didn't care about the money. She said she was sick of waiting for him to die. She would go away and start over with Sarah. Away from him."

"Sick of waiting for him to die." I repeated. "Think she plugged him?"

"She said he was alive when she left him."

"Did she say she heard a shot?"

"Claims not. Remember that pillow? It's better than a silencer."

I sighed and fiddled with the pebble in my pocket. I waited patiently, thinking Dick was going to tell me his theory on Carlton's murderer. Instead he said, "We'll cross-pollinate later. I think it would be a good idea if you gave me a key."

"For what?"

"For the office." He adjusted his tie and pointed to the door. "I don't want to keep breaking in."

That evening I pulled a new dress out of my closet for my date with Hidalgo: fuchsia roses on a black background that matched my new shoes. I showered and put them on then Devil Dog and I piled into my car. I stopped at Brookline Booksmith and picked up a Spanish Language tape which I played as I drove to Dorchester.

"Hoy es un dia muy importante en la casa de la familia Hernández, porque es el cumpleaños de Joselito."

I repeated it a few times. I was pretty good at languages. I already knew French and Latin, which admittedly I've mostly forgotten except for the legal jargon. And the church stuff which occupies a permanent place in my subconscious.

I repeated the Spanish phrase. If someone in the Gomez family were having a birthday today, I would be all set.

¡Felicidades, Joselito! ¡Feliz cumpleaños!" I looked into Devil Dog's eyes as I said it. He stared back at me with knowing attention. Maybe he was a Spanish dog. He certainly appeared more intelligent when I spoke Spanish to him. "We're here," I said, shooing him out the car door. *"¡Vamos a gozarnos!"*

Devil Dog wagged his tail enthusiastically and barked a few times as we walked up the stairs. Hidalgo met us before I even rang the bell. He opened the door and smiled, his perfect rows of white teeth dazzling me. He took the bottle of cheap, sweet wine from my hand and pulled me close.

"Querida," he said. "You brought your little dog."

He knelt to pat Devil Dog. "He's a very nice dog." Then he got up and kissed me, casually, as if we were an established couple who kissed all the time. My knees got weak.

He grabbed my hand and led me up the stairs. "Tonight," he said, "I am making *carne de vaca*. Do you like it?"

I nodded, smelling the heady aroma of roast beef, rosemary, and freshly grilled tortillas.

"Some potatoes and sweet carrots, roasted with the *carne*." He put his forefinger and thumb to his perfectly shaped mouth and kissed them. "Very good."

His mother greeted me with a handshake and took the wine from Hidalgo. She frowned as she read the label then smiled her approval. *"Muy bien,"* she said.

It was the sweetest *vino tinto* in the store. The stuff hangovers were made of.

His mother and aunt enjoyed a belly laugh at my birthday Spanish, and after Ines and I set the table, Hidalgo brought in the roast on a platter, ceremoniously, like he was bearing a treasure chest. Once again, Hidalgo's father doffed his straw fedora, said a quick prayer in Spanish, to which he added "and thank you for Swanson Herbinko," in tortured English. He'd probably practiced all day. I nodded at him appreciatively.

Ines didn't eat much. She was chattering about this and that in Spanish, while forks clanged against plates. Suddenly she turned to me and asked, "Have they found Señor Stubbs' murderer yet?"

I put my fork down. "The police think it might be a suicide. Have they spoken to you again?"

"Of course they've spoken to me. It would be so nice to blame the poor Latina. No papers. No money to buy off the judges."

"That's not exactly how our criminal justice system works."

"Ha! You are perfect. If I were accused, I would be given some poor slob public defender. What kind of defense do you get for the kind of money a public defender makes? I know I couldn't buy you for that kind of money." She looked at me slyly and when I didn't respond said, "You don't know anything about our family, Swanson. You should know about us, if, you know…" She cocked her head towards Hidalgo, and began.

"In 1845, we lived in Texas," she said.

"Not us, our great-great-great grandmother, Rosa Esparso," Hidalgo interrupted.

"It was us. What's the difference? The only difference was it wasn't Texas then, it was Mexico."

She looked at me to see if I understood the implications of this.

"The Texans stole our land," she said, impatiently. "It all belonged to Mexico."

"Anyway, that year, Rosa Esparso, our great-great-great grandmother, was kicked off her land. Winter was coming. Her family had disowned her because she was pregnant and not married. She had nowhere to go, so she went back to the ranch that used to belong to her family and waited until dark. Then she went into the granary and stole a sack of corn. She untied the rope of a palomino that was hitched to the post outside the house and led him away."

Ines stared at me to make sure I was paying attention. I was. So was the family.

Ines continued. "She was frying corn when the men found her at daybreak. Two *gringos*, small and skinny with mean eyes. They constantly fought with one another. They were frightened of her at first, thinking she was not alone. The one man nudged her with his rifle as though scared to touch her. She snarled and spit at them. It wasn't until they were sure she was alone that they became brave. Brave men with a pregnant woman! Slapping her. Pushing her onto the palomino. When they tied her hands behind her back and a cloth over her eyes, she knew they meant to hang her. The palomino did too.

"He twitched nervously from side to side. Rosa tried to calm him by relaxing her legs, *"Con calma, Caballo,"* she said, making clicking sounds with her tongue and teeth. She hadn't named him yet.

"She hadn't had a chance to name her baby either, thinking she would have plenty of time for that later. She had stolen her baby, too, from a *gringo*, another woman's husband, sleeping with him on the night of her saint's feast day. Neither of them would need names now.

"If she thought of the unfairness of the situation, that they took her family's land, not just a horse and some corn as she had done, she didn't think those thoughts then. The only thing on her mind was that her baby was pushing the oil and corn she had eaten for breakfast up into her throat. "You are going to be a Devil," she said, forgetting that soon they might both be Devils.

"She thought, 'I am being hung, but I am dying of indigestion.' She wanted to cross herself, but couldn't. She couldn't even cross herself. You are a Catholic, no?"

I nodded, understanding the implications of a Catholic, condemned to death, not being allowed to cross herself.

"Rosa felt woozy. There was no air. The sun and heartburn choked her. She could hear one of the men climbing the tree to secure the rope. Then the *gringos* started arguing again. One of them said something she couldn't understand. The other said something angry in return. Their fight got angrier and louder. She heard one gunshot, then another. She fainted and fell off the horse. She was awakened by a white woman removing her blindfold. Rosa could see now that the two men lay dead. They had shot each other. In the next minute, her baby—my great-great grandmother—was being born."

I looked around the table. Everyone had listened solemnly to this story, even Señor Gomez who couldn't understand English, and even though they had heard it a hundred times before.

During the whole story, Ines had never looked away from me.

"What happened to Rosa?" I asked.

"She became a servant to the *gringos* who stole her land. She washed their children and cooked their meals. Same as now. Nothing's changed. Now do you understand, Swanson?" Her gaze, hard and relentless throughout the story, softened. "We have a chocolate mousse cake for dessert, Swanson. We think you are fond of chocolate. Are we right? Hidalgo thinks you are getting too skinny."

I laughed self-consciously as the two old women wagged their fingers at me.

After dessert, the old women cleared the dinner table, and Hidalgo and I took Devil Dog for a walk.

"Don't believe we are all angry about things in the past," Hidalgo said. He held my hand as if it were the most usual thing in the world. "My sister can't let go of it. But I tell her, what about now? The *gringos*..." He bowed at me. "I meant no offense. But the *gringos* will still hold us captive if we allow our anger to rule us."

He was right about that. Look at my uncles who allowed their anger to ruin their partnership. At some point you have to release those chains, and ask yourself if you'd rather be right than happy. We had walked around the block several times already, and even Devil Dog was getting winded.

"What can you do? Go to war with the United States government?" He laughed at the absurdity of it. "Mexico."

"Rosa sounds like quite a girl," I said.

"I like her. I like strong women."

We stopped in front of my car and kissed our first real kiss. Hidalgo promised to teach me the entire Spanish vocabulary I would need to be in love with him. We made a date for my first lesson, at my house, not with the family.

Then Devil Dog and I drove off. I pushed the Spanish tape in and we practiced a few sentences. Me, laughing happily, and Devil Dog listening attentively.

"You are a Spanish dog, aren't you?" I asked. "Maybe we should name you *Diablo Perro*. No, that doesn't sound right. You're still Devil Dog."

My reverie was broken by my beeping telephone telling me I had a message. I sighed and dialed in.

Chapter 7

All Unhappy Families are Different

It was almost midnight when I left the Gomez's. The message was from Matilda saying to please use whatever legal muscle necessary to get Stone and her letters back from Bunny. "She's moved into my house and...what? She thinks she can have my life, too? Those letters are my personal property and I want them back." She paused. "Of course, there will be a little something extra in it for you."

I sighed. Well, it might be a good thing to catch Bunny off-guard. Reluctantly and sleepily, I drove to Harvard.

I parked my car in Matilda's empty driveway, got out and peered into the dark house. Nothing moved.

"Psst."

I turned and saw someone crouching in the doorway of the second floor of the carriage house. I walked over. The creature was enveloped in cigarette smoke. Her hair was straggly and unwashed. Pin pricks of light reflected off her dark eyes. It took me a second to realize that this wild woman was Bunny O'Reilly.

"Come here," she said in a stage whisper.

I wandered through the open door, an empty space with a dirt floor, used for a garage.

"Up the ladder," she said, and dropped a half-rotted, extension ladder from a hole in the ceiling.

"There's no other way?" I asked.

"It's okay, I'm holding the ladder," she whispered.

"Are you sure this thing is steady?"

"Yes, of course. I'm up and down all the time."

"Can't you come down?"

"No!"

Her feral eyes shone in the dark. She looked as if she hadn't slept in days. I shook the ladder with both hands, exhaled, and inched my way up, feeling my leather soles slip on the rungs of blackened wood. I was three-quarters of the way up when I thought about the trip down. But the die was cast. I pushed forward and popped my head through the hole in the ceiling.

"Give me a hand, will you?"

Bunny grabbed my hand and pulled me up, falling backwards as she heaved me over the top. She squinted at me through the smoke from the cigarette stuck in the middle of her mouth.

"Did she see you?" she asked.

I brushed myself off. It was hot as hell. There was no cross-breeze even though the windows, big enough for a cow to fly through, were wide open. Piles of boxes teetered against the walls. Old furniture and other junk filled up most of the floor. Bunny had cleared a spot in the middle of the debris around an old divan with stuffing dribbling out. Dust covered everything. "I don't think she's here. I didn't see anybody," I said.

Bunny laughed. "She's here all right. She never leaves. She's in there sawing everything in half. If she can't have it all, she doesn't want anybody to get anything. Anyway, I watch her. I know what she's doing."

"Bunny, I don't think she's here. Her car's gone."

She leaned back against the divan and looked at me over her nose. "She hid it in the woods."

Bunny had gone Howard Hughes. And now I was trapped up here, a rotting ladder between me and a quick escape to sanity.

"What are you eating?" I asked.

"At night in the garden." She lay down on her back and laughed. "She works all day in the garden and at night, when the lights in the house go out, I sneak down and eat everything up. Her precious tomatoes and cucumbers and radishes. I take a bite out of each then leave them. She thinks it's a raccoon." She cackled then started to cry.

I pulled my emergency Hershey bar from my purse and handed it to her. She examined it as if she had never seen one before, then tore off the wrapper and wolfed it down. She balled up the wrapper and smiled. "Thank you," she said, a glint of sanity returning to her eyes. Say what you will about chocolate, it's a proven life-saver.

"Are you okay?" I asked.

"Yes, I'm fine." She paced the tiny cleared area. "I'm scared she's going to find me. She's crazy, you know! She has a million knives and this idea that I want to destroy her. I just want what's mine."

"Isn't that the same thing?" I asked. "If you take what's hers, that is destroying her."

"But it's not hers. She's being selfish. If Carlton didn't want me to continue what he started, I wouldn't even be here. Do you think I want the money?" She held her palms out to me.

I thought she wanted the money.

"I'm in the prime of my life. I just want to do what Carlton wants me to do. He isn't interested in his money either. He wants to make sure his name is passed on to posterity. That's all." She grabbed a roll of papers from on top of a box and waved them in front of my face. "The waterfront development will prove his father wrong. Will prove Stone wrong. He isn't a fuck-up like they think. He just never had enough money to get started. Now with the money from The Trust going back to him, I can help him finish what he was trying his whole life to start."

"Bunny," I said, "Carlton is dead."

"He can't count on his stupid children to do that, can he? One's a dyke." She leaned and whispered, "The other's not even his."

I blinked. "That's a matter of speculation."

"It's not a matter of speculation at all. It's in writing. I've got the letters to prove it."

"They say that Tucker is Stone's child?"

"They say that they were in love. What else do you need to know?" She exhaled a long stream of smoke through her nose. "Stone was here. He was trying to buy me off."

"Buy the letters?"

She waved her hand around.

"They aren't your letters, Bunny. They're Matilda's and Stone's personal property."

"Possession is nine-tenths of the law."

I was getting tired of hearing that. "Why don't you just hand them over to me and avoid a lawsuit. You have enough problems. Isn't that what Stone wanted?"

"That. And pay me to forget about the waterfront development project. He said, Carlton is dead, and I should move on with my life."

"Carlton *is* dead, Bunny."

Bunny lit a cigarette from the butt of the one she'd just smoked. "Stone thinks he has it all sewn up. That he can do whatever he wants because he's Stone Stubbs. He's been buying up property on the waterfront for years. Just because he hates Carlton. You think he wants to develop the goddamned waterfront? He doesn't want to develop the waterfront. He just wants to make sure Carlton doesn't."

"Carlton is dead, Bunny."

"Everyone thinks Stone's so pure and Carlton is so evil. But they're alot more alike than people think."

"What did you tell Stone?"

"I told him to take his money and shove it. I'll find a way to do what Carlton wants. I could mortgage this place."

"Matilda might have something to say about that."

"Yeah, Matilda. She wants the money to put a plastic surgeon on retainer, that's what. Move him right into the house, so if she needs an emergency tuck he's right there. God, I'll never do that when I get old," she said, changing gears. "I'm going to age gracefully."

I didn't say anything. Despite my recent "*bonita*" accolades, I knew I wasn't a great beauty and would face my falling blossoms a lot differently than a woman renowned for her petals. How would Bunny feel in 20 years when she looked in the mirror? Unless she acquired some wisdom to go with the wrinkles, my guess is she'd ask Matilda for her surgeon's phone number.

"She would just waste the money, and Carlton wouldn't get to build the waterfront. Do you think Carlton wants the money?"

I thought Carlton wanted the money. I thought he wanted to be buried with it. Like a Pharaoh. And, like a Pharaoh, I thought he wanted to be buried with all his favorite things, like his mistress. Bunny looked like the walking dead.

"Look at this." She unrolled architectural drawings on the floor and anchored the corners with old paint cans.

The drawings labeled, "Stubbs Pier" were a design of the entire South Boston waterfront. Everything, including my uncles' home and their businesses would be razed, making way for one of the most grandiose sites I had ever seen. The way it jutted out into the harbor would block the light coming into the city for about a mile. It was the same landscape that Ulrike was painting in the background of Carlton's portrait. "Wow, this thing is…" I groped for an inoffensive word. "Amazing."

"Isn't it? It's going to happen. Everyone will have to acknowledge its existence. Do you know, it'll be visible from almost every corner of Boston?"

I gulped, thinking of the effect that would have on the morale of Boston residents.

She cupped an elbow in her hand and stalked around the room. "You never know what your role in life is going to be. Until I met Carlton Stubbs everyone thought I was just a pretty face, you know? A party girl from the projects. He gave me a vision. He was chosen for greatness and chose me to fulfill his dream. Seeing the Stubb's Harbor become a reality is my purpose in life."

Her purpose in life had certainly changed since high school, where, as the class fat girl, her big challenge was finding ways to skip gym class.

"Things change," I said, philosophically. "It's too bad that now this vision won't be realized."

Bunny laughed. "Don't be so sure."

"What if there's less money than you think there is?"

"People in this family will pay a lot of money not to have me broadcast what I know about them. I'll do it for Carlton if I have to."

"Look, Bunny. You should just try to settle with Matilda. Get her to give you some money for the salary Carlton owes you and get on with your life."

"You don't get it, do you?" she asked. "I'll never have anything this big fall into my lap again. If I don't capitalize on this, I might as well go back to the projects. How many times do you get a lucky roll?"

"This may not be your lucky roll, Bunny. A bigger one might still be ahead of you."

She knelt down to roll up the plans, as I pondered how to negotiate my way down the ladder.

Bunny dropped the ladder down and held my hands as I got my balance. Teetering on the balls of my feet, I made it down.

"Hang in there, Bunny," I called up to her, brave now that my car was within running distance. I took out my cell phone. "I'll order you a pizza. Do you like pepperoni?"

"Sausage."

Bunny pulled up the ladder and disappeared back into the hot hole of her dream.

No detective is interested in a cold murder trail, and due to lack of evidence, Carlton's murder investigation was stalled. Dick suggested I get on with my other cases. He would be in touch when things heated up.

It's a family tradition that both Swanson Hot Dog Emporiums close for vacation for two weeks in August. Part of the tradition is that I go with them as often as I could, and this year I did it gladly, happy to escape the tyranny of the Stubbs' problem.

The uncles take vacation together so neither gets unfair advantage and despite the risk that regular customers might find a new routine in the meantime. But the uncles are confident that the Secret Swanson Sauce will keep their customers loyal. And, so far they've been right. August first, both places fill up as if they were holding a grand opening.

It's not as if they take exotic vacations, either, where timing might be important. They go deep-sea fishing off Boston Harbor in their 15-foot cruiser, toting separate tackle boxes and bottles of gin disguised as 7-Up. They manage to avoid direct contact with each other on the boat, filtering a string of insults through me. It makes the experience more satisfying for both of them.

We leave before dawn, their theory being that fish are insomniacs, swim all night and hide when the sun comes out. They pick me up at the half-rotted pier by the Massachusetts Avenue Bridge. From there, you can see Cambridge and the ominous domes of MIT on the other side. The Gothic spires of Boston University are visible in the early morning haze up river. The Citco sign blinks its relentless psychedelic pattern over Kenmore Square. Early risers speed by on Storrow Drive on their way to work. A few overachieving joggers, taking advantage of the early morning cool, stride past on the tree lined Esplanade.

My uncles tied their boat to the pier. The engine was idling and both men were lost in the myriad of upkeep that even little craft demands. I called out when I saw them, and they lifted their heads in unison, waving at me. Devil Dog had never been near the water, so I didn't know if he could swim. I had bought a doggie life-jacket for him, and he resisted only a little when I put it on him. He barked at the water then jumped into the boat as though he had been shipping out all his life.

Uncle Joe had on a tank top, which showcased his lack of exercise. He throttled back and pushed off from the dock.

We began our gentle cruise down river. We overtook sailboats and sculls, the owners huffing with the effort of rowing. They paused with oars high as we passed, rocking in our wake. We raised our martini glasses to them. Isn't that what civilization is all about? Freedom from brute labor? I never understood the subculture that equates the labor of slaves with recreation.

"So that sonofabitch Carlton Stubbs croaks and now I'm stuck on Broadway forever," Uncle Joe said. "His brother isn't interested in doing a damned thing for the city or the state. They all come in talking big, but in the end they're out for themselves." He put an absurd looking plastic frog lure on the end of his line and cast it into the water, where it jiggled convulsively.

"You think a fish is going to be fooled by that thing?" I asked.

"You think fish are geniuses?" He pulled it back in and cast it out again. "You going soft on fish? You becoming an *ichthyophile?*" Joe laughed then looked at me sideways. "Well, fish don't think. I don't care what you learned in law school. Okay? They don't think. Some things you don't have to go to school to know."

My uncles were alternately awed and intimidated by my law degree. Even though they paid for my education and bragged to everyone about my (okay, so far modest) accomplishments, they didn't want to think that I'd outgrown them.

"Did you ever see Stubbs' plans?" I asked. "They were atrocious! You would have gone out of business in days."

"Who cares?"

"What? You want to be bankrupt?"

"Bankrupt? I'd be on easy street. Carlton would have paid me plenty for my shack and weeny roaster."

I looked at Uncle Stevie to see what he had to say, but he was playing with some weird radar device on the dashboard.

"You think I want to roast weenies all my life?" Joe said. "You think you're the only one with big plans?"

"You have plans?" I asked, surprised.

"Yeah, I have plans." He poured some of the contents of his 7-Up bottle into the cocktail shaker and swooshed it around. "Get the olives out of there," he commanded, pointing to a wicker basket as he refilled our glasses.

"Stubbs wasn't going to stop at the dog shack, he wanted to buy your house." I searched in the basket and pulled out a jar of onions. "You have these, too. Which do you want?" He took the jar of olives. "He was going to have everyone move into this project thing that ringed the auditorium. You would have been happy with that?"

He shrugged. "It would have never gotten that far. They would have bought all our businesses and houses for way above market value. In the meantime, I would have had a pretty penny from my Hot Dog Emporium and my share of the house, and I could be doing something that I want. I'm fifty-five years old. I think I want a change."

I sipped my martini and frowned. He was right, of course. Just because I never wanted my uncles to change, didn't mean that they didn't want to.

"What do you think I was doing before we got you?" he asked.

I had never thought about it. I was selfish about my uncles, like most children are about their parents.

"Steve and I had a regular restaurant. It was growing, but not fast enough to support a family. We got out of it and opened the original dog shack because it was a quick buck. Ah." He pulled the frog back in and cast it out again, smoothly. "It doesn't matter. I shouldn't have gotten my hopes up."

We passed the Museum of Science and got in line behind two amphibious tourist vehicles, the Duck Boats, waiting for the lockmaster to open the lock. The new suspension bridge towered over us. It was part of the Big Dig, a new artery that would re-route traffic into and around Boston. It would make the proposed Stubbs' Harbor even more valuable, as it would lead traffic right to it.

When we got the green light to pass through the lock, Uncle Stevie took the wheel and blew our horn. The sound echoed satisfyingly against the concrete walls, and then we were out in the harbor. *Old Ironsides* was docked on the left in Chelsea and three Coast Guard cutters were on the pier on the right. We headed out to the open sea.

"Now!" Uncle Stevie said. He fiddled with a little LCD screen on the dashboard.

I leaned in to examine it. "Find-a-Fish?"

"This baby changes everything." Soon, silhouettes of fish swarmed the screen. Uncle Stevie pointed to the seagulls circling overhead a little to the right. "See, I knew it." He steered the boat towards the gulls, the fish blips on the screen getting larger. Excitedly, he strapped himself in a seat facing the rear of the boat, cast a big line, and in seconds, pulled up a bluefish.

"I'll be a sonofabitch, look at that!" Joe started laughing at Stevie, who was struggling with the blue, still thrashing on the line. Devil Dog seemed impressed and started barking furiously. Joe winked at me. "That gadget actually works."

A series of small islands dot the water close to Boston. We rode to Bad Boy's Island, where they used to house juvenile delinquents in the nineteenth century. The property was now used for picnicking and corporate bonding. We docked there and got a fire going in a stone barbecue. Uncle Stevie cleaned the fish while Joe got a frying pan out of his boat. It would be the first time it had ever been used.

"I never thought I'd live to see the day when he'd actually catch a fish," Joe said.

"I never thought I'd live to see the day when you guys would actually eat together," I said.

It was the wrong thing to say, because they both became sullen as if they had lost some sort of a contest.

"It's too big for just me," Stevie said. "Wouldn't do anybody any good to waste food."

"I have to make sure he doesn't ruin it," Joe said. "He can ruin a simple hot dog. God knows what he'd do with a fish if I weren't around."

We fried the fish and ate it in silence. I wondered aloud if anything caught in the harbor was actually edible, but they ignored me and, truthfully, that fish was the best I've ever tasted. The secret sauce of Boston Harbor pollution. We sat on the grass, drinking dry martinis, alternating the olives and onions, so we would know how many we drank, and watched the hot sun cook behind thunder clouds. Any hope of reconciliation between my uncles was ruined, thanks to me. My appearance in their life caused them to give up their dream, and my wise-ass comments always drove them apart. As if following an unwritten script, we got up at the same time, cleaned the site, and headed back to the boat.

They sullenly rode to the other side of the island to check their lobster traps. They were empty except for tiny crabs, which were feasting on the rotting fish they used as bait. We turned towards home.

I watched the city skyline come into view and I was glad when we pulled up to the pier. I climbed out of the boat and drove back to Brookline to bury my sadness in work.

The office proved too hot to work in, so I dropped Devil Dog with Max while I went into Bunratty's to see the Sox lose the second game of a double header to the lowly Orioles on TV. An error by Brian Baubach, the klutzy left fielder, lost the game.

I finished my coke and walked outside into a hot, humid evening. It was 8 o'clock, but still light. And my nerves were on edge. I walked over to the Arcade to see the Russian hypnotist. The curtains in his storefront were drawn and a sign in the window said he was with a client, please call for an appointment. I banged on the glass and pushed the doorbell for a full 60 seconds. Finally he emerged from the inner room and opened the door. It was hard to tell how old he was because his hair and beard were like a frizzy gray bush. Two little black eyes squinted out from the undergrowth, looking at me disapprovingly.

"I am with client," he said. He tried to close the door, but I wedged my foot inside.

"I need help," I said, pulling out the pebble he gave me. "I forgot the phrase I'm supposed to say when I want a cigarette."

"You must pay me fifty dollar for last visit. You owe me fifty dollar."

I fished around in my purse, but only had a twenty. I handed it to him. "Here, take this. I'll give you the rest later."

He grabbed the twenty, pushed my foot out the door with his, and closed the door. He shouted through the glass. "Thirty dollar you owe me. Make appointment."

I walked out to the street and tossed the pebble in the gutter, but a superstitious feeling made me retrieve it and begin fondling it.

I picked up Devil Dog and went home. I searched around the lobby for my newspaper, to see if anything was happening with the

Stubbs Pier. But Fast Freddy, my newspaper delivery person, had let me down again. No paper. It wasn't the first time. A new concierge was asleep over his chemistry homework. I had missed the last condo meeting because I was having dinner with the Gomezes and so had forfeited my chance to complain. A well-thumbed Boston Globe was underneath his quart-sized Thermos. I made a lot of noise taking his paper, but he snored on, oblivious.

I opened the mailbox, which was stuffed with circulars and junk. Nothing interesting until a light blue envelope fell out, landing on my foot. Someone had jammed it into the tiny slot at the top of the box. Like the other one, it wasn't addressed, and like the other one, the message was composed of cutout letters from the newspaper. The note read: "IT'S PAY DAY". What did that mean? "IT'S PAY DAY"?

I coughed loudly and finally the concierge roused himself.

"Anything unusual happen around here today?" I asked, a little shriller than I intended. I breathed deeply and forced my voice down an octave. "Anybody suspicious hanging around the lobby?"

He sat up, trying to get his bearings, saw it was only me and seemed relieved. "Nah. Quiet as ever." He pulled his hat down over his face and went back to sleep.

I yanked the hat off his head. He looked up, terrified.

"Think hard," I said.

He straightened up, ran his hand over his head and pushed the visitor's log towards me. "See."

I scanned the log. Nobody I knew. "Do you make vendors sign in?" I asked.

"Nah. What's the point? They're not going into the building. Just the lobby."

I bent down to pick his up his hat and flipped it at him. "Look busy," I said.

I was still trembling when I unlatched the door to my apartment. I slid in, but left the door open behind me in case I had to make a quick escape. "Wait here," I commanded Devil Dog. I left him by the door as I made the rounds of my apartment. Nothing seemed out of place. I opened all the closets. Nothing but old books and clothes. Boxes of shoes.

I released Devil Dog from his post and closed the door. I turned on the air conditioner, as much for the cool air as for the noise that I hoped would distract me from imagining bad guys sneaking in all my windows. Hidalgo was coming over tonight and I was determined not to let my fears ruin my fun.

My stomach was killing me. I poured myself a big glass of cranberry juice mixed with Metamucil and Aloe Vera and sat down in the living room to assess what I had to do to get ready for the date.

Everyone has an idea of what romantic love looks like. Mine is this: a well-formed man who will talk to me about intelligent matters for about ten minutes, then spend the next twenty telling me, in specific detail, how wonderful I am. After making love to me, with breath-taking technique and tenderness, which he will swear is inspired by me and not years of experience, he will spring up and prepare a gourmet meal, chastising me to eat everything because I am getting too skinny. And he'll love my dog.

I subscribe to the theory that the first step in success is visualizing it, and so, in preparation, I examined the condo as if seeing it for the first time. I spent so little time there that if I closed my eyes I would be hard-pressed to describe it in great detail. The cleaning person, whom I have never seen, swiped the surfaces of tables and dressers in big swirls that left odd dust patches in every corner. The service, spoils in a divorce settlement in which my client got lots of things but no real cash, was payment for my work. Maid service for two years. I still had ten months to go on the deal. I re-wiped the tables and dressers, which made the streaks on the mirrors and windows more noticeable, so I took some paper towels to those as well. Which made the lamps seem sort of chintzy, like they were from a student's apartment. Which they were, actually, so I hopped in the car and went to Marshall's to get something more festive. I brought back two red ceramic beauties with clean white plastic-covered shades.

Satisfied with the living room, where I envisioned cocktails and dim lights, I turned a critical eye on the kitchen and found fault with everything. Mostly, that I didn't have cooking utensils. The truth is, I don't actually like to cook; I like to eat.

I got Devil Dog back in the car and we headed for Williams Sonoma in Copley Place Mall. It was more expensive than Walmarts, but it would last and I saw a new chapter in my life unfolding: a chapter where I had someone to come home to.

Clean apartment, stocked kitchen (I went to Bread and Circus on the way back from the mall) and then to my closet. I resolutely retrieved the red jersey dress from the back of my closet and tore off the tags. I hung it on the hook on the bathroom door to steam out while I took a bath. I always showered to avoid the self-scrutiny that a bath required, but now I examined my ripe body with shy appreciation. When I put on my red dress, I admired the way it clung to my curves. I put on a pair of black Audrey Hepburn-style pumps, applied war paint and waited for my partner in fantasy to arrive.

Which he did, right on time. I jumped when the doorbell rang. I was still on edge from the note in the mailbox.

"*Bonita*," he said, kissing me warmly.

It was better than the kisses I remembered. He pushed me away and looked at me. "*Querida*, what is wrong?"

I couldn't help it. I started crying. "I can't tell you, Hidalgo. It has to do with this case I took. It's just my nerves, I guess."

He took me in his arms and held me tight. "I will make it better for you, *Querida*. You will see." He smiled reassuringly and I daubed my eyes with a kleenex.

He looked around approvingly at the apartment. I saw, too late, that I'd left a price tag on one of the lamps.

"The little dog is here, just as I imagined," Hidalgo bent down to pat Devil Dog.

"He speaks Spanish," I told Hidalgo.

"Dogs speak all languages," he told me, looking gravely at Devil Dog, who seemed excited that someone appreciated his hidden qualities.

Did a man exist who was more charming than Hidalgo?

I poured us two glasses from the bottle of Château Mouton-Baron Phillip he brought. He definitely wasn't from the Manischewitz school of wine like the rest of his family. Come to think of it, he hadn't drunk any of the wine I had brought to his home last time. I was a little embarrassed.

"I'm sorry about the last time, the wine I brought..." I said.

"My father drank it all. He loved it." Hidalgo smiled and raised his glass in a toast. "This is a special occasion, no?"

"Yes. I'm surprised Ines couldn't make it," I said, joking. So far, she had been on all of our dates.

"You want Ines here?" He put his glass down and seemed suddenly proper. "She's working with Señor Stubbs."

I put my hand on his. "I'm kidding, Hidalgo. I was starting to think she was your shadow."

We drank and talked our ten minutes of serious talk, then he proceeded, as if on cue, to tell me in exquisite detail, how wonderful I was, and then, still following the script, he led me into the bedroom. He asked me to undress, which I did slowly. Not out of a desire to tease, but because I was shy about my bountiful attributes. I left my shoes on. I was proud of my feet, and I wanted to showcase them.

I pointed at my feet. "These are new..."

Hidalgo was at my side instantly. "Your feet are beautiful, *Querida,* but your lips and hips are..." He groaned, and I let myself go.

He made love to me, even making the donning of a condom seem erotic, and afterwards swore that I had inspired him and that it had never been like this with anyone else.

"And now," he said, springing up as if on cue, and pulling on his jockey shorts. "I will make you a wonderful meal."

I tumbled into that crevice that not even the jaws of life can pry you out of. That is, I felt myself falling in love.

"No, wait. Just a minute. Let's just talk." I patted his side (his side!) of the bed and he came back willingly. "If we're going to be friends...we're going to be friends, aren't we?"

"More than friends."

"If we're going to be friends, I need to know about you. About why you're not cooking professionally, about why you don't have immigration papers. I want to know everything."

I covered up my breasts with the quilt and he gently moved it down. "If I'm going to tell you, I need to see these. For inspiration."

We laughed loudly. Suddenly I heard Mr. Schwaizburg next door cough. I had never heard him through the walls before. I blushed, thinking that he must have heard everything.

"What first?" Hidalgo asked. "What do you want to know?"

"Well, how did you come here? Why don't you have papers if your family lived in Texas? What was your first job?" All I really needed to know was that Hidalgo had the smoothest skin, but hardest body I had ever felt on a man. But the curse of the litigious class is our need to know everything.

He smiled. "My first job in America. That's easy. It was in Hollywood."

"You were an actor?"

"I was an audience. The studios pay twenty dollars to sit through a show and laugh when the "laugh" sign lights up and clap when the "applause" sign lights up. You know? None of us spoke very good English, so it made it funnier than you can imagine. We had no idea what we were laughing at and applauding."

"How did you get to California?"

"Swam."

"The Rio Grande?" I was astonished.

"That's right, I'm a wetback. Want to feel a real wet back?" He turned around so I could touch his back. It was silky. I was glad nothing had happened to it in transit. "I carried my aunt. She couldn't swim."

He could tell I was becoming sad, so he smiled and said, "Now, I am really going to make you a meal. Like you have never had, I promise."

I put on a robe and followed him into the kitchen. Besides the wine and box of Kustom Klein chocolates, he'd brought steaks, which he marinated while baking a couple of potatoes. I sat on a stool by the counter and watched him, glad that I had bought all the cooking ware. Most people use one knife for everything. Not Hidalgo. He changed knives like a surgeon performing an operation. We decided to eat on the counter and forego the formality of the dining room.

"You know, Hidalgo, you should cook. Professionally. This is the best steak I ever had."

"I did, once. Now I am blacklisted." He said it as if it were of no consequence to him.

He told me about Mexico, where his family lived on Isla Mujeres. During the 1960's the island had been a Mecca for hippies and after that for tourists. In the eighties, an American company had built a clothing factory there to take advantage of the agile hands of the young girls. The Gomez family owned a restaurant and he was cook. A vacationing American chef gave him some free pointers and his card, telling him if he ever got to Boston to look him up.

But Hidalgo couldn't leave his family. Business was good. His sisters (he had two others still there) had found work in the sweatshop. Life was as good as anything they had reason to expect.

But then his sisters were blacklisted, because radical priests were organizing the workers, and they were devout Catholics. The American company kept lists of those who were strongly religious or strongly political, they made no distinction. Either could mean trouble to corporations that relied on non-unionized labor.

"It started to be very bad for us," Hildalgo said. "My sisters could no longer work. The armed patrols and the demonstrations were scaring away the tourists, so business at the restaurant was terrible. We had no money at all."

"So, then, you decided to come here?" I asked.

"Not quite then."

He told me about an American female executive tourist vacationing there one winter. By any yardstick, Hidalgo said, she wasn't beautiful. In Mexico, she was too pale to be considered beautiful or even exotic. But she pursued him and Hidalgo didn't resist.

They shared a few days of passion. He would leave her room tired, as if he had mated with a black widow spider.

"I forget her then, you know?" Hidalgo said. "I come to this country. I get a job in a Mexican restaurant in Copley Place and my boss there, he starts the papers for me. My father, my mother, my aunt, Ines are all here. When I get the papers, then I can do papers for them."

"For a green card?" I asked.

"Yes, for green card. And then, one day, I am coming out from work, there she is."

He saw her coming down an escalator, briefcase in hand. She looked at her watch then a second later looked at it again. He adjusted his chef's tunic and approached her.

"Miss Nancy?" he said.

At first, Miss Nancy didn't recognize him. When she did, she didn't seem pleased to renew their acquaintance.

"I was wearing, you know, a dirty uniform," Hidalgo said. "I should not have spoken to her in the dirty uniform. I embarrassed her."

It wasn't hard to get him fired. Carlos, the head chef, although he knew a set-up when he saw one, knew that if he didn't fire Hidalgo, he himself would be fired and there would be two senseless firings instead of one. Carlos told him that *gringas* sometimes misinterpreted a look of appreciation from Hispanic men. They viewed it as threatening. Especially these Boston women who tried so hard to look good, but treated you like a pig for enjoying the view.

"Carlos told me I was lucky I was only being fired," Hidalgo said. "I could have been arrested."

There was no malice in Hidalgo's voice as he told me this.

"We can start the paperwork again," I said. "Unless Mikey's doing it."

"No, Mikey won't do it. He likes me, but he doesn't want to get involved. He doesn't know if I was a criminal or something in Mexico," he said.

For a moment, he looked lost in his own problems. Then it was my turn to cheer him up.

"I'll sponsor you. Your family. Ines, too," I said, not knowing how the Bar Association would regard an attorney sponsoring someone so close to a murder.

Hidalgo started clearing off the dishes, but I shooed him away.

"My job," I said.

He laughed and then it was his turn to sit down and watch me work. He seemed to enjoy the view. "This is not why I am here, you know," Hidalgo said. "For the papers."

"I know. Bring your papers over next time. Let's see what you have. Then we'll see about the job thing. Copley Square isn't the only place in America to cook food."

He got up and kissed me on the cheek. He put on his clothes and took Devil Dog for a walk, while I finished the dishes. I don't think I've ever met a man who'd had more guff thrown at him but didn't turn bitter. There was a lesson in there somewhere. I thought of my bachelor uncles. They hadn't expected to have a child thrown at them to raise. Yet, they weren't bitter either. They, too, were just looking for the next opportunity. All three men were so unlike the vultures circling Carlton Stubbs' estate that they didn't seem to belong to the same species.

I dried the dishes and put them away, then, smiling happily, remade the bed in case Hidalgo wanted to stay over.

Chapter 8

What's a 7 Letter Word for Star-Crossed Lover?

Hidalgo left at 5 o'clock to go home and change for work. I was sinking back into a blissful snooze when Dick called.

"Get up," he commanded.

"No." I turned over.

"Get dressed."

"Why?"

"The paintings are missing."

He was waiting downstairs when I emerged 10 minutes later..

"Why do you need me?" as I climbed into his tan Taurus. "You didn't need me to visit Bunny. Hey, pull into that McDonalds. I need a cup of joe."

"Tucker is hostile to me. He hung up on me when I told him I was a private investigator. I need you to soften him up."

"Tucker? I thought we were going to see Ulrike."

"They're connected."

I ordered a McBreakfast to go with the coffee for the ride up. Who was I to discount Dick's hunches?

A Gentle Giant moving truck idled in front of Tucker Stubbs' farmhouse. Two wiry movers wrestled a crated painting through the front door, which was propped open by a dolly. Tucker appeared in the doorway to check us out then disappeared back inside. He reappeared with Stone.

They came down the stairs, followed by a bodyguard. Stone gave a curt nod to Dick and looked at me curiously. He whispered into his bodyguard's ear then climbed into a back seat of a silver Lexus. He opened the back window and Tucker leaned in to talk to him, looking over his shoulder at us once.

"Looks like he's getting rid of everything," Dick said.

"Maybe he had a big sale."

"To whom?" Dick seemed distracted.

We parked in front of the truck.

"You're staying in here, boy," I told Devil Dog. I didn't want him getting crushed.

We got out and I peeked in the truck. Six crated paintings were stacked inside.

"Say what you want about quality," I told Dick, "That boy certainly has everyone beat in sheer quantity."

Dick snorted. "I wonder why he's having a fire sale now."

"Times are tough," Tucker said.

We both started at the sound of Tucker's voice behind us. He pulled at his pony tail, noticeably agitated. He gave some directions to the men who were taking a break on the front step, wiping their foreheads and drinking Gatorade. Tucker took off his baseball cap. His head peaked in a ridge as if giant hands had done a poor job of fitting the two sides together.

Tucker saw where my stare had settled. His mouth stretched into an uneven curl. "You find it hard to believe that my paintings are coveted? That a private collector has an insatiable appetite for my work? He's having a party or something, and put in a big order. What could I do?"

"You don't have a reputation," Dick stated blandly. "Isn't that why investors invest? A reputation built on what the public wants?"

"The public has nothing to do with the judgment of art," Tucker said, testily. "If the public likes your stuff, you can pretty much guess it's irrelevant and not really art. Tourist painting. Over-the-couch mall paintings."

His passion surprised me. "So art is good only if no one likes it?"

He looked at me with disdain.

"Look, everyone loves the Impressionists today," Tucker said. "Yet, they were despised in their time. Monet couldn't give his paintings away. If he weren't independently wealthy, he wouldn't have been able to paint. I am in revolt against a public that ignores an artist who risks everything and later buys this same artist's works at auction for millions. And that lines up at blockbuster shows at museums to see this newly-beloved work. After the poor bastard is dead, of course, and can no longer profit from it."

Dick looked at him wryly. "That's a socialistic attitude for a rich kid."

"I was born an artist. I can't help the circumstances of my birth."

I pointed to the inside of the truck. "Where are they going?"

"Chicago."

One of the Gentle Giants came over. "We're set, Mr. Stubbs."

Tucker climbed into the back of the truck and checked the paintings against the manifest. He shook a couple of crates, making sure they were secure. His footsteps sounded loud in the trailer. Finally, he squatted on the edge and jumped down. "All set," he said.

After hanging around for a tip, which never materialized, the moving men consulted a map, jumped in the cab of the truck, and drove off.

Tucker showed us into the house. "I assume you want to ask me some questions, that don't concern my career. Although I don't know why I should talk to you at all."

The first time I was there, I was so keyed into the sound of flagellation and the shock of seeing a Dominatrix in action that I hadn't noticed the décor. The kitchen still had the plumbing and appliances of an old farmhouse; not the clever imitations some decorators like. Tucker turned on the water to wash his hands, and the sputtering water verified their authenticity.

"I can never keep all you official types straight," Tucker said. "What is your involvement in my life again?"

"I'm your mother's attorney. And Dick is my private investigator."

"Right." Tucker closed his eyes. He seemed tired. "Mummy."

"I gather we're not the first ones to ask you questions," I said.

"You must be third or fourth on the list. First there were the detectives trying to find out if I murdered Dad…"

"Did you?" I interrupted, then regretted my bluntness. "I mean, I can't really do anything to help your mother get her finances in order until the issue of your father's death is resolved. Murder or suicide."

"Sometimes," Tucker said, "I think, 'if only I had a different father'. I would be a famous artist. Or at least, a happy artist, if such a creature exists. But killing the father I had wouldn't give me another one, now would it?"

I shook my head.

"Look, I wish I could claim responsibility for killing the sonofabitch. God knows I would have felt like a man if I had. Dad was right about me. I never had the guts to go man to man with him. I don't think too many people did."

"So you hated him?" I asked.

"We were from different planets." Tucker looked mournful. "That's no reason to kill someone though, is it? If it were, we'd all be dead. Anyway, Dad was a presence. It would take an equal presence to take him on."

"And no one in your family had that kind of presence?" I asked.

"You've met them all. What do you think?"

He saw my surprised expression and said, "Look, it was probably a suicide. Dad always liked to call the shots." He allowed himself a smile at his own joke. "He was dying, and I don't think he wanted to be surprised. He wanted to know exactly when it was going to happen. Make an appointment. Pencil me in for Death!"

He laughed loudly. His cell phone buzzed suddenly. He pulled it out of his pocket, frowned when he saw who was calling and turned to speak.

"Don't be so impatient. Have I ever let you down." Pause. "I can't talk now." He put the phone back in his pocket without saying goodbye and turned to us impatiently.

"Where is Ulrike?" Dick asked suddenly.

"Meiner?" Tucker shrugged. "I haven't seen her in days. She works very hard. She's German, you know."

Tucker opened the car door for me.

"Why does it matter if Dad was murdered or committed suicide?" he asked nonchalantly.

"The murderer can't benefit from your father's death. And the people who are suspects will benefit. They can't be sure it was a murder, though," I said. "And if it's suicide your mother can't cash in her life insurance policy. It has a suicide clause."

Tucker tensed. "Too bad for Mother. I told you, it's a suicide. If you knew the man, you'd know it was the only way he would go." He turned to leave. The interview was over.

Dick put the car in reverse and backed down the driveway. When we were out of earshot, I said to Dick, "What's eating him?"

"Someone's putting the screws to him."

"What do you mean?"

"I mean, I think that his paintings are a cover for something else. And someone is waiting for the sale."

"Like who?"

"Ulrike Meiner."

"I don't see how."

We found our way onto a road that looked like a highway and headed south, frowning.

"They were old," Dick said, suddenly, banging the steering wheel.

"What was old?"

"The wood was old!" Dick said, excitedly, just realizing what was wrong with what he had been looking at. "Tucker's canvases were stretched over antique wood."

"Maybe he's frugal."

"More likely he's hiding old paintings by covering them with his own work. He's the cover."

I gulped. The missing masterpieces were right in front of us. "Why didn't you stop him?"

He looked at me as if speaking to a child. "You can't just yell 'citizen's arrest' over something as complicated as forgery. I could've blown everything."

"Why is he dumping them all now?"

"He probably needs the cash. He's being squeezed."

"Well, if Ulrike's forgeries were revealed, I guess Ulrike wasn't doing such a good job."

"On the contrary," Dick said. "She was doing a better job than the masters. She fixed their small mistakes. She couldn't leave the little imperfections alone. It's what confirmed them as forgeries. Of course, the Museum Director would have never volunteered that. He had already shown the Bates Collection three times. It would ruin his reputation if it got out he didn't catch the forgeries himself."

We drove in silence for a while. "So you think…" My mind grew blank as my blood sugar ebbed. "What do you think?"

He looked at me pointedly. "Stone can't afford a scandal in the family when he's running for governor. Matilda and Tucker are involved in an art hoax. That won't play in Attleboro."

"You got any proof for your theory?"

"None. We have to wait for the truth to reveal itself," Dick said.

We pulled onto Route 2, heading towards Boston.

"Is that your method of detecting the truth?" I asked, sarcastically. "Just hang around and see what happens?"

Dick was unfazed by my sarcasm. "I've spent twenty years dealing with people who were trying to subvert the truth for one reason or another. The only thing of which I am certain is that there's no way to force it."

I sat at the counter in Max's Deli picking up messages from my cell phone: a loving message from Hidalgo, a request from Uncle Joe for a 7 letter word for a star-crossed lover. A frantic message from LePage telling me that Sarah was on yet another binge, this time in a pool hall, and would I please "as a friend of the family" haul my ass over to Flat Top Johnny's and help out. And a call from a Mrs. Cornelius Clark. New business, I presumed from her desperate tone. I tried to recall if I'd ever met her. A blond, overly-surgeried woman came to mind. She could be any one of a hundred I had met in the last few years.

I wrote her phone numbers on an index card and decided to forget her and LePage for a minute and have a nice quiet lunch with Max, Devil Dog, and Howie Carr.

Max looked particularly spiffy. His white shirt was starched and he kept tugging at the collar. "What are you all dressed up for?" I asked him, pulling a plastic covered menu from the slot outside the napkin holder.

"Stone Stubbs is in Brookline today. I wrote him a letter and told him to try our restaurant. Free. Who can resist a free meal? It was Connie's idea." He pointed with a spatula towards the back of the room where Connie was peeling and slicing vegetables.

"Still mad about?" I cocked my head towards Howie Carr, who sat upright on her new dog bed in the corner behind the counter, politely sniffing Devil Dog. Howie still seemed shell-shocked from her experience at the track. It might take her a long time to trust her instincts again.

"Yeah. She'll get over it. She's a good woman, but she doesn't like animals. Thinks they're dirty. It's the way she was raised. In the city with no animals." He leaned over and whispered to me, "If you ask me, people can be a lot dirtier than animals."

"Tell me about it," I said. Is any creature nastier than a supposedly civil human being in the middle of a divorce? I buried my head in the menu. "What's good?"

"What's not good, tell me that?" He put on his reading glasses and showed me the special page. "Go for this," he said, pointing to the Blue Plate Special: boiled chicken and vegetables. He peered over his glasses, looking for my reaction. "Still on that diet?"

"Yes, no. I don't know." My weight didn't seem to be an issue with Hidalgo. I hadn't detected anything but admiration in his eyes.

"You don't need to lose weight," Max said, authoritatively. "But it's your business. I put this on the menu in case you want to, though."

I closed the menu and slid it back behind the condiments. "Whatever you recommend. I put myself in your hands."

Max smiled and called something to Connie in the kitchen. She came to the door with a knife in her hand. She gave me an evil look and stabbed the counter with the knife, letting it stand there, while she went to prepare my lunch.

I blinked hard and swallowed. "If Howie Carr isn't working out," I said to Max, "I can find another home for her."

"I love Howie," Max said, loudly enough for his wife to hear. "She's a very good dog. She likes everything I give her to eat." He turned back to me. "Don't worry about her. Her bark is worse than her bite."

He put a pot of boiled chicken and vegetables in front of me and watched me eat.

How do you know who is all bark and who would actually bite? Who just loudly hated Carlton Stubbs and who was capable of drilling a hole in his head? Dick was probably right. You had to wait for people to reveal themselves.

"Waddaya think?" Max asked.

I looked at him blankly. "Oh! This?" I tilted the bowl so he could see it was empty. "Delicious."

"It's a classic. I'd like to see them," he jerked a thumb at the Hammer and Pickle, "make boiled chicken and vegetables." He flung a dish rag in front of me, waving away my payment.

The door opened and we turned to see a man in a dark suit enter, followed by Stone Stubbs. Max was out from behind the counter in a flash. The man stood in front of Stone.

"Mr. Stubbs, what an honor." Stone must have said something to his bodyguard because he stepped aside and let Max through. Max clasped both of Stone's hands in his.

Stone smiled and took a seat at the counter. He turned and saw me. He pulled his bodyguard close to him and, not taking his eyes off of me, whispered in his ear. The guard nodded and came over to me.

"Mr. Stubbs would like to buy you a cup of coffee, Ms. Herbinko."

"I'm sort of busy," I said, surprised he knew my name.

"He really would like it," the man said, taking a hold of my arm—gently, but firmly.

Max saw me talking to the man and ran over. "Swanson, you should have told me you knew Mr. Stubbs."

I smiled wanly.

"Come here, Swanson. Sit by Mr. Stubbs. Or should I say, *Governor* Stubbs?" Max smiled obsequiously, pushing me into a booth. Stone got up and joined me quickly. He waved his hand and his bodyguard moved away. Max ran back into the kitchen.

Stone looked me in the eye across the table. "I feel as if I already know you, Ms. Herbinko."

"How's that?"

"Everywhere I go I find you've already been there."

"Matilda Stubbs is my client."

"You seem to have taken a broader interest in the Stubbs family than just Matilda."

"It's a pretty complicated case."

"Have you found out anything the police should know?"

"If the police should know it," I said. "I told them."

Max brought over a couple of coffees and, beaming, set them in front of us. He waited for us to order, but Stone's chilly silence made it clear that we didn't want any interruptions and he finally fluttered away.

"The police don't know who killed my brother," Stone said.

"The evidence was botched," I said. "If you're elected governor, maybe you can see that the police get a little extra training in crime-scene hygiene," I said, thinking of the night nurse who got away with the tape.

"Do you have any ideas?" he asked.

I looked at him. His eyes were navy blue, clear and steady, betraying nothing. I pictured him aiming a pistol at his brother's head. He must have seen what I was thinking, because he laughed.

"You think me?"

"Mr. Stubbs. I'm just trying to protect Mrs. Stubbs' interest. I'm not a detective."

"I understand someone had a tape player recording my visit with Carlton."

"That's true."

"I understand the tape is missing."

"That's true, too," I said.

"It's worth a lot of money to me to find that tape."

I gulped.

"I can't have a cloud of suspicion over my head." Stone leaned back against the booth. "Milton Baum told me your PI found out that I borrowed some money from Carlton's Trust."

I shrugged.

"I'm going to repay it before it comes due. It was just a loan."

"That's what I assumed," I lied. He seemed awfully nonchalant about stealing 125 million dollars. "It's due in a week or so, isn't it?"

"I have every intention of repaying it, even though Carlton forgave the loan."

I raised an eyebrow.

He looked at me, hard. "It would be disastrous for me, if erroneous information about my intentions with that money were leaked. And by extension, disastrous for you and your uncles. And it would be extremely beneficial to you and your uncles if nothing was said about this *loan* until after the election. Do you understand what I mean, Ms. Herbinko?"

I got up to leave. His bodyguard was at attention by the booth in a second. "I understand all too well, Mr. Stubbs."

I checked out the phone book before I left for Flat Top Johnny's. It was somewhere near Kendall Square in Cambridge. It astounded me that LePage felt no compunction about calling me to help bail Sarah out of trouble.

"Here we go." I lifted Devil Dog in my arms, pitched him in the back seat then drove to Cambridge. I rummaged in my glove compartment and found something suitable: "BIOHAZARD" with a red hologram atom swirling over the word. I might get a ticket, but no one would have the guts to tow me.

Flat Top Johnny's was in a new entertainment mall near Kendall Square. It was a yuppie square with the requisite brew house, Thai restaurant, and coffee house that catered to the overworked drones from the high tech firms forming like fungus around MIT. Flat Top Johnny's was a pool hall. Or rather, billiards club, as I was informed by a big kid in a navy polo shirt, who also told me that Devil Dog wasn't tall enough to reach the table and therefore had to be tied up outside. That was the rule: tall enough to reach the pool table.

"So an Irish Wolfhound would be okay? Or a Great Dane? This sounds like short discrimination to me."

"Just make sure he doesn't bite." The bouncer came back out with me and watched with his hands on his hips as I tied Devil Dog to a tree. "We don't need no lawsuits."

"Pee all over it," I whispered to Devil Dog, smiling at the bouncer. "Pee all over everything."

He glowered at me as I went back in. I wanted to growl at him, but then I saw a lone figure at the bar, LePage. She wore a neon pink shirt tied at the waist. One leg was crossed over the other, pumping furiously. I thought the mule at the tip of her foot was going to fly across the room at any moment. Two men stood nearby at the bar, talking nervously and looking at her. The obviously liked what they saw and were getting up the nerve to talk to her. I hurried over. The ice in the soft drink in front of her was almost melted, so I shimmied up the barstool, pointed to her drink and held up two fingers to the bartender.

"What the hell took you so long?" she asked, not exactly looking at me.

"Excuse me if I have to work for a living. Unlike some people."

"I always pay my own way."

"Inherited wealth is not exactly paying your own way."

"Inherited wealth is not all it's cracked up to be, honey. I'm earning every fucking cent. Believe me."

The bartender came back with the drinks. I sipped mine and winced. It had rum in it.

"Look at her," LePage said.

"Who?" I squinted into the dimly lit hall, my eyes adjusting to the darkness. Laughter came from a table in the far end, where Sarah waltzed with her cue stick, scoping her next shot. Three young men lounged nearby enjoying the performance as she bent over the table to shoot. Her dress couldn't be much shorter.

"I can't take much more of this," LePage said.

"Why is she doing this? I thought that you fixed it so you and Sarah were set for life."

"I haven't seen a nickel yet," she said. "Carlton was not only a bastard, he was a lousy businessman. I'm getting the vibe that there isn't much money to squeeze out of this family."

"So you love Sarah for the money?"

"Don't be an idiot. I just want her to get her due, if that's possible." LePage laughed. "Let's face it. If you see a bag of money in the street, you'd be a damned fool not to pick it up. That's what inherited money is. It's like a big bag of money you see laying in the street. Only you're not the only one who sees it. You're part of a pack of jackals."

"And in this particular case, someone killed the guy who was putting the bag in the middle of the street and tried to make it look like he ran in front of a car."

The bartender put a drink in front of her and pointed to one of the men who was standing at the bar. She pushed it away. "Tell him I'm busy. Look," she said, turning her attention back to me. "The cops ask me the same questions every day. Where was I? What was I doing there? Fuck, I live there!"

"What were you doing in his room, LePage?" I asked.

If she was surprised that I knew about her affair with the old man, she didn't show it. "I was breaking it off with him. That night. Honest to God, Swanson, I was breaking it off. Sarah found out about it. We dykes are pretty jealous."

"Well," I pointed out, "You were screwing her father. There're other principles involved."

"It was for us! He told me that he would leave the house to us if I were friendly with him. He had a thing for black pussy." She flicked her head back as if proud that she was able to turn her nubile body into cash. "You'd be surprised how many rich white guys do."

I wouldn't be surprised at all. "Then why break it off? You stop wanting the house?"

In one graceful movement, LePage drained the glass in front of her and began on the second. "Sarah said she would kill him if I didn't break it off. Then she would throw me out." Her eyes filled with tears. "After I've saved her ass a zillion times."

It was hard to believe that someone would throw away everything in a jealous rage, but define "everything."

"She only started gambling again after she found out about you and the old man, isn't that right, LePage? Her way to get some money so you wouldn't have to prostitute yourself."

She slammed her glass on the bar. "You think that's a reason? That's an excuse! She'll tell you that we all have our own way of trying to make it in this world. I use my body, she uses her luck. But those things only last so long. Her father's money would have meant security."

"Maybe she just didn't like how it was earned," I volunteered.

"There's no nice way to earn big money, sister."

She suddenly got up from the barstool. "That bitch! How much does she think I can take?"

Sarah was cozying up to two of the young men who were watching her play. She had planted her body right in front of the bigger of the two. He handed her a drink. The other one was moving a piece of hair that had fallen in her eyes.

"She's just flirting," I said. "She probably likes the attention."

"Hrmph! I can't believe you're so naïve. I gotta get a new best friend. One that ain't so stupid."

I let it sink in that I was now LePage's best friend. People like her have a strange concept of friendship: no reciprocity is involved. I thought a friend was someone who asked you how you were doing and occasionally waited for an answer. She was like other socially isolated people I had encountered—she needed witnesses to her life.

"Everyone flirts," I said.

"She's not flirting, she placing bets."

As if sensing that we were talking about her, Sarah put down her cue stick and came over. Sweat lined her upper lip. Her eyes had the colorless lashless look of a baby chick. She got in my face. "What are you doing here? Smell money?"

I stepped back. She reeked of cigarettes. "Is that what you're doing? Making money? I thought you were losing it."

"Hey, lay off." LePage stepped between us.

Sarah turned her white face coolly towards LePage. "These guys are chumps. Just see me through this one game." She spoke through her teeth as if scared that her opponents could read her lips.

She squeezed LePage's hand and I saw LePage's magnificence melt.

"Just one more, babe," Lepage whispered. "Then come home." She released Sarah's hand.

Just then the door opened and a tall, black-haired woman in all leather swept into the bar. It was Ulrike. She surveyed the room, when her gaze stopped at Sarah. I slid off the stool and ran after LePage who was running after Ulrike who was making a bee-line for Sarah. Sarah calmly put down her drink and chalked her cue, as Ulrike hissed something at her. Finally, she raised her gloved arm and slapped Sarah with the back of her hand. LePage grabbed Ulrike by the back of her hair and yanked her off Sarah.

"You got a problem with saying hello, lady?"

Ulrike turned nimbly and tripped LePage, who went flying onto a pool table. Sarah jumped on Ulrike's back and pounded her. LePage got up and she and Ulrike grabbed each other like wrestlers, going around and around, looking for an opening gambit. Sarah still clung to Ulrike's back, pounding her, until Ulrike collapsed.

The bouncer finally came over and threw all of us out. We stood on the sidewalk sizing each other up, breathing heavily.

"What do you think you're doing, bitch?" LePage yelled. "I should kill you."

"What is that bitch doing selling my paintings?" Ulrike pointed a finger at Sarah.

"Your paintings?" Sarah said. "They belong to my family."

"No one in your family likes art," Ulrike said.

"What does that mean?" Sarah said. "Is she crazy? And what are you doing stalking me? How did you know I was here?"

"Your brother tells me there are only a few places that his little sister would be," Ulrike said.

A cruiser car turned the corner, its lights flashing. As unobtrusively as possible, I walked towards Devil Dog. I turned around nonchalantly to see LePage arguing with the cop. She pushed Sarah forward and the cops suddenly let everyone go. Sarah and Ulrike continued arguing and LePage came up to me.

"You weren't much help." She looked disapprovingly at my new Audrey Hepburn-style pumps.

"I'm not much of a fighter."

"You might want to learn a few tricks. You're up to your eyeballs in this family."

"I do my fighting in court. What's that all about?" I jerked a thumb towards Sarah and Ulrike.

"That bitch thinks the Bates Collection belongs to her. Says Carlton promised it to her."

"It wasn't his to give away," I said.

"Yeah, well, I guess she didn't get the word." She walked with me. "You hear anything new from the cops?"

"No. They're getting comfortable with the suicide theory."

"Where's that damned tape, anyway? Can't they just search everybody's house?" LePage leaned against a street sign. "You know, girlfriend, if you think that Carlton Stubbs was murdered, aren't you scared that the murderer will come after you? You've been nosing around a lot. And there are a few people who wish you wouldn't."

"You're a suspect. Think I should be scared of you?"

"I'm saying it won't hurt to mind your own business." She went back to where Sarah and Ulrike were arguing.

The rum in the Coke made my head throb. Devil Dog lay still, his forepaws straight ahead, his head erect, like a Sphinx. I felt alert for unseen dangers, too.

"You can relax, boy."

As I untied him I looked around to see if someone were watching me. Then felt foolish for doing so. I wasn't James Bond, for God's sake, I was a domestic relations lawyer. No one would want me dead.

Still, LePage's words stuck with me and I opened the hood of my car, which was stupid because, unless it was labeled "Car Bomb," I wouldn't even know what one looked like. I jumped in, held my breath, and started it.

Devil Dog fell right asleep in the back seat. Breathing easier, I pulled out the index cards with the phone numbers on them. I decided to call Mrs. Cornelius Clark and immerse myself in her domestic disappointments. Dry her tears. Help attach her husband's income. Beat the brute into the ground. It would be a small vacation.

But before I could do that, my phone rang. It was Bunny.

"I got a cell phone," she said.

"I see."

"I need to see you. You told me to get legal counsel. So I did. I want you to tell me what you think."

"Think about what?"

"What you think about my choice in attorneys. We're going to be going up against you and Milton Baum."

"You're not fighting Milton Baum. He's on your side."

"My attorney advised me that he is not. That he's on the Stubbs' side. And while our interests may coincide, he's not my lawyer and will not represent my interests."

I didn't say anything. I saw 3 billable hours slipping away as I wasted them with Bunny.

"Just come here and meet them."

"Them?"

"I wanted them to check on each other."

I laughed and found myself liking Bunny. Despite our conflicting interests, I had more in common with her than I did with Matilda.

I hung up, thinking I should see Matilda anyway and get her up to date. After all, she was paying the bill.

Chapter 9

Behind Every Great Fortune There's a Crime

The next evening, I picked up some vegetarian chili from The Hammer and Pickle and headed to Harvard under the cover of darkness. The air was oppressive, the house dark, and Matilda's car nowhere in sight. The carriage house, though, was lit up as if it were burning. I drove through the double doors and parked. Overhead, footsteps tromped back and forth.

I stage-whispered up into the hole in the ceiling. "Hey, Bunny!"

A young man in a navy blue suit bowed his head through the hole. "What do you want?" he asked.

"I want to see Bunny? I'm a...friend." I held up my carton of vegetarian chili. "I thought she might be hungry."

The man disappeared. In a moment, Bunny appeared overhead. A cigarette dangled from her lower lip. She squinted, trying to make me out in the darkness. "Oh, it's you, Swanson."

The ladder slammed down and I wobbled up the rungs. With Bunny was the guy in the navy suit and a clone in an identical suit who grabbed my arm and dragged me over the top. The place was cluttered with pizza boxes, empty cola cans, and crumbled Marlboro packs. It reeked of sweat and rotting food.

Bunny was even dirtier than the last time. Her hair hung in limp, greasy strings. Her face, bloated from junk food and soda, had lost its chiseled look. Her belly draped over low-rise jeans. She was beginning to look like Tommy O'Reilly's fat older sister again.

"Jesus," I said.

"Good to see you," Bunny said. She stuck out a hand for me to shake, which I did, then wiped my own surreptitiously on my skirt. She gestured towards the clones. "This is my legal counsel."

The men nodded in unison.

"Where did you get them?"

"Milton Baum referred them."

We shook and introduced ourselves. They let it "slip" that they graduated Harvard Law. Ivy Leaguers always find a way to introduce their pedigree within two seconds of saying hello. Anyway, they didn't need to tell me. Only Harvard lawyers would wear blue wool suits on a sultry summer night to visit a client in a dirty loft. Each clutched a briefcase, old and battered accordion types that appeared to be heirlooms. They were too young to have been practicing for more than a few years. Milton Baum was stacking the decks with amateurs.

"We're going ahead with plans for the redevelopment of Stubbs Pier," Bunny said. "We've already begun Phase I."

"Which is?"

"The buy-out," one lawyer said.

"The buy-out," Bunny said, as if he hadn't spoken. "Here look." She opened the rolled-up plans on the table and jerked her head for me to come over. "This whole area will be demolished. Then we can start construction. When the people see how much their neighborhood is improved, the rest will go without a hitch."

I looked down at the map and inhaled sharply. The area within the red circle contained my uncle's house and their businesses. "How can you be sure these people are going to volunteer for your experiment?"

She pulled her head away from her cigarette smoke. "Already have. It's a done deal."

"It's a done deal," one of the lawyers repeated. If I looked closely, I could almost tell them apart, like twins. I wondered how much she was paying these guys. Probably a lot more than I was paid so far by Matilda.

"Where are you getting the money?" I asked.

"Well," Bunny said, excitedly. "Tristan here," she pointed to one of the lawyers, "was looking into Carlton's business deals and found out that Carlton's businesses in Mexico are very lucrative. Ramirez and Betancourt, that's the Mexican law firm that handled Carlton's Mexican finances, was trying to find me. We crossed paths looking for each other." She laughed.

"Trying to find you for what?"

"Carlton put the manufacturing plants in my name." She leaned in to me. "I told you he loved me. That must've been why he wanted to honeymoon in Isla Mujeres. To show me what he was going to give me. Anyway, I went to Fleet Bank and they made me a loan, based on those earnings."

I looked at her blankly.

"They thought I was a very good risk." She licked her lips. "I mean, the Stubbs name is like collateral, for God's sake. They're going to make a lot of money on this, too, don't worry."

I wasn't worried about Fleet Bank making money. I was worried about Matilda getting her due. I would have Dick check all this out before I broke the news to her.

I gave Bunny the bag of chili. "I brought you this. I was going to bring you some Swanson Dogs, but I didn't have time. Swanson Dogs. My uncles make them. They're named after me," I added, wanting to make Bunny's attorneys realize that I was a woman of substance. I had a hot dog named after me.

Bunny put her nose in the bag and inhaled the aroma, closing her eyes as if she were enjoying a private delight. "Wonderful! Thank you, Swanson. You're such a good friend."

I pulled her close and whispered. "Bunny, do you really need two attorneys?"

She looked surprised. "They keep each other honest. Each one has a different opinion on what I should do." She flicked the ash off her cigarette then squashed the butt on her soda can before pushing it inside. "Anyway, I can afford them now. I have access to all this credit. Fulfilling a great man's legacy is the most important thing in the world," Bunny said. "And it's going to be my legacy, too."

"You think this complex is a legacy?" I asked. "What about his family?"

She laughed. "His family? You've met them. Think they're a legacy?" She looked over at the twins and they laughed too, taking their cue from her.

"After he got sick, he had time to rethink his life," Bunny said. "Rethink what's important. How do I want to be remembered? That's what he asked himself all the time. What do I want people who aren't even born yet to think when they hear the name 'Carlton Stubbs.' I started to ask myself the same question, Swanson: What do I want people who aren't born yet to think of when they hear the name "Bunny O'Reilly!" She banged on the rolled out architectural drawings. "This is Bunny O'Reilly!" She leaned closer, her cigarette breath overpowering me. "In a year, everyone is going to know the name 'Bunny O'Reilly'."

I left her there to plot with her two counselors, and lurched back down the ladder. Quickly it was dragged back up. What were the chances she would pull this off and anyone would think of anything except the word "deranged" when they heard the name "Bunny O'Reilly"? Of course, maybe all captains of commerce had to be a little deranged to take the risks they did. I just didn't know what to make of it.

I went over to the main house, peering through the screen door to see if any life stirred. Matilda still had barricades up to divide the house in two. All the knives in the kitchen were stuck in a cutting board on the counter, like a dog baring its teeth to the enemy. Even a woman as entitled as Matilda Bates Stubbs had to fight for a piece of the pie. Her own pie. I left.

Bunny hadn't lied when she said she had already bought up Broadway. When I drove down the street the next day, the neon lights were off over both Swanson's Doggie Emporiums. Big orange and black "Closed" signs covered the doors. Uncle Stevie's door was padlocked, but Uncle Joe's wasn't. I entered. Uncle Stevie was drinking coffee at Uncle Joe's counter as if he did it every morning. Uncle Joe was wrapping coffee mugs in newspaper and packing them in a cardboard box. The place was almost bare. The empty doggie cooker sat motionless, like a Ferris wheel in a condemned amusement park.

"So, it's true," I said.

"She made us an offer we couldn't refuse," Uncle Joe said, winking at me. "An *ultimproffer.*" He wrote it down.

"Jeez, that's the worst one yet," I said.

"I'm losing my edge," he admitted and crumpled up the paper.

I took an unwrapped mug and poured myself some coffee, then sat at the counter next to him. "Your place too?"

"Packed up," Uncle Stevie said. "Ready to go."

"You're going into that complex? I can't believe it." What I really couldn't believe was that the entire neighborhood was going to be gutted and buried under a granite mausoleum. "What about the house?"

"Sold. Everything sold. We couldn't wait to be driven out of business. We'd lose big time."

"You could fight it," I said.

"Little people don't have a chance when big money steps in. All you can do is get out of the way. Anyway, we wanted it. We were tired of...things." They looked at each other warily.

"I'd like to see the house one more time. I grew up there you know." I felt suddenly miffed that no one had thought to consult me about selling my childhood memories.

"You have time. It won't be torn down for a month, at least."

A month! Bunny was certainly in a hurry.

"What are you going to do? Where are you going to live?" I was afraid to ask what made them start speaking to one another again.

They looked at each other. "You tell her," Joe said.

"No, you."

Joe smiled. "We're going back to school."

"School! At your age!"

Stevie looked hurt. "We wanted to do it before," he said, "but you know..."

"Oh!" I stirred my coffee. Putting me through law school had come first. I felt ashamed of myself for being so selfish. "For what? What are you going to school for?"

"You tell her," Joe said.

"No, you."

Joe said, "Cooking school. We're going to the Cordon Bleu in Paris."

"Cooking school! The Cordon Bleu! Paris?"

"We want to open a Reuthenian restaurant."

Our family was Reuthenian, although beyond a few holdover traditions like ornate Easter eggs and Slavic superstitions, it meant nothing to me. I was third generation and raised in the white pudding melting pot of South Boston. Older Reuthenians, keepers of the culture, had either died or were living with their children in the suburbs. I couldn't even imagine what Reuthenian cooking was. I racked my brains thinking of ethnic food I was subjected to as a child and came up with only hot dogs.

"What the hell is Reuthenian cooking?" I asked.

"You tell her," Joe said.

"No, you."

Joe smiled. "That's the beauty! No one knows!"

"No one knows?"

"We can feed people anything, tell them it's Reuthenian, and charge them an arm and a leg. Ethnic food is very big. Very big." Joe looked serious. "And no one has anything against Reuthenians."

"Not until they find out they've been hoodwinked by you two." It was such a harebrained scheme, I had to laugh.

I picked up my things to go. "But why Paris?"

They looked at each other and shrugged. "Why not Paris? If it can be anywhere, why not Paris?"

Why not Paris, indeed.

Since I hadn't heard from Matilda in days and since she wasn't in Harvard when I saw Bunny there, I was beginning to worry about her. Then she left me a voice mail saying that she had temporarily moved into a house in Cambridge. She wanted me to review a business venture she had hatched.

She left unclear directions and told me to meet her there that afternoon. I grimaced as I looked at my watch. It was four o'clock. I would never find a parking place. Of course, mundane considerations like that would never occur to Matilda.

After circling Harvard Square a number of times looking for even an illegal parking spot, I outwitted a bleached blond driving a navy blue Saab convertible who was waiting to back into a metered space that was being vacated in slow motion by a Volvo station wagon. She put the car in reverse to parallel park, but I nosed my car in as the Volvo left. The result was not a pretty parking job, but I was in there.

The blond was out of her Saab with the velocity of a weasel. "You can't do that! It's illegal to park like that!" She stomped on the curb, calling me names.

I calmly flipped through the parking cards in my glove compartment until I found the appropriate one: Dean of Harvard Divinity School.

"You're supposed to parallel park, not do what you did!" she screamed.

I put the card in the windshield. "I was here first and you know it." I pointed to the bogus Divinity School sign then rolled my eyes heavenward. "More importantly, He knows it."

"You're just a bitch!"

"There's no law that says you have to parallel park," I told her.

"How would you know? Are you a lawyer?"

I opened the windows a little, locked Devil Dog in the car and looked around for the address Matilda gave me. "As a matter of fact, I am."

"What now? Lawyers for Jesus?"

Before I could walk away, the blond was dragging over a meter maid, a middle-aged black woman who looked tired of our argument before she even heard it.

"Take your hands off me." The meter maid shook the blonde's hands off her and squinted through the windshield at my Dean of Harvard Divinity School sign then at me. A smile flickered across her face. "Good morning, Dean."

I nodded reverently.

The meter maid put her ticket pad in her pocket and put her hands on her hips officiously. "Now, what's the problem here?"

She spoke directly to me, but the blond piped in. "She took my parking place. I was waiting to parallel park, and she zipped right in and...."

"Excuse me," I interrupted, "but I have a very important meeting which I am missing because of this most interesting conversation. Could you please just tell me if I am legally parked or not?"

The meter maid bent over, closed one eye to line up the center of the car with the curb, then said, "It's legally parked Dean. If you have a meeting, I suggest you not miss it."

She winked at me and I smiled, leaving her to collect an earful from the blond.

I looked for the address again. Nothing on the street looked swank enough, but I rang the doorbell of the house matching the number Matilda gave me. It was an old frame house, probably dating from the Revolutionary War. The window frames were so rotted that one violent Nor'easter would blow the windows out. I rang the bell again. A voice yelled, "It's not locked!" so I went in.

A whirring floor fan stirred around the humid air. The curtains were closed in an effort to keep out the heat. Within the muggy gloom, I could make out two figures entwined on an old-fashioned sofa. Pins of light seeped in through the drawn curtains, dotting their faces.

"Matilda?" I asked.

"Hello, Swanson. Come on in. I want you to meet Attila."

"Attila?"

"He's my hairdresser."

"Hairdressers make house calls?" I stuck my hand into the darkness in the direction of the figure that was not Matilda. A large warm hand grabbed it and pumped it vigorously. He said something I didn't understand.

"Attila is Hungarian. He doesn't speak English," Matilda pulled the man's face close to hers and kissed him. "It's his best trait."

"How do you do?" I said, enunciating every syllable. As my eyes adjusted, I saw that Attila was very handsome. He was tall with chiseled yet pleasant features. His thick black hair was pulled back from his high forehead into a ponytail that ended below his collar. His open shirt revealed a muscular, hairless torso. He was a swarthy Fabio. I glanced at Matilda's mutilated face and wondered who started the myth that money couldn't buy you everything.

Attila reached out and touched my hair. Apparently he didn't like what he saw and felt, because he began speaking excitedly. I assumed I was being accused of hair abuse. It was a fair assessment. My method of hair maintenance is to color my naturally blond hair brunette, perm it, and wait for the ends to break off without intervention. It was a grim cycle started in my student days when my salon was the punk Blaine Beauty Career School in Kenmore Square. Attila reached for a felt roll-up from which he pulled a comb and a pair of scissors.

"Keep him away from me!" I screamed.

"Isn't he darling?" Matilda asked. "He'll do wonders with your hair, Swanson, even if you don't know what he's saying."

Attila pushed me down on a desk chair and began to snip, chattering away in Hungarian. He obviously felt he had gotten to my mop in the nick of time. I watched in horror as long swatches of dark brown fell to the floor.

"How do you know he's not a madman?" I asked nervously, although I had to admit that Matilda's hair looked wonderful. No longer a classic helmet-do, it feathered in wisps around her face. It softened the effect of her plastic surgery, making her look more exotic than deformed.

"Don't be so provincial, Swanson. Isn't your inamorato Hispanic? Oh yes, don't look so surprised. Do you think I wouldn't have my attorney checked out?"

"Checked out?" I asked. "For what? By whom?"

"Dick, of course."

"Dick? My Dick?" I rose from the chair, but Attila pushed me back down. "You hired my private detective to spy on me?"

"Who would be in a better position to know what you do?" she asked.

"What?" I asked. "You don't trust me?"

"Of course I trust you, Swanson, especially now that I know all about you. It's your example that made me ask myself: why not go for an adventuresome man? A real man! A man who wants to start something."

"Attila wants to start something?"

"He wants to own his own salon. It's nothing to me, of course. But to him, it's the world. He shows his gratitude most satisfactorily." She chuckled and stood up to pour herself a drink.

"What about Stone?"

Matilda shrugged and looked away. "Stone and I have an arrangement."

Attila, meanwhile, held up a mirror. He had cut off three inches from the back and layered it around my face. I looked like a different person. He pointed to my roots and wagged a finger at me. I shook my head.

"I'll make an appointment," I promised him, getting up from the chair.

Attila held my shoulders and smiled at me. A little too friendly, I thought. But, his fidelity wasn't my problem. His desire to deplete my client of liquid cash, however, certainly was.

"Do you think it's wise, Matilda," I asked, "to go into your cash reserves right now? Don't you want to wait until the life insurance pays out? You'll have more to play with."

Matilda rattled the ice cubes in her drink and looked up at me with her unnatural doe eyes. "*Carpe diem*," she said.

I nodded. She apparently didn't know about Stone's "loan".

"How is the murder investigation going?" Matilda asked. "When am I going to see this mythical cache of cash?" She laughed at her own pun, and Attila laughed along although he couldn't possibly know what she was saying. Or maybe he did. Maybe he spoke English. Maybe he wasn't even Hungarian.

"They're stalled," I admitted. "They can't find the tape. They're starting to conclude it must have been a suicide."

"Nonsense!" Matilda fought to keep her face calm. "It was a murder. Get some one! Get Ulrike or Ines. Stick it to them. Ines is illegal anyway, for God's sake. And wasn't it Ulrike's gun? For God's sake, arrange the evidence so it's convincing. You people know how to do that."

I inhaled, appalled at what Matilda was suggesting.

"If the police have somehow bungled the evidence linking the murderer to the murder, fix it. You're smarter than they are, Swanson. Just speed up the process. There will be a little something extra in it for you, of course."

"Of course." I thought Matilda was being sarcastic, but she wasn't smirking. Of course, with the tailoring job on her face, it was hard to tell what she was feeling.

"How much do you think you'll need for…" I cocked my head towards Attila, who was busy sweeping my hair from the floor.

"I think $450,000 to buy the building and equipment."

I blanched.

"It's a small investment for my happiness, Swanson. I don't owe you an explanation. You know what it's like to be lonely and what price you'd pay to stop being that way."

I stifled my urge to ask her what price she thought I was paying. Anyway, I thought that Stone was taking care of her loneliness.

"I have some cash, you know," she said, ruefully. "Stone is very generous with his money. With his family, anyway."

"Is Tucker his?" I asked.

Matilda pulled back. "How is that pertinent to this?" she asked sternly. Then she shrugged. "The ambiguity is useful sometimes. It'll pay for a beauty salon. Someone should benefit from our bad conduct. An innocent bystander." She gestured towards Attila, who wasn't your archetypical innocent bystander.

"You might have some cash. But, if there's a snafu in probate or in the murder investigation, or," I swallowed hard, "The Trust, your non-liquid assets will be tied up forever. I'm just saying to watch your cash flow."

"I'm not worried about myself. I'm concerned though, for Tucker and Sarah. They are ill-equipped to make it through life on their own. It's my fault, I know. I didn't teach them fiscal responsibility. Frankly, with all the money in our family, I didn't think they would need to know those things. And their friends are dreadful, aren't they? Where do they pick up those culls? We're not great judges of character, are we?" She looked at Attila and scrunched up her face. "And Bunny? What community outreach program did my dear late husband fetch her from? You know, I'm tired of being a Stubbs. Maybe I should change my name. How would 'Matilda Szilagi' sound?" She laughed.

"You won't have to change the monogram on your towels," I said. "But you won't have to if you marry Stone either."

"Hmm."

One day in the not too distant future Matilda was going to wake up and discover that Attila Szilagi not only knew English, but had quite a deft hand at bank transfers. I told her that.

"You think he wants me for my money?" Matilda said as she saw me to the door. "Probably. Why else would he even look at me? I may no longer be beautiful, but I'm not a fool, Swanson. At least I know what I'm getting into. Do you know what you're getting into with the Gomez family?"

I assumed she would be smiling if her taunt skin would allow it.

"You can call off Dick," I told her. "Probate's the day after tomorrow. I don't think you'll find out anything new about me before that."

"People always surprise me, Swanson. But you have to give them time to reveal themselves." She closed the door.

I went to my office happy, for once, to see the light on. An evil glee overtook me. I wanted to rip the disloyal tongue right out of Dick's head.

I pushed the door open. "What's the idea of spying on me for Matilda Stubbs?"

He looked up from my desk. "You'd rather she hear about you from an unfriendly source?" he asked calmly.

"What do you mean?" He was going to be reasonable, a trait I hate when I get mad. "It sounds pretty unfriendly to me when a detective I have on retainer gets paid by my client to spy on me. I guess you're finally revealing yourself."

"The word isn't 'spy', Swanson. It's 'investigate.'"

"Don't patronize me, Dick. Why did you take the assignment?"

"I didn't just take it. I suggested it."

"I can't believe you would betray me like that!"

"Swanson," he pointed to the chair with a pencil, indicating that I should sit down. "I worked with Matilda on the Isabella Stuart Gardiner Art Museum theft 15 years ago. Do you remember that?"

I shook my head. "Vaguely. I was a kid."

"Well, she knew me from that, and so she trusts me. She asked me if she could trust you."

"She asked you that? You're lying! I have a great relationship with Matilda Stubbs. We understand each other."

"Look, she didn't know you. She got your name from some society luncheon, where you handed out your card. Be realistic. She has a lot to lose in this probate, and she wanted to know if you were everything you appeared to be."

"So you volunteered to find out?"

"Would you rather some thug from immigration find out about the Gomezes holding jobs that should be going to Americans?"

I dropped my head. "No."

"I didn't tell her everything, Swanson."

"My private life is my own. You told her about Hidalgo, too. What possible concern of hers is that?"

Dick looked at me as if I were a third grader caught cheating on a test. "Ines Gomez is his sister. In case you've forgotten."

"And your point is?"

"She was Carlton Stubbs' nurse. She's a loose canon, Swanson. You've gotten yourself involved in a rather questionable liaison." Dick sat back in my chair. "All I can tell you is, if you're getting close to her, watch your back. She might be using you."

He watched me. "And what about your uncles and their Hot Dog Emporiums and their connection to the Stubbs Pier?"

"For God's sake." I left in a huff, stood out in the hall for a minute, then stormed back in. "It's my office, buster," I said.

"Do you want me to leave?"

"No, I have an appointment." I shoved some files into my briefcase.

"I'll leave if you want me to."

"That won't be necessary."

At least my refuge, Hidalgo, remained constant. He listened every night when I called with the day's perplexities and adventures. And we were meeting at my apartment, I looked at my watch, in one hour.

I took Devil Dog for a walk. Fed him. Showered. Tried on some dresses and realized that everything looked better with my new haircut. I decided to stop taking fashion advice from boys wearing tongue studs and let Attila dye my hair back to its original blond. Barter might be my only payment for the rest of the case after Attila got finished running through Matilda's money. A year of haircuts and hair coloring. I sighed. The phone rang, and I thought it might be Hidalgo telling me he was going to be a little late, but it was Dick.

"Twice in one day, Dick. To what do I owe the pleasure?"

He exhaled loudly into the phone. "Are you sitting down?"

"Yes," I lied.

"I verified that Carlton's Mexican factories were profitable and that he had indeed given Bunny majority stock in them. But there's more."

I sat down.

"He's mortgaged all his houses to the rafters. Harvard. Louisburg Square. Louisburg Square is worth a cool 4 million alone. There's others, apparently. He pumped all that money into his Mexican factories."

Matilda couldn't have known how badly she was about to get screwed. I looked at my watch. Hidalgo would be here any minute. My brain was pounding. "You know, Dick, I really can't process this right now."

"You remember what Balzac said?"

"Please, Dick, no French aphorisms!"

Dick continued as if I hadn't spoken. "Balzac said, 'Behind every great fortune there is a crime.'"

It was hopeless. There was no way to reroute that money back to Matilda. I felt sick. "Could Matilda have known what Carlton was doing and popped him. Could she?"

"That's what you're paying me to find out. They finally got search warrants for that tape. Now we're getting somewhere." He hung up just as the doorbell rang.

Hidalgo stood there in a sharkskin suit with a white tee-shirt and spit-polished black shoes, holding a cardboard packing box. I let him in and when I began to say something, he covered my mouth with his. "You look beautiful." He broke away, put the box down, and looked at me, spinning me around. "What's wrong?"

"New haircut. Do you like it?"

"Very much." He nodded his approval. "But what is wrong, *querida?*"

I couldn't confide in Hidalgo. "Lawyer-client confidentiality," I said.

He was thoughtful for moment, then brightened. "Tonight we are going dancing."

"Dancing?" I hadn't been dancing since the Spring Swing in law school. "I'm not a very good dancer," I confessed.

"Yes, you are. A woman as beautiful and graceful as you is a good dancer. I will teach you."

Despite the evidence, I allowed myself to believe that I might be a good dancer. We petted Devil Dog good-bye. I pushed the cardboard box into a corner. "It's my family's legal papers," he said to my raised eyebrows, and off we went to Hot! Hot! Hot! a new club in Dorchester frequented mostly by Dominicans.

I learned the Rhumba, the Samba, attempted a little Salsa. Love made me light. Love made me see the world through a crystal where people were good and didn't try to atone for past sins by committing new ones.

Chapter Ten

Sloppy Seconds

The alarm went off at six fifteen. Devil Dog was asleep on my feet. Hidalgo mumbled something in his sleep and inched closer to me when I touched his back. I luxuriated in his warmth before jumping out of bed, making a cup of instant coffee, and writing him a note. By seven thirty I was in Cambridge, knocking on Matilda's door.

Attila answered, bathrobe open, holding a cup of tea. He said something in Hungarian.

"In here Swanson," Matilda called from the kitchen. "Have a cup of tea. We stopped drinking coffee." Attila bent to kiss her. She ran a hand through his hair. "As you can see, we are very health conscious. In the beauty business, we have to be."

I waved off her offer and plopped down in a chair.

"So what's so important it couldn't wait until a civilized hour?" she asked.

"I have bad news, Matilda."

"He didn't commit suicide, Swanson. I don't care what kind of evidence they have."

"It's not that." I took a deep breath. "It appears that Carlton wasn't as bad a businessman as we thought. He had some lucrative enterprises in Mexico."

"Is that right?" Matilda sat up, interested. "People always surprise you, don't they?"

"Always. But the point is that he isn't the majority stock holder in these companies."

"Who is? Me?"

"Bunny O'Reilly."

Matilda froze. "Bunny O'Reilly?"

I nodded.

"I see."

"There's more. Two months ago, Carlton mortgaged Louisburg Square, Harvard and several other properties and plowed the money back into these factories." I held my breath and waited for her to scream.

Matilda stared at me for a moment. Then, she opened a cupboard over the sink, brought out a bottle of Tanqueray, and poured a fat shot into a juice glass. So much for her health kick. "This must never get out," she said.

"What?"

"No one must know. Don't we have a confidentiality agreement?"

"Some publicity might pressure Bunny to do the right thing."

She smiled bitterly. "The right thing." She pinched Attila's cheek. "No one is to know. Do you understand. We're going to probate as if nothing happened."

"Did you hear me?" I was incredulous. "You don't have a house."

Her face turned hard. "If this gets out, I'll ruin you."

It was as if Matilda had been raped but was ashamed to report it.

"We're going to go through probate as if nothing's happened. I have my reputation to protect, Swanson. And Stone's." She laughed. Attila joined in.

"Whatever you say, Mrs. Stubbs." I picked up my briefcase to leave. "You're the boss."

"That's right."

Later that morning, I was debriefing Dick on my conversation with Matilda when a tawny paw poked out from behind my desk. It was Howie Carr.

"How did you find Howie Carr?" I asked him.

"Is that his name?"

"Her name." I bent down to pet Howie. She allowed me to touch her but responded like a creature who has known the hollow taste of success. "It's a female."

"She was tied to the door with this note on her collar."

I opened it and read: "It was either Howie Carr or Connie. Sorry, Max. P.S. I have some new chicken soup for you to try. Secret ingredient, you'll never guess it."

"How would you like a dog, Dick?" I crumbled the note.

He brushed Howie Carr's hair off his trousers by way of reply.

I reminded Dick that we had a confidentiality agreement with Matilda.

"I understand," he said. "She wants to keep up appearances, as Stone's future wife. However, the police are no closer on the Stubbs murder. They searched everyone's home for that tape and couldn't find it. The murderer must have taken the tape."

If they didn't charge someone with the murder, it would remain a possible suicide.

"Maybe we can get back some of Matilda's paintings," I said, hopefully.

Dick went to the window and put his hands in his pockets. He hadn't changed his shirt or tie. Circles were under his eyes. "I have a friend in Chicago," he said, "FBI. He's on the lookout for the moving truck with the paintings."

"You look like hell, Dick. What do you do all night?"

"The same thing you do. I'm investigating you, remember?" He ran a hand through his hair. "I'll shower later. I think we should visit our boy Tucker."

"Do you miss him?"

"The kid's a good artist. I don't want him to throw his life away bolting like a scared rabbit until we find the paintings."

"I didn't know you were a philanthropist," I said. "What makes you think he's going to bolt?"

"I think Ulrike's blackmailing him and he's blackmailing Stone."

"Oh, dear."

"'What a tangled web we weave when first we practice to deceive.'" Dick said.

"Who said that? Shakespeare?" I asked, taking a shot at esoterica and grabbing my purse.

"No." He closed his eyes and sighed. "Sir Walter Scott. Let's go."

We drove to Vermont. The mailbox was stuffed with several days worth of mail and Tucker wasn't there. Naturally, Dick picked a lock and walked in.

"Where did you learn to do that?" I asked.

"The Boy Scout's." He ran up the stairs. A second later, he ran back down. "Everything's gone. Something's wrong."

Without bothering to re-lock the door, we ran to the car and headed to Manchester, to see if Tucker was with Ulrike's in her Little House of Horrors.

"You know," he said, on the ride up. "Matilda's father never liked Carlton."

"You knew old man Bates?" I asked, surprised.

"I told you I worked with Matilda on the Gardiner Museum robbery. She was on the board of directors. No one thought a robbery on that scale would ever happen in Boston. But after that, she was petrified that someone would try to steal her father's collection. Or deface it. She had it in storage, but Carlton insisted she hang some of it in Beacon Hill. The paintings made him feel important. His family was Texan oil-well money, remember. More money than pedigree."

"I wonder what Bates would think of the paternity suit."

"It's pointless to speculate. Gossip, really."

"Yes, Dick, I know." It was a trait I was coming to respect in him.

"But," he continued, "I know Bates didn't like Carlton, because Carlton was a playboy. He thought Stone would be a more reliable husband. He wanted Matilda to marry Stone."

"Why didn't she?"

"That, I do not know," Dick said.

I pulled into Ulrike's driveway. Tucker's beat-up van was parked alongside the house. A new red BMW convertible was parked beside it.

"Let's just forget Ulrike and go swimming," I said, glancing at the cold blue Atlantic. It looked pure and good, unlike what I was sure awaited us inside.

"Are you scared, Swanson?"

"Scared of what?"

Dick didn't bother ringing the doorbell. He peeked in a front window and pushed the door. It was locked. I followed him around back, through a thick bramble, which snagged my pantyhose, and onto the porch. The kitchen door didn't give way to his shove so he got out his Mastercard.

We went to the cellar door. Dick pushed it open and I followed him down the stairs. The bottom step groaned, and we froze, peering into the basement, lit only by a bare incandescent bulb.

Tucker was bound to an examining table, an electrical clamp attached to his penis. Ulrike wore a skimpy nurse's uniform and swayed on a pair of white five-inch heels. She fiddled with some controls, turning up the current on Tucker's electrode. His moan became a shriek broken by gasping sobs and whimpering.

Another woman in a black cat suit, complete with mask and little pointed ears, sat by his side. She held a cartoonishly huge hypodermic needle, which she brandished in his face. "Don't you know what we do with bad boys?" she admonished him.

Ulrike nodded her approval. "Very good, Mistress Noir. Soon you will fly solo."

"Unlike this piece of scum," Mistress Noir jabbed the needle almost into Tucker's eye. "You can't do anything right. Where is the money you were supposed to get from Stone? Huh? You've kept us waiting."

"That's right," Ulrike said. "He is completely *vortless*."

She spun the knob on the control panel higher. Tucker shrieked. "He hasn't given me any money, Ulrike! I told you!"

"You are such a *vuss*," she said. "A bourgeois *vuss*."

Tucker screamed again. "You greedy bitch!"

She slapped him. "Did I tell you to speak?"

Ulrike stalked around the examining table. "You are a very bad slave." She scowled down at Tucker then tightened the knots binding his hands and feet to the table. His skin swelled around the rope.

"He told me he borrowed the money. You'll get it soon, Ulrike. I told you," Tucker said.

Ulrike hissed. "We'll get our share out of him some other way! You bourgeois always have hidden money. You are *wortless*."

I clutched Dick's arm. "For God's sake!"

Tucker screamed. "At least I'm a real artist, Ulrike! You're not!"

"Ha! Is that what you *tink*? Your paintings are wrapping paper."

Ulrike threw her head back and laughed. Mistress Noir joined in the hilarity while holding the syringe to the light to tap out air bubbles.

"At least the wrapping paper is original. All you can do is copy."

Ulrike slapped him. The first sign of real emotion I had ever seen from her.

"I can think of nothing else to do with you," Ulrike said. She cranked up the power again. A sickening burning smell wafted up towards us. Tucker was getting enough voltage zapped into him to power the entire town of Manchester. He stiffened, then seemed to pass out.

"You pig, don't you die on us," Ulrike shrieked, a note of real concern in her voice. "Administer the antidote!" she commanded the cat lady.

Mistress Noir obediently emptied her syringe into Tucker's thigh. He remained inert. Both women slapped him, screaming obscenities until finally his eyelids flickered. His lips curled in a wan smile.

Dick took my elbow and steered me up the stairs. It seemed superfluous to say goodbye.

The sea air and light startled me. I leaned over the porch railing, to catch my breath and let my nausea subside. But it didn't. I threw up.

Dick looked away.

"What the hell was the point of that?" I asked.

Dick didn't ask me if he should drive. He took the keys and buckled me into my seat. I was too upset to protest that he was taking over even my car. We found our way to Route 128 and headed back to Boston.

"Tucker's never gotten any of the money," Dick said. "I thought perhaps Stone was using some of the money to pay Tucker to play along with the paternity suit. But he wasn't. Tucker knows his uncle raided The Trust. It's a volatile situation."

I imagined myself in the witness box telling an enthralled jury about the scene I had just witnessed. How would I explain the fact that I was there in the first place?

I roused myself. "You think he's okay? They weren't going to…kill him, do you think?"

"No. That's not how those scenarios play out," Dick said. "And like I said, I don't think Ulrike's the one he has to worry about."

The Stubbs' sordid life was turning into an abrasive immorality play, which I didn't have the stomach for. Anyway, we couldn't count on Tucker to help Matilda get her paintings back. He had his own problems.

LePage called me that night to tell me she was dropping all claims against the estate. I found her the next morning in her rented space in a Cambridge antiques mall.

"It was a long shot anyway," she said, defensively, as she arranged some Stubbs family china in a glass display case. It was Royal Doulton, the India pattern. Trees and organic motifs scrolled across the plates, cups and saucers. Shades of Anglo world dominance.

"You don't want to keep even the dishes?" I picked up the serving platter. "They're pretty."

"I'm counting on certain people thinking they can buy a pedigree." She took the platter from my hands, slapped on a price sticker, and placed it in the case.

I whistled. "Is that for the platter or for the whole set?"

"Platter." She surveyed the display. "That letter Carlton gave to me didn't give me anything but the house in Louisburg Square." She sighed. "Which has so many liens on it, I can't afford to inherit the beast. What a booby prize! We'll go back to Virginia after we sell this garbage."

"How did you find out about the mortgages?" I asked. Matilda would be furious if she thought I had leaked the information.

"What do you think I am? Stupid? I did a title search. I figured there might be back taxes. I never thought mortgages. What a prize pig Carlton was. I don't think there's going to a big pot of gold at the end of this rainbow. We're out of here as soon as we sell this stuff off."

"It might not be over for you, LePage. Sarah sold one of her mother's paintings."

"Matilda can take that up with the fence," she said, examining a cup and saucer in the India pattern before putting it next to its siblings in the case.

"How much do you think you'll get for this stuff?"

"I already cleared ten grand."

"Where's Sarah?"

LePage smiled broadly. "Twelve-step program. Meeting this morning. Meeting this afternoon. Meeting every damned minute I can get her to go."

"Gambler's Anonymous?"

"That's right. She's getting her shit together."

"Does that stuff work?"

"Who knows? It gets away her from the puppies and the pool hall. That's all I care about."

"Maybe she should find an interest, a hobby," I suggested.

"She already has one. Gambling."

We shook hands, and I wished her luck. Without a legal entanglement drawing us together, there was no reason to see her again. Anyway, for best friends, we didn't have much in common besides a highly suspicious regard for rich people.

"You take care of yourself, girl," she said, solemnly. "Watch your back."

She made a gun out of her fingers, closed an eye as if aiming at me, then pressed down her thumb. Goose bumps rose on my arms. I waved goodbye, uneasily. Devil Dog barked at her individually, then at the whole place, and we left.

I prepared for probate halfheartedly, knowing that at the end of the rainbow there would be no pot of gold: just a lot of debt as Matilda paid off the mortgages on her properties. It was a mystery why Matilda wouldn't fight the injustice that had been done her. Or at least try to retrieve her stolen paintings.

Instead, I put all my energy into the one thing in my life that promised a payoff: my relationship with Hidalgo.

I threw myself into making the Gomezes real Americans. The technicalities of becoming a citizen were one thing. I could take care of that by calling in my (admittedly meager) chips with the DA's office. What the Gomez family really needed was a crash course in Americana.

"We already have a culture," Ines said, imperiously.

"And I'm sure it's a fine culture in Mexico, but in America you have to learn how we play the game."

"Have they settled Señor Stubbs' will yet?" Ines asked suddenly.

"It's not that big a deal. Sometimes rich people have a lot of things, but no real money."

This information didn't make her happy. She still thought that something should be in it for her. "Who cleaned up his poop? Tell me that? No money in the world is enough for that. What about his brother, Señor Stone, huh? Why doesn't he give me some money?"

"You're working for him now, Ines," I said.

"I took care of his brother for him," she said.

"You were paid for that, too," I said.

Hidalgo squeezed my hand sympathetically. As more time elapsed since Carlton's death, Ines seemed to be getting more agitated.

"So I thought maybe we could go someplace really American. Is there anyplace you want to go?" I asked.

Ines shrugged.

Hidalgo sighed, exasperated. "Well, what do you want to do?"

Ines smiled evilly. "I want to go to a bowling alley. I saw it on television. Candlestick bowling. I want to do that."

"There are other things we could do. Community Boating is right on the Esplanade. We could learn sailing."

Ines laughed. "Bowling. Candlestick bowling."

Hidalgo kissed my cheek. I felt slightly mollified. It's easier to be a martyr if you have witnesses.

"Candle*pin* bowling," I corrected her as we headed out the door. For 30 years, I had managed to avoid learning how to bowl. My record was about to be broken.

We went to Tidy Bowl in Sommerville. It was a time warp. The giant marlin that hung over the refreshment stand suggested an era when Sommerville had a clean body of water to fish in. Pictures on the wall showed teenagers in the 1950's jitterbugging and holding up candlepin bowling trophies. Candlepin bowling is a unique New England sport. The pins and balls are smaller than regular bowling.

"Having fun yet?" I asked her, after she rolled eight straight gutter balls.

"I'm just nervous, that's all."

We watched Hidalgo stare at the pins for a long while. With one swift movement his right arm swung the ball in a wide arc and it slid down the center of the lane. All the pins dropped. I jumped up and yelled like a high school cheerleader. Hidalgo looked pleased, but Ines smirked as if she had caught me red-handed.

I sat next to her as she marked the scorecard. She smoked a Camel non-filter and sipped beer from a plastic cup.

"I didn't know you smoked." I picked up the pack and played with it.

"I just started. I like it."

"I like it, too." I put the pack down resolutely. "It's really hard to stop liking it."

"Look at these people," Ines said, an edge in her voice.

I looked around the Tidy Bowl. Mostly blue-collar workers.

"The Stubbs of the world destroy everything for these people. Putting industries in foreign countries where labor is cheaper, so prices can come down in America." Her eyes narrowed. "I don't see prices coming down, do you? My sisters used to get 40 cents a day making jeans. It cost two dollars to make a pair of jeans that sell for 50 dollars. Who makes out in this deal, tell me that? Give me a farm with pigs and chickens. At least I'm not locked in a room, chained to a bench."

Ines picked up the cigarette that burned the edge of the Formica table. "Why Carlton Stubbs? Why does he get to dole out money, even when he's dead, when others cannot have human dignity?"

"I don't know, Ines," I said. "Life isn't fair."

Hidalgo rolled another strike. Ines snorted. "We allow it to happen. We do the choosing, Swanson. We are victims of ourselves."

Ines finished with a perfect score, if you count straight zeros a perfect score. Which she did. Around 8 o'clock, Hidalgo and I dropped her in Dorchester. She said she had to be at work early, cleaning Stone's condo. Then we went to my place.

Since that time I heard Mr. Schwaizburg coughing through my wall, Hidalgo and I turned on the TV loud when we were making love, hoping it would drown us out. We had just finished when the Late Movie on channel 68 came on: *The Treasure of Sierra Madre*.

"Oh, no," I moaned.

Hidalgo sat up, interested. "What?"

"Turn the channel. You won't like it."

Hidalgo shrugged and grabbed the remote, flipping through the channels, when Stone Stubbs picture flashed on the screen.

"Wait! Go back!" I yelled.

The announcer was just finishing a news flash: "There was no apparent motive and no suspects to date. Once again, Stone Stubbs, candidate for the Republican nomination for governor of Massachusetts and his body guard, Sebastian Toner, were found shot to death in Mr. Stubbs' home on the waterfront."

I pushed the forward select button on the remote looking for more news, but could find none. It was midnight. I called Dick.

"What?" Dick sounded like he was asleep.
"Didn't you hear? Stone Stubbs is dead. Someone shot him."
"Where are you?"
"Home."
"Alone?"
I glanced at Hidalgo. "No."
"Get over to your office right away. I'll meet you."

I hung up, then made Hidalgo promise to feed the dogs if I was gone too long, kissed him goodbye and was out the door.

Dick got there at the same time I did. We ran up the stairs, panting. I unlocked the door and we sat down to catch our breath.

"What should we do?" I asked.

"I'm not sure you're safe, Swanson."

"What do you mean?"

"This is obviously the work of a madman. You are so involved in the case, I'm afraid whoever did it might lash out at you."

"Are you going to tell me who you think did it?"

"No."

"No?"

"I only have suspicions, Swanson. No facts. It wouldn't be right to prejudice you."

"So now what?"

The ringing phone startled me and I jumped. Dick answered it. "Yes, yes. Okay." He hung up. "We can go over now."

I groaned. "To the crime scene?"

"Yup."

I grabbed my purse. "Any suspects?"

"Nope."

"So, whoever did it could be waiting in the bushes for me?"

"Are you scared?"

I exhaled and squared my shoulders. "No."

We sailed across town and were at the waterfront in 15 minutes. I blinked, trying not to envision a maniac lurking behind every bush with a pistol in hand. A body bag was being carried out the front door when we arrived. The place was crawling with police. Dick conferred with the officer in charge. He let us in and resumed questioning the security guard at the front desk.

"Whoever it was had to be familiar to the guard or have access some other way," I said as we stepped into the elevator.

Dick nodded. "Eleventh floor," he said to the elevator operator, a different one apparently from the one who let the murderer in. That one was down at the station. The elevator opened on the eleventh floor directly into Stone's apartment.

It was decorated in a modern style—beiges and charcoals. Three uniformed cops passed us on the way into the elevator. One of them nodded to Dick.

"Over there," Dick said, pointing to a room with the familiar yellow tape pasted across the door jamb. "Wait here."

I stood in the foyer, looking at myself in the mirror that hung on the wall over a sleek console. Dick returned in an instant.

"It's pretty gruesome," he said.

"I can handle it." I jutted out my chin and prepared myself. But it was even worse than I imagined. Blood was everywhere. Someone had smeared blood across the wall where it suddenly and dramatically dipped into the bathroom. I gagged and turned away.

Dick put an arm around my shoulders. "The police think it was a lover's quarrel."

"Matilda....?"

"Stone and his body guard were both naked."

"What?"

"His bodyguard was his lover. His gun is missing."

I turned and leaned against the wall.

"There's more."

"What?"

"The bodyguard isn't dead. He's in a coma, but he isn't dead."

Dick accompanied me to an early morning cup of coffee at Max's Deli and escorted me home.

"Get some sleep," he commanded.

"You," I said.

"I'll call you if anything happens."

It was ten o'clock. The concierge was asleep, my newspaper wasn't there and another message, on pale blue stationary, was in my mailbox. This time, the message read: "BETTER TAKE CARE OF BUSINESS. YOUR OWN BUSINESS."

I tried to say something, but the sound got caught in my throat, and I coughed instead. It woke up the concierge.

"You okay?" he asked, pushing the brim of his hat up from his face to get a better look at me.

I thought I smiled, but the concierge stood up, concerned. "Should I call someone for you?"

"No!" I stuck the note in a file in my briefcase. "I'm fine."

Chapter Eleven

Love is All You Need

Hidalgo had already left for work. A note on the table told me he had walked the dogs and put coffee in the maker, ready to go.

"*Querida*," he said in the note, "Call me as soon as you come in. Don't make yourself sick over other people's problems."

I folded the note and put it in my lingerie drawer. I heard every noise in the building and imagined figures in black cat suits trying to break in.

"Stop it!" I said aloud. Devil Dog snapped to attention. "Not you." Howie Carr cast a sad eye on me and put his head down between his paws. I made the coffee and drank two cups. I wasn't any more awake, but I was wired. I turned on the television to see if anything else was happening with the Stubbs' murder.

Howie Carr (the canine Howie Carr's namesake was on Channel 5) was practicing his specialty: bashing the rich and famous.

"In this day and age," he was saying, "It seems odd to hide something like your sexual orientation. It makes you wonder what else Mr. Stone Stubbs was hiding."

The camera shifted to the front of Matilda's house in Cambridge. Attila opened the door, smiling. He had his bathrobe tied in a neat knot for the occasion, but otherwise seemed oblivious to the camera on him. He was very telegenic.

I put my head in my hands and groaned. "Oh, no."

Attila beckoned into the house for someone to come out. He pulled a slender hand into view, but it snapped back suddenly. Attila grinned.

"The once and would-be Mrs. Stubbs seems a little shy," Howie smirked. "Could she have had anything to do with," he leaned into the camera, one eyeball as large as a whale's, "murdering her fiancé?"

Attila succeeded in dragging Matilda, clad in only an op art print robe and feather mules, into view. A gleeful Howie Carr wasted no time shoving the microphone in her face. The light from the cameras drained her color. She looked pale and helpless. But suddenly, she clutched onto Attila's arm, reared back, and kicked Howie Carr in the shins.

"Hey, ow!" he said. "What did you do that for?" He rubbed his shin vigorously, looking pleadingly into the camera. "I just want to talk to you."

"Talk to my lawyer!" she said and wheeled around back into the house.

I turned off the television and went to my closet to pick out something that would make me look feminine, yet professional, on national TV. Then I got in my car and drove to Cambridge.

Attila, now dressed in pleated dark pants and a white silk tee shirt, let me in.

"You certainly took your time getting here," Matilda said.

She was still in her robe. An open bottle of gin was on the end table, a half-full tumbler was in her hands.

"The police said they didn't want you till this afternoon."

"Well, here it is. Afternoon."

"Get dressed, Mrs. Stubbs, and I'll take you down."

"It's funny, isn't it?" she said. "Now that the whole world knows I don't have money, nobody makes house calls. I have to go to them. Ha!" She laughed bitterly and pushed herself out of the over-stuffed chair.

I followed her into her bedroom.

"What shall I wear? I don't know my part. Am I a widow or a cockold?" She laughed and rifled through a rack of clothes.

I sat on a plump dressing chair. "You're a suspect. That's your role."

A noise came from the closet.

"You didn't know he was gay, did you?" I asked.

She emerged from the closet and dropped her head to her chest. A little chirping sound came out of her. "I was so in love with him. You have no idea."

"But you had an arrangement?" I jerked a thumb towards the other room where Attila was.

"I thought it would make Stone jealous. We tried to make love once, but it was a disaster. I guess I should have known then. I guess I did know, but didn't want to believe it. I told myself he had too much to drink. That's when we agreed to be husband and wife in public. He said he wanted me to be happy. What he didn't understand, is that I loved him and he couldn't give me what would make me happy." She sobbed. "God, I hate him."

"I thought you loved him."

"Love. Hate. If you ever find love, you'll know what I'm talking about."

Attila came in and pointed at his watch.

Matilda nodded and grabbed a navy blue dress with white collar and cuffs, slid it over her head and slipped into a pair of backless pumps.

Through the long window panes on either side of the front door, I could see at least two news vans from local television stations, as well as one from NBC and one from CBS. I reached into my purse and gave her a Life Saver.

She put it in her mouth. "Food's always the answer for you, isn't it, Swanson?"

"Look, Mrs. Stubbs," I said, grabbing her elbow. "You are a suspect in this murder. Everyone knew you were in love with Stone. They think you found him in *flagrante delictco* and shot him and his lover. So, your job now, is to pretend you didn't."

She looked shocked. "I didn't."

I breathed easier. "Good girl. Smile for the cameras and let me do the talking."

There wasn't much to say. I pushed through the gaggle of reporters. Matilda and Attila walked arm in arm behind me—Attila armed with his lack of English and Matilda with the sense of entitlement endemic in her class.

Reporters threw questions at me and I answered each with, "Mrs. Stubbs has no comment at this time."

Howie Carr, an evil grin on his face stepped forward. "Swanson Herbinko, since when do the likes of you get involved with the likes of her?" He tilted his head towards Mrs. Stubbs.

"Have a heart, Howie," I said, sheepishly.

"I should file assault charges against her."

"She has enough problems without you hounding her," I said.

"I'll say. Tell your uncles I said hello."

I nodded. Matilda and Attila piled into the back of Matilda's Town Car.

I turned once more to nod respectfully at several questions and answered each the same way: "Mrs. Stubbs has no comment at this time."

I scanned the group of people warily, thinking any one of them could have killed Carlton and Stone. And they could now be gunning for Matilda. Or me.

Just because Matilda was a major suspect, didn't mean she was the only suspect. LePage, Sarah, Tucker, and Bunny were waiting to be interrogated. Ulrike was prominent by her absence.

"Round up the usual suspects," Tucker said as I walked in with his mother. He looked a little thinner than I remembered him. And tired.

He and Sarah both got up and kissed their mother affectedly on the cheek.

"Sebastian still hasn't come to," Tucker told me.

"Sebastian?"

"Uncle Stone's body guard."

"Oh right." I had forgotten his name.

"In the meantime, we'll be subjected to this nonsense."

A small Hispanic woman, whom I hadn't noticed at first, raised her eyes shyly to look at me and Matilda and Attila, then lowered them resolutely to her clasped hands again.

"Maria del Carmen," Tucker said, by way of introduction. "Daddy's nurse."

"The night nurse!" I exclaimed before I could stop myself.

"*Nolo tape-o?*" I asked in what I hoped was Spanish.

She shook her head violently and began ranting in some Indian dialect I couldn't begin to understand.

"She's El Salvadorian. Part Indian. I can't understand her either," Tucker said. "Neither can the police. They're trying to find a translator now."

Perhaps because of her rank, the police beckoned Matilda to come in first. The detective, an older man with a distinctly gray pallor, blocked my entrance with his arm.

"I'm her attorney," I said.

"It goes a lot faster when we're alone," he said.

"So I hear," I said, pushing my way in. A younger detective with a bull neck and a crew cut was rubbing his hands together.

They seated Matilda at a small gray desk. The young detective pulled a chair close and motioned to me to sit. He started by asking Matilda the usual: her name, relationship to the deceased, etc.

"Fiancé," she said with no apparent irony. And what she was doing on the evening in question. "I was with my business associate, Attila Szilagy. We were planning our new venture: a beauty parlor and health spa all in one. I think it's a fabulous idea, don't you? Body wraps, manicures, pedicures, massage, hair services all in the same afternoon." She dug in her purse and pulled out some business cards. "Give them to your wives," she commanded.

They men obediently pocketed the cards.

"Mrs. Stubbs," the older detective asked, "Did you visit your, ah, fiancé, last evening?"

"No, I did not. I was deeply involved in the financial calculations of my new venture."

"Were you aware of the sexual orientation of your ah, fiancé?"

I leaned forward. "You don't have to answer that, Mrs. Stubbs."

Matilda looked triumphant. "I don't have to answer that." She patted my hand.

They asked some more questions, which I told her she didn't have to answer, and so she didn't. Reluctantly, they released her.

"There," she said, emerging from the room. "Can I please now get on with my life?"

Attila rose to take her arm. Her children rose and kissed her perfunctorily on the cheek goodbye. And that was that.

Tucker was reading a magazine. "Where is Maria del Carmen?" I asked.

"In there." He pointed to a room with glass walls where a tearful Maria del Carmen was speaking to two detectives through a translator. She showed an inordinate interest in the tape recorder they were using. "Apparently she taped everyone's conversation. It was her way of trying to learn English. She says she began to tape the conversation between Stone and Carlton, but she fled when they started to argue. She never went back to the house and she doesn't know what happened to the tape. She was trying to get home to El

Salvador. She has six children still there. They caught her at the airport."

"Wow," I said. "How do you know all that?"

Tucker cupped his ear in his hand. "Listen."

You could hear every word coming out of there. "Could you hear us?"

Tucker smiled. "I don't have to answer that."

I drove Matilda and Attila to Cambridge then called the clerk to see if the pretrial to contest Bunny's codicils had been cancelled considering the new developments. He assured me that it was still on.

"If you're not comfortable, Mrs. Stubbs," I said to her on the phone, "We can postpone. No one would think any of the worse of you."

"Let's get it over with," she said.

I called Dick several times, but I only got his voice mail. I wouldn't blame him if he were asleep, but I could have used a little emotional support. I wanted to make sure he was going to court with me tomorrow.

I called Hidalgo and assured him that I was okay. Called my uncles and told them the same thing, then unplugged and sat down on the bed to watch some television and promptly fell asleep. When I awoke it was seven o'clock in the morning.

In my business, I was used to running after the facts. This time they came directly to my door, delivered by my paperboy, Fast Freddy. The name was a marketing gimmick, because Fast Freddy was slow. Most mornings my paper hadn't arrived before I left for work. Sometimes it wasn't there when I came home. And Fredericka insisted on being called a paperboy, instead of papergirl.

"It's tradition," she told me. "You don't mess with tradition."

She eschewed feminism, claiming it put women in a separate class. "All I want is equal pay for equal work," she said. "Only weak people need special favors."

That morning, Fast Freddy arrived as I walked down the steps of my building. She stopped her bike, balancing on one foot, and handed me a Globe.

"Good morning, Miss Herbinko," she said.

I was about to respond when I caught the headline at the bottom of page one: "Art Forgery Embarrasses Experts". There were two pictures of a Corot painting side by side. The forgery was in the Boston Museum of Fine Arts. The FBI had stopped the truck carrying the original when it pulled into a warehouse in the outskirts of Chicago. I smiled. I frowned. Matilda's damage control was unraveling. I even found myself worrying about Tucker.

"Miss Herbinko?"

Fast Freddy opened a small leather pouch she wore across her chest. She pulled out a sheet of worn graph paper, grimy with newsprint.

"You haven't paid me for three months."

"Send me a bill."

"I can't send you a bill. Stamps and stationary cut into my profit margin. Plus my time. You have to pay paperboys when they collect."

"But you never collect," I said. Where was a 12 year old was learning about profit margins?

"You're never here when I collect."

I found my wallet and fished around for some big bills. All I had were singles. "I'm kind of low."

She thanked me, made a note on her ledger then pedaled away. When I was in my car I remembered I hadn't tipped her in three months. I cursed my association with rich people. I was picking up their habits.

I was disappointed Dick wasn't at the office, even though there was no reason for him to be there. Matilda and I were challenging Bunny's codicil to Carlton's will in pretrial, and I would have found his presence reassuring. He was probably giving a press conference. I took out the Globe and read the entire article. No mention of Dick. He wasn't taking any of the credit. Add "modest" to his list of virtues. I stuffed the paper in the wastebasket then shoveled the files I needed into my brief case.

Matilda's pretrial was scheduled for nine o'clock with Judge Finsterwald. I moaned. Judge Finsterwald treated probate court, over which he'd presided for the last ten years, as his personal naptime. He would lean back in his leather judge chair, hands folded over his chest as if he were pondering the intricacies of the case, when he was in fact fighting sleep. It was a battle he often lost. His own snarfing would startle him awake and as he woke up, he would fling his arms out to the side like a referee calling a first down. Regaining his composure, he would say sonorously, "Proceed."

It could work for you, if you knew how to keep him awake longer than the opposition. My plan was to have Matilda mesmerize him with her new face. He hadn't seen it so it had untapped shock value.

Outside the courthouse, I kibitzed with other lawyers who were waiting for their clients, having a smoke, or hoping to offer services to people who hadn't thought until that very morning that they needed counsel. We sweltered in our navy blue suits. I leaned against a cement column and closed my eyes, pretending I was on the Titanic with the cold sea air ruining my make-up and Leonardo DiCaprio holding me upright. I felt a tug on my sleeve. Reluctantly, I left the doomed luxury liner and opened my eyes to see Bunny, Tristan and the other lawyer.

"Are we late?" she asked nervously. Her eyes darted left and right.

Although she still looked on edge, she had cleaned herself up. Her hair was washed and pulled back in a chignon. Without the grease and dirt, it was blonder than I remembered. She wore a sleeveless black shift and looked rather elegant.

"Show hasn't started yet." I nodded at Tristan and the other lawyer, whose name I never did learn.

They put down their brief cases and began talking to the other attorneys.

"I didn't want to be late," Bunny said. "It makes a bad impression."

The timer watches of several of the lawyers started beeping simultaneously, signally nine o'clock. I looked around for Matilda. Technically, it didn't matter if she appeared as long as I did. But she figured heavily in my plan to keep the judge awake.

"Go ahead," I told Bunny, "I'll see you in there."

Bunny and her entourage filed into the building, while I squinted against the sun searching for Matilda. Reluctantly, I went inside too.

There wasn't much of a crowd for a contested will. I half-expected to see Ines, who, I worried, was going to appeal to the court for damages for cleaning up the deceased's poop. It was only Bunny and company, the clerk, me and Judge Finsterwald, who appeared to sleep walk as he emerged from his chamber. We rose to greet his entrance. His head was so shiny you could see the blue veins mapping the upper layer of his skull.

He sat, we followed. Slowly he pulled reading glasses from his pocket and put them on, reading the depositions in front of him. He read for a very long time. Bunny looked over at me and smiled. She didn't know Finsterwald had gone to sleep.

Finally, the clerk went over to him and whispered something. Finsterwald's arms flew out to his sides and he looked up, like a scared rabbit caught in a hunter's sight.

Suddenly, the side door opened and Matilda walked in, black veil pulled over her face, clutching Attila's arm. She waited until all eyes were on her, then pulled back her veil dramatically, revealing the carnage beneath.

Judge Finsterwald snorted. She had gotten his attention. He couldn't take his eyes off her. I smiled and raised a hand to Matilda, gesturing that she should sit next to me. She and Attila glided over and took their seats. The judge made a judicial noise, banged his gavel needlessly and straightened to make an announcement.

"I see we have one will here," he said, stating the obvious.

I rose. "Yes, your honor, but it is being challenged."

"What?" He examined the pile of papers in front of him, and found what he was looking for. "Oh, yes. So what is the substantive difference?"

Tristan rose. "My client has control of all of the deceased's real estate assets in the company's name, which the deceased's wife is now claiming is personal property. As you can see, my client has a codicil, which wills the company's property remain at the disposal of my client in lieu of payment of wages for the years she was in his employ. It was written just two days before Carlton Stubbs died."

"Stubbs died?" the judge thundered.

"Yes, his is the estate in question," Tristan said. "My client has the codicil. Properly witnessed."

"Ah." The judge turned to the last page of the codicil and noted the witness signatures. "Have you checked these witnesses?"

"They are legal signatures," Tristan replied, reading their names. "Maria del Carmen Reyes and Ines Gomez."

"But they are not legal citizens," I said, trying a risky tactic. "Both are illegal immigrants." Technically, it didn't matter if the witnesses were citizens or not.

"Ah, illegals." He shook his red face and the movement in the veins in his head accelerated. It was the first time he had been asked to think in a week, I guessed. The novelty made his entire body shake.

"Your honor," Tristan said, "I don't know what bearing the immigration status of a witness has on the legality of a signature."

"I don't either," the judge admitted, his jowls quivering with the effort of prolonged speech, "But I don't like it. I don't like it one bit. Do they speak English, I wonder? If they don't speak English, it might be possible that they didn't witness a damned thing!"

We stared at the judge.

"Well," Judge Finsterwald said, "do they speak English or don't they?"

I waited for the other side to hang themselves. Or reveal themselves, as Dick would say.

"Your honor," Bunny's lawyer said, "I hardly think it's relevant what language the witnesses did or did not speak. In fact, with all due respect, I don't think you're allowed to ask that question."

"Not allowed to ask that question? What kind of a remark is that? If someone is ignorant, because of language or any other damned thing, like a physical impairment, it renders his judgement suspect. And another thing, young man," the judge said, clearly upset at the upstart questioning his judicial pronouncements, "If I say something in my courtroom is relevant, it's relevant. Is that clear?"

Tristan bent his head and nodded.

"So, it's relevant. Now," he said, "were the witnesses, or were they not, legal residents of the United States of America?"

"They were not," I answered.

"Then the codicil is invalid." He hit his gavel and dismissed a stunned Bunny and her lawyers. They filed out like ducks following their mother.

The judge turned his attention to us. Matilda was trying to force her immobile face into an expression of supplication.

"Counsel," he said, looking at me, alert for the first time that I had known him, "is this will in order?"

"Yes, your honor."

"Good job. The will stands without the codicil. Please file your papers." He slammed his gavel and the three of us got up. The next case was already lining up, ready to come in.

"Congratulations, Mrs. Stubbs," I said, shaking her hand. "You're at least 5 million in debt." I wondered if Bunny knew how lucky she was.

"I have my pride," she said.

"They recovered some of your paintings."

"Oh, that." She shook her head in disgust. "It's not pleasant to be constantly reading about yourself in the paper."

I nodded. "You could sell them."

"Six paintings don't exactly make a collection, do they? They're worth more as part of the Bates Collections."

"I don't know," I said.

"Of course you don't. Well, it's back to Harvard and the life of a poor country mouse." She took Attila's arm. He was wearing an Armani suit. Since my association with Dick, I could pick out an Armani suit in a line-up.

I shook Matilda's hand and gave Attila a wary look. "I'll be in touch. Call me if you need me."

They swept out of the courtroom. The place was filling up with the participants in the next case. A man sat on one side, a woman on the other. Both sat rigidly, neither looking at the other. A divorce. I sighed and put my files back in my briefcase and was ready to go when I heard a "psst" coming from the entrance to the judge's chambers. Judge Finsterwald's head and hand curled around the half-open door. He beckoned me to come over, which I did.

"Yes?" I asked.

He pulled me inside and closed the door.

"So, Carlton Stubbs is really dead?"

"We just read his will," I reminded him.

"And that man Matilda was with, what is his relationship to her?" he asked.

"Business associate," I said.

He smiled. "I waited a long time for Carlton Stubbs to die. I've always been a little in love with Matilda. She looks more beautiful than ever, don't you think?"

"Do you?" I asked.

"I think I'll call her," he said, beginning to pace. "How long has that sonofabitch been dead?"

"A couple of weeks." Carlton's death was headlines for a week. I wondered if he knew Stone had been murdered.

A few weeks was clearly not a proper season of mourning, but the judge shrugged and said, "She's a fine looking woman. At our age, you can't wait till society clears you for take-off. Why should that sonofabitch Stubbs always have the luck?"

I left him staring out the window, oblivious to the packed courtroom that awaited him. He was more alert than I had ever seen him. That's what love will do for you.

"Thanks for coming," I said to Dick sarcastically. I put my briefcase by the coffee table, which was now my desk.

I smiled at him for the first time. "Congratulations, Dick. That was a good piece of detective work. And now?" I took off my shoes, and put my feet on the coffee table. "What'll happen to Tucker?"

"They're going to take him into custody this afternoon."

"Ulrike?"

"They have a warrant out for her arrest. She wasn't in Manchester this morning. She's probably petrified the people she sold the paintings to are gunning for her too, thinking she'll talk."

Ulrike in prison blues and spike heels would give a whole new meaning to the phrase, 'good behavior.' "There's no nice way to earn big money."

"Who said that?" Dick asked, intrigued.

"A friend." I sighed and pulled a file from my briefcase. A blue note fluttered to the ground. I picked it up and tried to hide it.

"Did you get another one?" Dick asked, alarmed.

"You know about them?"

"I've seen them in your mailbox. They weren't even sealed," he said.

"Didn't the concierge stop you?"

"Sleeping Beauty?"

"Maybe it's just a creep."

He pursed his lips.

"But you don't think so."

He shook his head.

Truthfully, I was scared that someone who had such easy access to my mailbox could slip past the concierge and into my condo. I gathered up some files.

"I have two appointments. Then I'm seeing Hidalgo tonight."

"Do you think that's wise?"

"To see Hidalgo?"

"He is Ines' brother."

"Do you have something against me seeing a Mexican? Does it bug you?"

"Is that what you think, Swanson?"

"What I think is, I'm in love and you could at least pretend to be happy for me. I'm going to walk my dog, take a long bath, treat myself to a pedicure and get ready for my big date. If you want me, I'll be at home."

I got up to leave.

"Be careful, Swanson," Dick said.

"It's a date, Dick. With the man I love. Some big danger. A date. Or have you forgotten what it's like to be on a date?"

It was mean and I was sorry I said it, but I wasn't going to allow him to ruin my happiness. I got in the car and drove off pretending I didn't care, but I was sad that Dick wouldn't wish me well.

Later that afternoon, I opened my mailbox and sorted through the junk. Bills, bills, advertisements enticing me to buy more stuff so I would get even more bills, bills, bills. I was relieved not to see another threatening note.

When I opened the door, Devil Dog jumped up my legs. Howie Carr didn't move. I threw away the advertisements and put the bills in an overflowing basket. An envelope fell to the floor and I bent to pick it up, my heart beating fast. I recognized the blue stationary. Shaking, I opened it. The message, like the others, was spelled out with cut out letters from The Boston Globe. This one said, "LAST CHANCE." I stared at it, trying to divine the identity of the sender. I was getting too close to…what? I felt icy. I toyed with the idea of calling Dick then decided not to. I was a big girl.

The ringing phone startled me. I dropped the note and inched over to the phone as if it were a bomb. Tentatively, I picked it up.

"Swanson, go to your office right away." It was Dick.

"What are you talking about? I have a date, remember?"

"Cancel it!" Dick screamed into the phone, "And meet me there! Take Devil Dog and Howie Carr and get out of that apartment. Right now! Don't ask questions."

"Dick," I asked as calmly as I could, "What's going on?"

"Tucker's been murdered."

"Tucker? Who...?"

"They don't know. Just get out of that apartment right now. Don't call anyone. Just move. Are you moving?"

"I'm moving," I said, heart racing. I picked up Devil Dog and led Howie Carr out of the apartment as quickly as I could.

I slammed the door, my hands shaking as I fit the key and locked it. "Okay, boys and girls," I said, "Let's move." We ran down the stairs on our unevenly matched legs, past the sleeping concierge, and onto the street. We jumped into the car and I sped to the office. I parked and we ran up the stairs of the Arcade. When we got to the top of the stairs, the dogs, absorbing my excitement, pulled me forward. But I yanked them back. They sat, docile and whimpering, while I tried to compose myself. Calmly, I pulled out my cell phone and dialed Hidalgo.

"Something's come up," I explained, trying to sound lighthearted. "I'll call you when it's resolved. No, no, of course, I'm fine. Why wouldn't I be?"

After assuring him that sometimes my job kept me late, and that I would call him the next day, I took a deep breath. "See, it's not so hard," I said to the dogs.

It was as if the Stubbs were being murdered one at a time. And, as Dick said, my close association with them made me a pretty tempting target. I had every intention of going into to my office, to wait for Dick. Instead, I tied the dogs to the cast iron chair outside the beauty salon, wrote a note for Dick, and left hastily for Harvard to make sure Matilda was okay.

Chapter Twelve

Cat (and dog) Fight

It was about seven o'clock when I pulled into Matilda's driveway in Harvard. A big mosquito landed on my leg and I squashed it in mid-suck. Rubbing the blood off my hand and leg, I knocked loudly on the kitchen door. LePage yanked open the door. She'd been crying.

"Yo," she said.

"Are you okay?" I asked.

"I'm okay. She's in there." She pointed to the living room.

"Is Attila here?"

"He was clearing out when we arrived. He said we'd be hearing from his lawyer."

"In English?"

"Yeah, why?"

"No reason."

I went into the living room. Matilda was on the sofa. Tears were streaming down her face and her nose was red. When she saw me, she stopped crying and came over to me.

"Who hates us?" she asked. "What have we ever done to anybody?" She grabbed my wrist with her bony fingers and exhaled high-octane gin in my face.

This was the first time I had seen her lose her composure since the whole messy affair began. "Have you seen the body?"

She slapped me, and I recoiled. "It's not 'the body,' Swanson, it's my son. It's Tucker." She started to cry again, the seams on her face turning an angry purple.

"I'm sorry. Of course. It's Tucker." I eased her into the hall so LePage couldn't hear us. "Have the police questioned you?" I asked.

"Of course they questioned me. As if I knew something. What could I know about it? He was a grown man, he had his own life."

'Did he have enemies?' they ask me. Well, of course he had enemies. Anyone with any blood in his veins has enemies. Just don't ask me who they were. He was a talented artist and people are always jealous of talent."

"Did they ask you to identify him?"

"I went up there this afternoon." Matilda put a wrist to her eye as if to block out the sight. "The head and the chest. I couldn't look. The sonofabitch shot him in the head. The sheriff said it was close range. How can you look someone in the eye and kill him?"

I guided her to a bench in a corner and put my arm around her while she sobbed. There was no doubting that Matilda's heart was broken. I was used to consoling women who had lost 25 years of their lives to a failed marriage, but they had hope of another life. I didn't know what to say to a woman who had lost a son. I searched in my bag for a candy bar. I put my hand on it, but finally left it there.

She looked up at me suddenly. "Swanson, I have to tell you something." She led me out a back door to the garden, and she looked around furtively to see if anyone could hear us. I could smell the gin on her breath. "We still have that confidentiality agreement don't we?" she whispered.

I nodded.

She started crying. "I think I may have had something to do with Tucker's murder."

"What could you possibly have to do with Tucker's murder?" I put an arm around her.

"Listen," she hissed. "Those paintings he sold weren't the originals."

"What?"

"When the people he sold them to found out they were fakes, they had him killed." She laughed drunkenly. "Those paintings that Ulrike copied weren't the originals. I had the originals copied myself years ago, after the Isabella Stuart Gardiner theft. The originals are in storage in...." She whispered in my ear.

I gasped. "All of them?"

She nodded.

"Who knows?"

"Dick. Now you."

"Dick?! Dick knows those paintings aren't original?"

Matilda snorted. "He should know. He advised me to do it after that robbery. Carlton wanted to show off and hang the Bates Collection at the house. But it made me nervous. Dick said to have them copied, like my jewelry. He knew someone." She twirled her rhinestone ring. "No one suspected. Not even at the Museum. And who was I hurting? No one."

"When the Museum Director told me my paintings were fake, I panicked, Swanson. I thought I had been found out. But Dick," she laughed. "One look at what they had, and he knew something was fishy. He suspected Ulrike right away."

"And Tucker," I reminded her.

"Tucker was just her stooge. He had too much integrity to copy other people's work. But those people he sold the paintings to thought he knew they were fake. I know he didn't. Now he's dead and it's my fault."

I led her back in the house and motioned to LePage, who glided over, replacing my arm with hers. Matilda put her index finger up to her lips, and I nodded.

Sarah was in the kitchen, washing some glasses as I passed through to leave. She wore her usual madras shift, her hair disheveled. I smiled at her, but she glared at me.

"I'm terribly sorry about your brother," I said, offering my hand. "And everything."

She refused it, keeping her own hands in the running water. "You people are like vultures, aren't you?"

It was the second complete sentence she had spoken to me, and it was no friendlier than the first. She turned away, and I opened the door to leave.

Dick left a couple of messages on my voice mail, but I didn't even listen to them. I just decided to go to my office and see if he was there. It was 10:00 at night when I got back there. No lights were on, the door was locked, and the dogs were gone. I assumed Dick had left and taken the dogs with him.

"Hello," I said into the darkness, for no reason. The moonlight seeping through the windows reflected off the white papers strewn across my desk. I threw my briefcase on top of them. Then I froze.

From a darkened corner came a faint gurgling sound. Slowly turning, I flicked on the light. It took a second to make sense of what I saw. Dick struggled on the sofa in a macramé cocoon. A red rubber ball bulged from his mouth. His eyes popped, almost as large as the rubber ball. "What?" I gasped.

He tried to say a whole sentence through his nose, before it finally occurred to me to pluck the ball from his mouth. His speech was slurred as if he had been drinking. Even in my most sordid conjectures, I could never imagine him so out of control. "Ulrike," was all I understood.

"Ulrike, here?" I asked, my heart pounding. "How did she know where to find me?"

More words slobbered out. "Ulrike…on the lam. Ulrike…Madame Kabalevsky."

"Ulrike? Madame Kabalevsky?" I sounded like a parrot. "Ulrike is Madame Kabalevsky?"

"Wants to escape…go underground…Madame Kabalevsky." I concentrated to follow his words. They must have had a few drinks before the fun began.

"Ulrike is Madame Kabalevsky?" I asked again, unable to believe it. "She must have been surprised to see you here."

"Not… happy." Dick squirmed in his cocoon.

"Does she know this is my office?"

"Scissors…cut me." He caught his breath and slobbered before the word "out" emerged.

"Oh, yeah, that." I rummaged through the top desk drawer. No scissors. "Those knots are like a work of art," I said, appreciatively. "How did she subdue you anyway?"

"Hurry."

"Dick, where are the dogs!?"

"Ulrike…Manchester…"

"Ulrike took my dogs?"

Dick exhaled and closed his eyes.

"How could you let her take my dogs!?"

I grabbed my bag.

"Don't." Dick whimpered.

"I have to find Devil Dog and Howie."

"Get…me…out…Chinese finger wrap…just gets tighter."

"I don't have time, Dick."

"Swanson, no!" he called as I closed the door.

I drove wildly, not knowing what to expect.

Ulrike's house was dark. I killed the motor and coasted into her driveway. The surf masked the sound of my tires on the gravel.

I got out of the car. On the second floor, a flicker of light, perhaps a candle, passed from one room to another. I crept towards the house and tried the front door. Unlocked. Gently, I pushed it open. I breathed loudly and went in, my heels clattering on the hardwood floor. I smelled a whiff of Paul Gaultier perfume.

"*Wer ist da?*" Ulrike called from upstairs.

"It's me. Swanson Herbinko."

"*Ach, du.*" A clicking sound on the stairs and there she was, in full regalia: white bustier, white stockings, and white, lace-up, five inch Walter Steiger shoes. She carried a taper in a candlestick, the kind with a hook for the thumb. She seemed to be in a trance. "What are you doing here?"

"Where are my dogs, Ulrike? I want them. Now."

"The greyhound, he has no spirit. You are a very bad mistress for those dogs."

"It's a she." Devil Dog came running into the room. "Hey, boy!" I stooped to pet him and let him lick me. He ran over to the cellar door and began pawing it. Ulrike went over to lure him away with baby talk.

"*Kleiner süsser Hund,*" she purred. But Devil Dog wasn't buying. He growled.

"What's the matter Devil Dog? Is something wrong?" I asked. "Where's Howie Carr?"

"You can't go in the basement," Ulrike said.

I ran to the door and opened it. Devil Dog scrambled down on his stumpy legs. I followed, apprehensively. It was dark and I didn't have a flashlight. The moon filtered through the basement window and reflected off bits of metal: locks of cages and tips of brass adorning the cat-o-nine-tails, and the one remaining revolver on the peg board. Devil Dog stared at the second blank spot on the wall.

Ulrike's heels clicked behind us on the stairs. "I told you not to come down here." She thwapped a white riding crop across the palm of her hand. A white bull-whip coiled, like an exotic snake, around her wrist. She followed Devil Dog's gaze.

He stared, accusingly then began to lap water from a bowl. I tried to be cool.

"Where's the revolver, Ulrike?" I asked.

"Where do you think?" She laughed, her lips pulled back over her gums.

Before I finished examining her dental work, her bullwhip furled overhead then whipped around me, pinning my arms close. I wriggled to get free, but it pulled tighter. "For God's sake, Ulrike," I said.

"Sit down," she commanded.

The examining table stretched behind me. I slumped on the edge.

"You are too nosey, is that how you say it? For your own good."

"That's how you say it." My calm amazed me. I've heard that in time of crisis you revert to your strong point. My strong point is the law, but, realizing that it would be more helpful to fight than litigate, I jerked my foot, slamming a spike heel into her knee.

"You bitch!" she screamed. "You want to play?"

"I've seen you play."

She backhanded me across the face, gouging it with her rings.

"You will learn how to serve me. Don't think you will leave here without learning that." She spit at me.

I glanced at the last revolver and prayed it wasn't loaded. I didn't have a chance against hardware like that. Howie Carr appeared out of nowhere, and sat down under the pegboard, stiff as a statue. Devil Dog had fallen asleep. No help from them. "Why did you kill Tucker?" I asked, fishing.

She didn't hesitate. "The bastard! He turned me in. He sacrificed me to save his own heinie."

"What do you mean he turned you in? Weren't you blackmailing him? Anyway, you were already turned in." As soon as I said it, I realized my mistake.

Her eyes got small, dripping with hatred. "*Du!*"

She circled me slowly. "It was you who gave the police information for the warrant. Bitch!" She kicked my shins with her pointy toes.

Her blow broke the skin. Tears ran down my cheeks.

"What do you have against me? What have I done to you?" Her riding crop lashed across my face.

"In your circles, killing people may pass unnoticed, but civilized people don't like it much." I tried to inch off the table.

"Or is it, that you *tschust vant* to play? Why else would you be coming back here again and again. I think you like it, no?"

"No!"

She opened a drawer and pulled out the giant syringe Mistress Noir had used on Tucker.

"I'm allergic to everything," I screamed.

She filled the syringe from an ominous looking bottle, not bothering to tap out the air bubbles, and scanned my arm for a plump vein. I leaned in and bit her ear. I chomped down as hard as I could, and, revoltingly, a piece of ear was in my mouth.

Ulrike screamed and reached for her ear, dropping the syringe and bull whip. Blood ran down her pale neck. I tried not to gag as I maneuvered it out of my mouth and spat it onto the floor. Ulrike screamed again and stooped to pick it up. I kicked her in the chest, knocking her down, disentangling myself from the whip. She flailed helplessly on her back like a turtle trying to right itself. Her five inch, lace-up heels scuttled futilely against the floor. As she turned onto her stomach to push herself up, I jumped on her back, spiking her kidney with my heel.

"Give it up, Ulrike," I screamed. "Dick knows I'm here. He's on his way." She laughed into the dirt. "You're counting on your Dick? He took his medicine. He won't be going anywhere."

Ulrike turned and grabbed my ankle, bringing me to the hard dirt floor. My head slammed against the edge of a cage. I forced my eyes to focus, fighting for consciousness. Ulrike reached for the syringe. Devil Dog had roused himself and was licking my face. His licking revived me and I wobbled up. Ulrike and I faced each other.

She lunged with the syringe. I backed away, kicking at her feet, trying to unbalance her again. But she danced away, mocking me. We circled the table. She jabbed with her syringe.

"You know you want it," she taunted me with the needle.

On her third lunge, I grabbed her arm. She grabbed my hair and yanked.

"Bitch," she said, "Take your medicine. Be a good slave."

I couldn't lean and hold her arm much longer. I was in too much pain. But I had to get back to Dick. God knows, what "medicine" she had given him. I bit her arm until she released my hair, then I ran to the steps. "Come on, kids," I yelled at the dogs. They roused themselves to follow me, but when I pushed the door, it was locked.

My adrenaline went berserk. I pounded my head against the door. Ulrike laughed softly behind me. I turned and kicked, but she caught my foot.

"Too late, *Liebling*," she muttered. "You are too late." She aimed the needle at my inner calf when Howie Carr, remembering some primal programming, sprang. Her jaws clamped around Ulrike's thigh. Growling and thrashing her head, Howie dragged her down and shook her as though she had finally caught the rabbit of her dreams.

"*Halt Hund! 'Raus!*" Ulrike commanded. She clutched the steps and tried to beat Howie off, dropping the syringe, which bounced down the stairs and rolled into the shadows. Howie had her in a death grip. I kicked Ulrike's face, and she tumbled down the stairs. I staggered after her, pulled the revolver off the peg board and aimed it at her head.

"Not the head, please," Ulrike begged.

"Why not? It was good enough for Carlton Stubbs," I said, fishing again. "For Tucker."

"Not Carlton," Ulrike said, whimpering. "I didn't kill Carlton."

I reached in my bag for my cell phone and dialed 911, directing them first to my office, then to the cozy basement in Manchester by the Sea.

Aiming the gun at her head, I ordered her to crawl into a cage. I found my other shoe, put it on, and petting my newly-brave Howie, waited for the police.

Chapter Thirteen

Till Death Do Us Part

I visited Dick the next morning in the hospital. The curtain around his bed was closed, but Dick's voice, giving terse instructions to the orderly bathing him, carried over the flimsy divide. A grumpy man, cursing softly in Spanish, pulled the curtain back and peeled off his latex gloves. I went in the room. Dick, newly washed, combed, and shaved, sat upright, an unread Boston Globe on his lap. His breakfast plate and coffee cup still had their warmers on. I sat down on the foot of the bed, purposely messing up the neat arrangement.

"Feeling better?" I asked, breezily.

"Swanson, the next time you see me in dire straits, call for help immediately. You should have a card with important numbers, ready for emergencies."

"I didn't realize it was an emergency. I thought you were having fun."

He sat up even more erect. "You think I enjoy being bound, gagged and drugged?"

"I didn't know about the drugged part."

"For God's sake, Swanson, I could hardly talk! What were you thinking?"

"I thought you were drunk."

"Drunk? Have you ever seen me drunk?" He reflected a moment. "That woman could teach the Turks some tricks. I checked with the police this morning," he said, suddenly changing gears. "Ulrike's being arraigned this afternoon."

"Is her name really Ulrike Meiner? Or is she Madame Kabalevsky? Or someone else?"

"The FBI is finding out. It doesn't matter what she calls herself, unless she's connected to other murders." Dick looked pensive. "Which she may well be."

"It's funny how someone who could create beauty, could also create such ugliness," I said, thinking about the forgeries I glimpsed in her hidden gallery.

His face reddened. "She didn't create beauty. She created chaos. Her paintings make a mockery of real creativity."

"She would be livid if she knew the truth about the paintings," I said.

"Matilda told you?"

I nodded. "You advised her, I understand."

"I never dreamt it would unravel like this."

"So, what about you? Assault and battery, attempted poisoning?" The nurse had told me that Dick had enough Thorazine in his system to paralyze an elephant.

"I'm not pressing charges. What good would it do? She'll be out of the way for the next few lifetimes at least," he said. "I heard you held your own with her." His eyes were laughing.

I blushed. "Howie Carr rallied. She found her doggie spirit. She's going to be insufferable to live with from now on."

"No less hairy," he said with distaste.

The orderly came in and told me I had to leave; they wanted to conduct some tests on the patient.

"I'll follow up this afternoon on the loose ends. We'll cross-pollinate then," Dick said. "I should be out of here by noon. Isn't that right?" he asked the orderly.

"*¡Espero que sí!*" the orderly muttered.

"*Yo tambien,*" Dick answered then looked at me. "He says, 'I hope so'."

I raised and lowered my eyebrows. "Did Ulrike confess to Carlton and Stone's murder, too?" I asked.

"No." Dick shooed the attendant who was trying to tie the johnny to hide Dick's fanny before putting him in a wheelchair. "She claims Stone killed Carlton so he wouldn't let it out that he raided The Trust. Tucker must have told her."

"Have they found the tape yet?"

"Nope."

"What about Stone?"

"She claims that Tucker was livid when he found out how his uncle had betrayed him. He went there that night to demand his money."

"What do you think?"

Dick sighed. "All I have are suspicions. But she admits to killing Tucker. The police will stick with that. Until they find the tape or Sebastian Toner comes out of his coma."

I felt the hairs on my neck vibrate.

"Be careful, Swanson."

"I have my guard dogs."

"What a family," I said, trying to laugh it off.

"All unhappy families are unhappy in their own way," Dick said, one hand up in pontification, as the orderly pushed him down the hall, IV hangers wobbling above him like royal appointments. "Tolstoy," he called over his shoulder.

"Too bad you can't say that in Russian," I called after him, glad, for once, to have the last word.

The orderly gave me a disgusted look as he pushed Dick into the elevator.

As I was turning to walk back to the nurses' station to find out when they planned to discharge him, Dick's voice emerged before the elevator shut. "*Dos vedanya, Tovarisch.*"

I prepared the final bill for Matilda and delivered it personally to her in Harvard—along with the news about The Trust.

"I knew it, Swanson," she said. "I knew it all along. I just didn't tell you."

I laughed to myself.

"Of course, I naively thought if I married Stone, The Trust wouldn't matter. I thought Stone was richer than God. Milton told me all he had were debts."

Dick had found out the same thing. There was such a long line of creditors in front of Stone's door it was possible Ines wouldn't even get paid for her cleaning stint. I didn't want to witness her rage when that piece of information was delivered to her.

I handed Matilda the envelope with the invoice. She put it in her purse and I groaned inwardly when she said, "I'll give it to my accountant."

"What's next for you, Matilda?" I looked around the living room. "Are you going to stay here?"

"I never liked this house," she said. "I like it less now. But before I decide anything, I'm taking a vacation. Chad Finsterwald invited me on a cruise."

"*Judge* Finsterwald?"

"We have the same friends." She smiled. Her scars were healing nicely, and she could actually move her face. "In my circle, the only thing worse than having no money is not having a husband. And all the eligible men run after much younger women. Who can blame them, really? It must be nice to tell the same jokes you've been telling for 30 years and have someone pretty laugh at them." She smiled wryly. "Chad thinks I'm beautiful. It's funny. When someone thinks you're beautiful, you feel that way. It's a nice feeling."

"I know what you mean."

We shook hands.

"Take care of yourself, Swanson."

"You too."

I handed her some business cards to give to her friends, and left, hoping my invoice would find its way to her accountant.

Back at my office, I daydreamed about a secretary for awhile then tried to forget the whole nasty business of the Stubbs. I cleaned up a few no-fault divorce referrals from a seminar I gave at Boston Center for Adult Education ("How to Plan Your No-Fuss, No-Muss Divorce"), pleased that no dead bodies had shown up, and prepared for business-as-usual.

First stop was the hairdresser. Out of loyalty to Matilda, I snubbed Attila's spa and patronized a grade school classmate—Carla's *New Fangled Tangles* in Southie. I had my hair dyed back to its original blond.

"Like the wheat fields of Reuthenia," my Uncle Joe said when I dropped by the house to say good-bye to the wooden structure that held so many memories. The partitions were still up.

"How do you know what the wheat fields of Reuthenia look like?" I asked. "You've never been there. I did some research, and there is actually no place called Reuthenia. Reuthenians are a people not a place."

Joe reddened. "It's too late. I already had posters of Reuthenia made for the restaurant."

Ever since the idea for the Reuthenian restaurant hatched in their brains, the uncles had been obsessed with their heretofore-uncelebrated ethnic roots. I hoped they weren't going to start dressing in costume. I had seen pictures of Reuthenian folk costume, and frankly, unless you rode a cow, it was a pretty silly look. I certainly hoped they wouldn't make Hidalgo wear a stupid hat.

That was the other thing we discussed: a place for Hidalgo as a cook in their new enterprise. They'd requested an audition, and he was cooking for them tonight at my apartment.

Uncle Steve and Uncle Joe had agreed to sponsor him when they came back from France. At least some things in my life were falling into place.

I took a bubble bath, painted my toenails a new shade of red, Frostbite Tomato, from War Zone, the punk cosmetic company that Fast Freddy had turned me on to a few months ago when I was still paying my bills. War Zone added a gunmetal frost to all their colors, giving the wearer an instantly hip, if slightly decomposing, look.

I slipped into a honey colored dress I had bought specifically to accent my new hair color and right at seven the doorbell rang. Hidalgo smiled as he made his way past me with bags of groceries, plopping them on the kitchen counter. Hidalgo had insisted on buying the food himself. "A good cook always selects his own food," he said, kissing me distractedly. I was in on the birth of a new cuisine: Mexican Reuthenian.

"I am so happy, Swanson." He took both my hands in his and pulled them to his lips. "You have made my life livable. Is that the way to say it?"

"That's the way to say it," I said, breathlessly, wanting to forget the meal and make love with him right there and then.

He felt it, too, but said. "We will have lots of time for that, after..." He reached in his pocket and pulled out a black velvet box, fumbling only a little, and handed it to me. "If you will marry me."

"Hidalgo!" I started to cry.

"Here," he gently took the box from my hand and opened it.

It was a square cut garnet, set in silver. Two little balls of silver shone on each side of the stone.

"That's my birthstone," I said as he slipped it on my fourth finger. It took on a new brilliance the moment it was on. It was the most exquisite ring I had ever seen. Life with Hidalgo was going to be magic.

Hidalgo turned solemn. "You have answered with your eyes and your heart, but not with your lips."

I looked at him. "Yes. The answer is yes, yes, yes." I kissed him gently on the lips, and he responded then pushed me away.

"For our future, I have to make this just right. This dinner for your uncles has to be perfect."

I sat on the kitchen stool while he got out pots and pans, knives and mixing bowls and began preparations. I noticed the box of his family's legal papers that I had shoved into the corner a week ago. They had slipped off my radar. Soon I could devote my time to making the Gomezes legal, law-abiding citizens of the United States of America. A job I could enjoy.

I set the box on the counter and began pulling out papers, admiring the deep resonance of the garnet each time it flashed on my finger, giving half-attention to the papers that I held in my hand. Most were in Spanish. A few were in English, like the lease on their Dorchester apartment and bills of sales for old automobiles. Birth certificates, almost everything else was in Spanish. They would have to be translated. No big deal. My mind kept shifting from legalese to the prospects of actually getting married. I had never considered a church wedding, but now I saw myself in ivory silk and some very cool new shoes dancing the polka (the Salsa?) with my Uncles.

I pulled out a tape. It wasn't labeled. "Hey, Hidalgo, there's a tape in here. Mind if I listen?"

He stuck his head out of the kitchen. "Everything in there is for you to decide," he said. The smell of roasting garlic permeated the apartment.

I popped it in my stereo where I usually listened to my Spanish Language tapes. I heard some loud rustling and then some voices. It was LePage and Sarah telling someone they were going to the movies. Sarah said, "Good night, Father." A deep male voice that I didn't recognize said, "Good night." The sound of heels echoed off the wood stairs and then they were gone. There was the patter of a woman speaking Spanish in the background, talking to herself it sounded like at first. Then another voice, Spanish speaking too, came on. It was Ines. The two women spoke for a while. The sound of more heels on the stairs and then, for a while, nothing. Then the sound of someone opening and closing drawers, when another deep male voice said, "Hello? Anybody home?" It was Stone. This was the tape! My blood ran cold.

My phone started ringing, but my heart was pounding too hard to answer. Hidalgo came out of the kitchen. "Your phone."

I shook my head and pointed to the speaker. Stone and Carlton were having an argument. Hidalgo shrugged and ducked back into the kitchen.

"I'm going to replace it, Carlton. It was just bad timing. And some bad luck. No one's luck stays bad forever. Just give me another 60 days," Stone said. "You know what that's like."

"Look," Carlton said, "You've been fucking around with me my whole life. I want what's mine. If that money isn't back in The Trust in 30 days, I'll tell everyone you're a fucking queer. I don't care. You want my wife, you want my son. I'm tired of your games."

They argued some more, loudly, then silence. I half-covered my ears expecting a gunshot to ring out. But it didn't. Then the sound of heavy male heels on the stairs. My phone started ringing again. Hidalgo came back into the living room and made a motion that said, "Should I pick it up?" I shook my head and he retreated to the kitchen. For a while silence then more footsteps. I strained to listen. It was Ines, but I couldn't make out what she was saying.

Suddenly her voice got loud. She was reciting the story of the Gomez family, which I had already heard, except in this version, the Stubbs' family were the villains. The Stubbs family stole their Texan lands, their labor in Mexico and finally blacklisted her sisters in Mexico. I closed my eyes to think when the doorbell rang, startling me.

"It's probably Ines," Hidalgo said, shouting from the kitchen. "I wanted her to share in our happiness."

I opened the door to see Ines glaring at me.

She slipped past me and pulled Hidalgo into the kitchen and began speaking rapidly. I couldn't understand the words, but I could tell she was very angry. Hidalgo's voice rose.

I stepped into the kitchen. "Is something wrong?"

"You got what you wanted, didn't you?" Ines hissed. "Now, who is going to support my family? Eh? You don't need a man, but we need him. Strong American women don't need men. You don't even need them to make babies. You get them right out of a bottle. What do you want with Hidalgo? You are just another greedy pig! Taking everything that is ours."

I looked at her, trying to remain calm, wishing I understood what she had told Hidalgo. "I am not taking him, Ines. He will always be your brother."

She threw her head back and laughed. "Yes, and it will always be our farm. They told us that, too. We could live there forever as servants. All of our sweat would belong to the *gringos*. Great big, fat greedy pigs. We would clean up after them, nurse their babies, be their slaves. They forced us from our land. But that wasn't good enough. They followed us to Isla Mujeres and enslaved my sisters, enslaved my family with their stupid factory, making college sweatshirts for *gringo cerdos*."

"And then, they had my sisters fired because of my politics. They didn't know me personally, of course. I was just another Ines Maria Gomez. There are thousands of us in Mexico. They made sure that none of my family could work in his town. Their farm, their town. They have taken what wasn't theirs. They got what they deserved. I am happy I found him before he died. And his brother too." She paused. "And now, you are taking what isn't yours."

"Ines," I said, steadily, "What are you talking about? Hidalgo is a grown man. He's allowed to choose the life he wants."

She snapped. "All I know is that you are taking my brother when we need him the most. Who will support my sisters in Mexico? Who will support my mother and my father and my aunt? After you get married, he will give everything to you. The *gringa* gets everything. We get nothing." She spit in my face.

I slapped her. "I don't want anything you have, Ines Gomez."

We jumped at the hollow sound of a gun being fired, it's sound muffled, as if by a pillow. I had momentarily forgotten the tape was playing. I swirled around to turn it off.

"Ines!" Hidalgo shouted.

I turned to see Ines pointing a pistol at me.

She raised it to my face and cocked it.

"Ines! *Que haces?*" Hidalgo threw himself in front of me as she squeezed the trigger. He fell on top of me and we both crashed to the floor.

"Get up, Hidalgo," I said, trying to push him off. I could see past him to Ines, who still pointed the gun at me, waiting for a clear shot. Beyond her, in the open door to my apartment, Dick appeared.

"She has a gun!"

Ines turned to see who I was talking to and fired wildly. Dick winced and clutched his arm, bending over.

Dick ran into the apartment. Ines aimed the pistol at Dick. "Drop it!" he yelled, "Police!"

Ines looked confused, the gun fell from her hands. "She's a thief," Ines said. "They are all thieves."

I whispered into Hidalgo's ear. "It's okay, dear. You can get up." I pushed him off my legs, but his torso seemed glued to me. My hand on his back felt warm and moist and sticky. I rolled him on his side and saw that his eyes were blank, unseeing.

"No!" I screamed.

Dick tied Ines hands together with the trussing string that Hidalgo was about to use on the game birds. He planted a foot on her and dialed the police. "Homicide," he said sternly into the phone. When he hung up, he closed Hidalgo's eyes and lifted me to the sofa. "I'm sorry, Swanson. I tried to warn you before, but I wasn't sure. Sebastian just came out of his coma. He said it was the cleaning girl. He didn't even know her name. He said she got the gun from his holster, which was draped over a chair and shot them both. I got some information from the Mexican police in the last hour that implicates Ines in a political murder in Oaxaca. Why didn't you answer your phone?"

I nodded, unable to speak. My Hidalgo was dead. His brown face, so dear to me, was right there, but his spirit had fled. Devil Dog, that coward, came out of hiding to lick his face.

"You killed him, you pig," Ines screamed at me. "You took him away from us."

A knock on the open door interrupted her. Uncle Stevie smiled in the doorway holding up a bottle of wine. "Are we late? We wanted to get a really nice bottle for the celebration."

Hidalgo had probably asked them for my hand. My heart cracked along a thousand lines.

"Oh, Jesus," Uncle Joe said coming over to me. He took my head in his hands. "Jesus."

The police were there in five minutes, reading Ines her Miranda rights, asking questions, replacing the chicken trussing on her wrists with handcuffs, leading her away. Police photographers came and took pictures of Hidalgo. Finally, someone came and scooped him up in a body bag. The whole numbing procedure took about four hours, but the time passed as if it were a minute.

My uncles insisted Dick leave to go get his arm tended to, assuring him they would take care of me. Then they stayed with me, not talking. Just sitting there. Me in the easy chair. Uncle Steve and Uncle Joe on either end of the sofa. We drank the wine they had brought for dinner, and eventually I passed out.

When I awoke, Devil Dog was sleeping on my lap, Howie Carr sat at my feet, staring straight ahead. My uncles were snoring, heads touching in the middle of the sofa.

It was light and for the first time in weeks, I could feel a breeze make its way in from the ocean and gently caress my face. This time it wasn't a dream.

Chapter Fourteen

Game Over

In the beginning of September, I went to Broadway to watch the destruction of the old neighborhood. By the time I arrived, wrecking balls were moving through like giant pendulums. Trish stood in the window of Dunkin Donuts watching the demolition of her old office. She gave me a thumbs up, holding her jumbo cup of coffee in salute. I waved, trying not to think of a certain employee of Mikey's garage who couldn't be here today. I blinked away the tears, but I couldn't shake the ache from my soul.

Bunny O'Reilly was overseeing the project management for the harbor redevelopment herself. She said, and she was right I'm sure, that if it was going to have her name on it, she wanted to personally guarantee the quality.

"O'Reilly-Stubbs?" she asked me, "Or Stubbs-O'Reilly? What do you think?"

The ballpark would remain where it was—in the Fenway—but the rest of the project looked exactly like the plans Bunny had shown me that hot night in the barn.

She looked natural supervising the work. She wore a hard hat, striped engineer' suit and steel-toed work boots. She had a roll of plans under her arm and an air of authority that was more becoming than any outfit she could put on. She saw me, smiled, and came over.

"Can you believe Dunkin Donuts is holding out," she asked, indignantly. "What do they think they're going to get for that dump if we get eminent domain to put a road through here? And believe me, we will."

The Dunkin Donuts shop stood alone in pink splendor on the almost flattened street. Seven hundred square feet of American culture holding out against big money.

"Wanna get some coffee?" Bunny asked, jiggling the change in the pocket of her jumpsuit. "I owe you."

I stared at her blankly.

"Matilda and I made peace. She even gave me the paintings they recovered from Chicago. Can you believe it? She wants to contribute them to the Pier. We'll hang them in the main rotunda."

"You're kidding."

"People always surprise you, don't they?"

"More than you know." It was the first time I laughed in a month.

"Coffee?"

"Let me tell my uncles where I'm going. I'll join you."

The uncles were standing at attention while the wrecking ball went for the first of the Swanson Hot Dog Emporiums. It crumpled like a house made of Popsicle sticks.

"The end of an era," I said.

"I don't think that damned building was ever up to code," Uncle Joe said. critically. An *analegal-domicile*."

"That's not a word," I said.

"It is if people use it. And a lot of people are going to be using when they see how these buildings were made." He gestured to his former Emporium. "Look at them run!" A family of rats scooted off then disappeared down a hole. If Bunny had realized how little the buildings were actually worth, the Reuthenian Renaissance in America wouldn't even be a dream.

I felt a peculiar freedom, like a release from the past. "I'll catch you guys later." They waved at me absently as I went to join Bunny in the Dunkin Donuts.

She was engaged in vigorous debate with the owner, a slight, intense man with horribly out of style eyeglasses.

"Final offer," she said, tapping a manicured nail on the table between them.

"I don't know. This is my life. You don't have enough money to buy my life."

I'd never stopped in Dunkin Donuts, and so had never noticed that the women behind the counter looked just like the owner himself. They were his relatives. He was right: It was his life.

I ordered a Coffee Coolata and Bunny indicated that I should join them. "This is my attorney," she said, offering no names in either direction. "Now that you're not working for Matilda, you can work for me." She had the look I had seen CEOs get when they rearrange reality for their own convenience.

"Unless you want a divorce, I'm not sure it would be a wise use of your money," I said.

"You did a good job for Matilda. That wasn't just a divorce. Anyway, one of the things Carlton taught me was to always have the biggest sonofabitch working for you." She turned to the owner. "She'll be in touch with you," she said. "Give him your card, Swanson."

I obeyed, stunned at my new status. We shook hands, eyeballing each other as if we were about to go to our corners then come out fighting. He looked down at the card. "Swanson Herbinko? You know Joe and Stevie?' He jerked a thumb towards the destruction outside.

"They're my uncles."

"You're Swanson," he looked at the card then me again, a smile breaking across his face. "You didn't charge her for this, did you?" he yelled to a woman behind the counter. "This is Swanson! Give her a chocolate donut. You like chocolate donuts, don't you?"

I told him I liked them very much, and we bonded over a paper plate full of them while he told me that he was Doctor Albert Saad from Lebanon. He had published nine books about Arab history in his native country and had come to this country to teach. But no one wanted to learn about Arabic cultures. So instead he opened a coffee shop, where intellectuals could come and debate the issues.

"But they only want to talk about the Red Sox," Doctor Saad said, looking around his Dunkin Donuts sadly. "Where are the intellectuals? Maybe I should sell."

A man in Native American dress came in, and banged his spear on the ground. With his headgear full of feathers, he looked at least 8 feet tall. He scrutinized each face in the room, until his gaze landed on Bunny. He thrust his spear at her.

"You!" he said.

Bunny stood up, standing on tiptoe so as not to be at a disadvantage. "Yes," she said coolly. The time in Matilda's bunker had hardened her.

"You are disturbing an Indian burial ground. You cannot dig further."

Once some tribe claimed the land was sacred, development would be tied up for years. Between the Indian burial ground and the Dunkin Donut holdout, Broadway would look like a disaster movie for as long as I lived. I moaned silently and tried to slip out the door, but Bunny caught me.

"This is my attorney," she told him, pushing me in front of her. "Give him your card, Swanson. God," she whispered, "I am so glad you're here."

I smiled stonily, handed him my card and went out the door, just as a petite, auburn –haired woman was entering.

"Excuse me, miss, do you know where I can find a Miss Bunny..." She squinted down at her card. "That's all I have. Miss Bunny?"

"She's in there," I pointed to the counter. I looked the young woman over. Besides her unnaturally cheery attitude, she seemed normal enough. "I'm her attorney," I said, succumbing to fate. "Is there something I can help you with?"

"Her attorney? Good." A smile lit up her face. "She's going to need one." She handed me her card, which read, "Joanne Barry, Army Corps of Engineers."

"What's the problem?"

She pulled out a bound report from her bag, a third-world affair made of brown mud-cloth. "It's pretty technical. Chemical levels, evidence of PCB."

She looked at me to see if I understood. I did. The land was polluted and would need a major clean up before construction could proceed. All I had to do was find out what companies had been doing the polluting, sue the bejeezus out of them to fund the clean up, and get on with it. I had a plan.

"Any idea whose mess this is?"

"As a matter of fact." She took back the report and flipped to a page in the middle. "C&S Enterprises. We couldn't find out much about them, but we're working on it. It was supposed to be cleaned up with the Superfund, but since the Bushies drained that fund, C&S Enterprises, whoever they are, is responsible."

I smiled weakly. I had no doubt who C&S Enterprises was. Leave it to a professional sonofabitch like the Stubbses. I was still very much an amateur in the sonofabitch department.

"Excuse me," Joanne said, politely, "but I have to tell the owner of this Dunkin Donuts the bad news."

"He has to close?"

"He has to be informed. Do you have a card?"

I handed her one and walked down the street. There was commotion around the second Swanson Hot Dog Emporium. An anti-development group was picketing the site.

Uncle Stevie and Uncle Joe were getting in their rented Jeep, escaping the scene of the crime, heading towards the airport and France. I smiled. We had shed tears together at Hidalgo's funeral and said our good-byes, so there was nothing left to say, except "see you in France." They both had encouraged me to visit them there. Take a long-needed vacation. Even if the Stubbs brothers had screwed their own family, they had financed my uncles' dream and perhaps my vacation. Before I started mucking around in Indian burial grounds and Dunkin Donuts coffee grounds, I would need the succor that only authentic chocolate éclairs could bring.

Devil Dog and Howie Carr were waiting for me in my new car. I had leased an indigo Miata and put the BMW up for sale. I couldn't bear to drive it, knowing that Hidalgo had worked on it. We were driving to my office when my cell phone rang, and I almost caused an accident while I scavenged through my bag looking for it. I found it and breathed a hasty, "Hello!" It was a bad connection, but through the crackling line, I heard LePage's distinctive voice. She didn't say hello. She just started talking as if we were in the middle of a conversation that had been cut off.

"And so," she said, "they're going to reinstate me as a Specialist Four."

"Who's going to reinstate you?" I asked. The car in front of me stopped suddenly and I had to downshift to avoid hitting it.

"The Army. I reenlisted."

"I thought you told. You know, 'don't ask, don't tell."

"It's okay to tell now. You still have to be ready to beat up every bastard who has a problem with it, but legally they can't touch you. So, I'll be a Spec Four. I'm cool with it."

"Why a Specialist Four? Weren't you a Sergeant before?" I jammed on the brakes at a red light. A cab swerved around me, tires squealing, the driver hurling invectives at me out the window.

"That little incident on the firing range," she said.

"But you were found innocent!"

"Nevertheless."

"What about your house in Virginia?" I asked.

"Hah. That bastard Stubbs mortgaged that too. He's one prize pig. That's why I'm in basic green again, honey."

"Well, good luck. Take care of yourself. And Sarah."

"I will."

"Roger and out," I said.

"That's so wrong, Swanson," LePage said, laughing.

I hung up. She wasn't good at good-byes. Neither was I.

I had promised my uncles I would take care of their boat, so I spent the next two weeks ignoring Bunny's repeated phone calls and taking the dogs for rides on the river. While peaceful, it allowed me too much time to think, and soon I was looking forward to getting back to work. I scheduled some seminars to drum up new business. I finished up the few cases I still had pending and thought about going to France. Unfortunately, I couldn't go anywhere until Ines' trial was over. I would get through by becoming so busy I wouldn't have time to think about Hidalgo.

I parked in back of my building and looked up at the office to see if the lights were on. They weren't. I hadn't seen Dick since Hidalgo's funeral and I had no reason to expect him here now. Until I scared up more business, I didn't need a PI.

I wrapped the dogs' leashes around my hand and led them up the stairs. I picked up circulars and mis-sent mail that someone had dropped in front of my door and unlocked it, peering into the dark office. A figure was sitting in the guest chair.

"Hello?" I ventured.

"Swanson."

I clicked on the light. It was Dick.

"What are you doing here?" My voice sounded gruffer than I intended.

"I wanted to give you these." He held out the keys to the office. "Have you heard from your uncles?"

"They're experts on béchamel sauce. Not that I think South Boston needs any experts like that. They said half their class at the

Cordon Bleu is Chinese. I can't imagine that the Chinese need béchamel sauce either." I was rambling.

I felt the tears coming and looked away. Talk about cooking reminded me of Hidalgo. Dick politely examined his fingernails then bent down to pet Howie Carr.

I sniffed. "You don't want a dog, Dick, do you?"

"Too hairy." He brushed some of Howie off his navy trousers.

"I thought so." I blew my nose. I was where I started at the beginning of the Stubbs' brouhaha. Net one dog. I was turning into one of those eccentrics with a menagerie of animals and no humans in their lives.

"Here, Swanson, I found this in Ulrike's basement." He pushed my black pebble towards me on the desk.

I picked it up. I hadn't even missed it. "It's out of mojo," I said.

"It never had any. It's all up here." Dick tapped his head. "Are you going to be okay?"

He tried to be nonchalant, but I could tell he was concerned. At the funeral, every time I looked up he was watching me, giving me a nod of encouragement.

"You don't have to give back the keys," I said, "It's not that I trust you. But Bunny asked me to represent her. It turns out the Dunkin Donuts isn't going to sell, and the Corps of Engineers found toxic waste there, and they found some Indian remains under Stevie's Hot Dog Emporium…"

Dick threw back his head and laughed. "You're kidding!"

"I am not. I'm going to need you to help me get to the bottom of all this. You know how naïve I can be about corporate shenanigans." I didn't tell him Bunny's assessment of me as a sonofabitch. He would have gotten too much mileage out of that. "Have I revealed myself yet, Dick?" I asked.

"Revealing yourself is not necessarily a bad thing, Swanson," he said, quietly.

"I know where we can get some chicken soup," I said.

"Lead me to it."

I dangled the keys in front of him. "I think you'll need these."

He waved the keys away and closed the door behind us, being careful not to get too close to Howie Carr. "Locks only keep out honest people."

So, I was net one dog and one PI. The Red Sox didn't make it to the playoffs, but the Yankees were beaten by Annaheim in four games. That's some consolation.

September turned quickly to October, then November, and while my grief for Hidalgo never stopped, eventually I was able to push it down to where it smoldered instead of burned. I still wear the garnet and silver ring he gave me the night he died. I'll take it off when I meet a man who loves me as much as he did.

I'd started going to work later in the morning, and one day I caught sight of Fast Freddy slipping something into my mailbox, then pedaling madly away, the weight of the papers making her bicycle sway. The concierge was already asleep.

And Fast Freddy hadn't left a newspaper. Then I opened the mailbox and found a note, cutout letters from the Boston Globe pasted onto pale blue stationary. It read: "GAME OVER."

ABOUT THE AUTHOR

Bathsheba Monk is the creator of the Swanson Herbinko Mystery series. Read more about her on her website: www.bathshebamonk.com

Made in the USA
Charleston, SC
18 August 2016